MAGIC REVEALED

THE MAGIC OF THE HEART SERIES

MISHA McKENZIE

ICASM PRESS
SAVANNAH

This book is a work of fiction. The characters, names, events and places are fictitious and products of the author's imagination or are used fictitiously. Any similarities to actual persons, living or dead, places or events is entirely coincidental.

Published by Icasm Publishing LLC
5710 Ogeechee Rd. Suite 200 #278, Savannah, GA 31405
www.icasmpress.com

Library of Congress Cataloging-in-Publication Data

McKenzie, Misha
Magic Revealed / Misha McKenzie
    p. cm.

ISBN-13:978-1-9423180-2-6
ISBN-13:978-1-9423180-3-3 (ebook)
I. Title

Printed and bound in the United States of America

10 9 8 7 6 5 4 3 2 1

ACKNOWLEDGEMENTS

I wanted to take a minute to thank everyone who made this possible.

To my cousin, Traca. Without you, The Magic of the Heart Series would probably still be sitting in my computer. So thank you, thank you, thank you. I will never be able to repay you for what you did.

David – You'll never know how much getting your email asking to look at Magic Found again meant. They say it only takes finding the right person to get you started. You were that for me. You're patience and guidance has been invaluable. Thank you for taking a chance on me

Mandi – Thank you for all your help and lessons in grammar and sentence structure. I swear I'm trying to learn the rules and keep them straight, lol. It might take a while, though, so bear with me. Thank you for letting me vent and bitch when the characters refused to do anything but sit on the page. I've really enjoyed working with you and consider you a good friend. Maybe someday we can even meet face-to-face.

To everyone else who has had a hand in getting these books ready for the readers. Thank you for all your advice and hard work. Without each step of this process this series wouldn't be what it is, so thank you very much.

PROLOGUE

Gideon Marquand took his eyes off the road long enough to look over at the woman lying unconscious on the seat beside him. He still wondered if he should have told Fate to go fuck herself.

What had The Powers That Be been thinking when they'd paired him up with this damaged and broken woman?

Hadn't they kicked him in the teeth enough? One by one, they'd separated him from everyone he'd loved, leaving him to fend for himself at just two years old. Had they even cared that he'd been alone and scared? *Hell no.*

Despite being so young when it had happened, his memory was still clear and fresh. Every last detail of that night was etched into his brain. Maybe it was the magnitude of power he carried. But really—what did it matter? That terrifying night was burned into his mind and had changed his life forever.

~~~

He could hear the fighting and the blasts of magic as Roanik, puppet of the coven, attacked his family and home. He could see the urgency in Maria, their nanny, as she whisked him, his baby sister, and his cousin out of the nursery and through secret passages. Their little legs had trouble keeping up as she rushed them down to the garage where she hastily buckled
~~~

them into their seats. He sat through the frantic drive to where they kept the boats, and then the mad dash across the water. Once on the mainland, they were strapped into another car. He could hear her crying as they drove away when finally, exhausted, he'd fallen asleep.

Until he was awakened by more screams when the nanny lost control and they spun. When the car came to a stop, it rested against a group of trees. Branches had smashed through the windshield. One had reached all the way into the back seat and had left a long gash across Aiden's arm.

Gideon looked for Maria but couldn't see her. He was strapped in directly behind the driver's seat and couldn't see around it. But he could feel her pain and knew she was hurt badly.

They needed help. He fought to unbuckle the belts which held him, but his little fingers weren't strong enough. Sitting back, he concentrated on the buckle with his still-developing powers. It took a couple of tries, but it finally gave way, and he was free.

Gideon jumped down and scrambled over the seat to see what had happened to Maria. He found her slumped over the steering wheel. There was a lot of blood. Too much.

"Ria?"

No answer.

Through his magic, he could tell she was still alive, but no matter how many times he called to her, she wouldn't wake up. That really scared him. He wanted to sit down and cry for his parents, but he knew Maria was in trouble and needed his help.

Gideon looked back at his sister and cousin. Marissa was just a baby, and since Aiden was injured too, it was up to Gideon to go alone.

He slipped back around the seat and tried the door where he'd been sitting. It wouldn't open. Using his gifts, he pushed at the door. It didn't move. He looked over his shoulder at the one next to Aiden. Carefully he moved to the other side, ducking under the tree branch. He tried the door handle first, and when that didn't work, he put some power to it.

The door opened a little bit, but then stopped and wouldn't go any farther.

Aiden started to whimper in pain. Gideon looked up at him. "I get help." He gave up, turned to the front of the vehicle, and looked out the broken windshield.

Weaving his small body in and around the tree limbs, he crawled into the front passenger seat. From there he could reach the dash. Mindful of the shattered glass, he crept through the windshield and across the hood. He turned to lie on his belly and slowly slid down until his feet touched the bumper. Once he was on the ground, he took off running.

~~~

That had been the last time he'd seen any of his family.

Gideon again wondered why he was letting Fate jerk him around by the shorthairs. He had all his power back now; he didn't need to put up with her shit. Then he looked at the willowy redhead next to him and saw again what this one small woman would mean for his future.

She was his, for better or worse. And Gideon knew that for quite some time, it would definitely be for the worse. He was aware of everything that had happened to her and understood how deeply ingrained her training had been.

It was going to take love, kindness, patience, and a whole hell of a lot of fighting to bring her back to the woman she was meant to be—before she was betrayed by the one man who was supposed to love her.

To repair the damage done to her, he was going to need time and privacy. Both in short supply when you were being hunted.
~~~

Gideon just hoped the place he'd prepared would be secure enough to keep them hidden, and strong enough to remain standing when two witches went to war.

1

Stacia came back to consciousness slowly. From long habit, she didn't let on that she was aware until she took stock of her surroundings. She'd learned the hard way that having even a small advantage was better than nothing.

She was lying on a soft, comfortable surface. A bed maybe, but definitely not her own. How long had she been out? The heat on her skin and the light glowing behind her closed eyelids told her the sun was up.

Had it been hours, or days, that she'd been unconscious? The last thing she remembered was that Marquand bitch stealing the powers intended for her. There was a battle, and then it had all gone black.

Where was she, and who had taken her?

Using her magical senses she reached out, searching for any sign that someone was in close proximity to her.

She felt nothing. Taking a chance, Stacia opened her eyes just a crack, and seeing no one, sat up. She found herself in a nice-sized bedroom. Rough-hewn logs made up the walls, and the floor was wide-planked wood of some kind. Someone had scattered rugs around the room—maybe in an attempt to add a touch of color or warmth? She rolled her eyes. Only the soft and pathetic needed that kind of bullshit.

She swung her legs off the right side of the bed. Straight in front of her was a wall of windows. Outside the floor-to-ceiling glass was a grassy area leading to a sandy beach and then a large body of water. Lake? Ocean? It was too hard to tell.

Stacia stood and stepped closer. She searched the beach as far as she could see in each direction, but saw nothing that would tell her where she was. She did see land out in the distance, but it was almost impossible to tell how far away it was. Since she didn't spot watercraft of any kind, swimming it would be her only choice. A water escape was an option, but until she knew how far it was to the opposite shore, she'd leave it as a last resort.

Switching her attention to the windows themselves, she studied them carefully. They seemed to be just ordinary double-paned glass. Shouldn't be too hard to shatter one. She backed away a few paces and looked around for something to use.

Her gaze landed on the bedside table and the solid-wood lamp standing tall upon it. With just a flick of her hand, she sent it hurling towards the window.

The bulb exploded on contact, and the neck of the lamp snapped in half. But the glass remained intact. She left the debris where it landed on the floor and searched for something else.

She spied a grouping of thick pillar candles. Scattered around the bases were medium-sized river rocks. One by one she sent them flying. She applied more and more force, but they just bounced back like a tennis ball off a jail cell wall. This glass was either made of the strongest material known to man, or someone had spelled them. Her guess would be the latter. So that meant her captors had power. Something to keep in mind.

Frustrated, Stacia twisted back to examine the rest of the room. She briefly took note of the bed she'd been lying on. It was one of those old-fashioned wrought-iron styles with lots of bends and loops. She sneered at the sunny yellow paint someone had used on it. The bedding was also done in a mix of yellow, blue, and white.

Who the hell *were* these people? Who lived like this? Everything all matching, bright, and girly.

Turning away from that nauseatingly happy and cheerful sight, she spied a closed door. It was probably the way out, but she decided to hold off on that for the moment, at least until she had a better grasp of her situation. Without knowing more details about who held her or how many of them there were, she'd be better off biding her time and gathering information. And chances were good the door had the same seal as the windows.

Turning to the right, she saw the open doorway leading into the bathroom. Next to that was another closed door. She was pretty certain that one was the closet, but she checked anyway. It never hurt to be thorough when planning an escape route.

Pulling it open, she stood and stared at the clothes hanging inside. Whose room was this? Had to be a woman's, judging by the décor and styles of clothes. Curious, she grabbed a shirt at random. Whoever this woman was, she was small like her. The garment in her hand looked like it would fit. She checked the tag. It was her exact size.

A sick feeling began to take root in Stacia's stomach. Not that many women were five foot three and thin as a stick. She threw down the blouse and snatched out a pair of pants, over and over until most of the contents of the closet were strewn across the floor. They were *all* her size.

This didn't bode well for her release. Did these assholes plan on keeping her here forever? Well, not if she had anything to say about it, they didn't. Fuck waiting—she was getting out of this prison. *Now.*

Before she could formulate a plan, someone spoke inside her mind.

"This isn't a prison, and you're in no danger. Come to the kitchen when you're ready. Just follow your nose; I have food waiting."

It wasn't the fact that someone had been in her head that startled Stacia most. It was that the smooth, deep, sexy-as-hell tone was familiar to her.

She'd been dreaming about that voice and the tall, handsome man it belonged to for the better part of two years.

The dreams had played out like a movie, each one a continuation of the last. They didn't come every night—not even every week. But off and on over the last couple of years, she had watched a relationship bloom between her and this mystery man as she'd slept.

They'd journeyed from the initial meeting between strangers, to the first stages of affection, to whispered words of love. The last one had shown their bodies entwined and sweaty. She'd awoken, wanting and unfulfilled.

Stacia had never told anyone about the dreams. She'd kept them a closely-guarded secret. Neither Uncle nor her father would have taken well to her allowing such nonsense to distract her from her mission. She'd been taught a long time ago to push away everything but the quest for vengeance. Her punishment for any lapse in that rule would have been swift and severe had they ever found out.

Besides, that happily-ever-after fantasy shit was never meant to be hers. Revenge was her life. That's all there was. So the fact that just hearing his voice had made her ache was of no importance. It couldn't be.

She ruthlessly shoved all those thoughts out of her mind and crossed to the door. She jerked it open with such force it banged into the wall behind it.

Wrapping herself in the familiar blanket of rage, Stacia set out to find her warden.

By the time she emerged from the hall and into the dining area, hunger was overriding her anger. The aroma of whatever he'd cooked had saliva filling her mouth. That weakness, on top of everything else, sent her temper over the top. She mercilessly bore down on the man standing with his back to her.

"Who the fuck are you, and where the hell am I?" Stacia snarled.

"We can get into that while we eat," he answered with annoying calm as he turned to face her.

Hearing his voice earlier should have prepared her. But it hadn't. The shock of seeing his tall, muscled frame, sun-tipped dark blonde hair, and gorgeous sculpted features nearly took the breath from her lungs. Stacia forcibly hardened her defenses and held firm. She refused to let any man affect her this way.

"Look, asshole. You can forget sitting down to a civilized meal. I'm not taking anything from you."

His cool green eyes were appraising.

"You've been out of it for over thirty-six hours. I know you're hungry. You need to replenish your energy." And with that, he turned and walked back into the kitchen.

Shocked, she stared after him in disbelief. Was he stupid? Didn't he know not to turn his back on his enemies? That she could kill him by barely lifting a finger? Or maybe he just didn't care.

Deciding to use his negligence to her advantage, Stacia magically emptied the block on the counter and launched the entire arsenal of knives at the broad expanse of his back.

Only to have every last blade halted in mid-air, several inches from sinking deep. Seemingly of their own accord, they turned themselves around and found their original resting places.

Stacia was stunned. He'd done all that without having made a single move. He hadn't acknowledged her attack in any way.

She was quickly reassessing her options when he came back, two plates of food in hand. He looked at her with a spark of amusement in his eyes. "Are you finished?"

"Not even close."

The complacent grin was back as he brought the food to the table. "Are you at least done for *now*, then?"

That know-it-all smirk of his made her want to slap his arrogant, self-important, patronizing face. Who the hell did he think he was? He was obviously very gifted magically, but that didn't give him—

All at once, everything clicked. The group she'd fought...The green eyes...The mind-blowing power. The answer slammed into her brain.

Oh, shit.

"Yup," he confirmed, setting the plates on the table. "Give the girl a prize."

So this was the infamous Gideon Marquand.

Stacia had done endless hours of research on him and his family. But she'd never known what he looked like. She'd had no pictures of him, even as a child. At one point, she'd considered merging photos of his parents to come up with a possible likeness, but there were just too many variables.

And now here he stood. The most powerful witch born in over two centuries. The heir apparent. The man she'd vowed to destroy.

And the man she'd been having hot, sweaty sex with in her dreams.

A thought suddenly struck her. Had *he* done that? Made her have those fantasies?

Knowing who he was and what he was capable of, it was a definite possibility. The more she thought about it, the more sense it made. How would she have known precisely what he looked like otherwise? He had to have planted those images in her mind. Stacia began to wonder just how long he'd been playing around inside her head.

But why would he do that? What would be his motive?

To sway her way of thinking, Stacia concluded. Use her subconscious to make her develop feelings for him. That way, when they finally did face off, she wouldn't be as inclined to take her revenge.

Well, she'd die trying.

His family had cost her everything. All her life, she'd been preparing for this one purpose. To become strong enough to put an end to the coven that had murdered her family. The Marquand coven.

When the old witch had died in her sleep, Stacia had known her time had finally come. Without the spells to cloak them, the lost ones would be out in the open and unprotected. But first she'd needed to make herself unstoppable. Uncle had told her that once she'd gathered enough power, he would let her have her vengeance against them.

It was her duty to put a stop to the monsters that had taken her loved ones. All her training had been leading up to this. When she'd veered off track or gotten distracted from the main goal, the punishment had brought her focus back to where it needed to be.

And now, this most coveted Marquand was standing right in front of her. She may not have access to the magic she'd been gathering, but she still had her own and her training. She'd use whatever she had in order to even the score.

"If you're done plotting my demise, come eat." He sat and picked up his burger.

"Stay out of my head," Stacia demanded.

He took a huge bite. "I don't need to be," he said around a mouthful. "Your face is easy enough to read. And I know very well what your orders are. Sorry. *Were*," he quickly corrected.

Seeing him enjoying the food brought Stacia's hunger raging back. She was starving. She wanted to snatch up the other plate and devour everything on it, but she forced herself to remain still. This wouldn't be the first meal she'd missed.

"What do you mean, 'were'? If there's one thing you should know about me, it's that I won't quit. Not until the ones responsible for killing my mother and older brother pay."

He popped a potato chip into his mouth. "You've got that mixed around a little. Your father and brother *are* dead, but your mother is very much alive."

"Lies!" Stacia took an involuntary step forward in her fury. "*Your* greedy family killed them when they tried to take our power. They came into *our* home and attacked us when my father was away. My mother and brother were killed when they fought back. I was only three years old, but I knew enough to hide. I stayed hidden until my uncle found me. He took me to my father, and he sheltered us."

Gideon laid his food aside and was suddenly serious. "No. Your *uncle* took you from your family and gave you to Santino Mylos. They systematically tortured and brainwashed you, until you became their own personal weapon."

Stacia shook with rage. She took another step and gripped the back of the chair in front of her. She held it with such force that her knuckles turned white, and her nails dug crescent-moon shapes into the wood.

"No. He took me in. He trained me—made me strong. He gave me the chance to avenge my family. And nothing will stop me from doing just that. Not you *or* your lies. Not your power-hungry coven, and definitely not your stupid dreams. It'll be a son for a son, and a mother for a mother before this is over." A subtle lift of her finger upended his plate into his lap. As a distraction, it worked perfectly to hide her main objective. The carving knife on the counter.

As Gideon jumped back from the table to dodge the descent of food, Stacia summoned the weapon to her hand. When the hilt found her palm, she moved fast. Rounding the table, she got within striking distance. Her first slash sliced deep into the outside of his upper arm, biting deep through cotton, skin, and muscle tissue. She smiled victoriously at the gush of blood that ran free to drip from his hand.

This is turning out to be easy. Stacia moved in to finish him. She could already picture the shocked expression on his face when she sank the knife hilt-deep into his chest. Felt the blood covering her hands.

She adjusted her grip and drew her arm back. She'd just started the deadly downward arc, when the blade was ripped out of her hand by unseen forces. Undaunted, she quickly prepared for some hand-to-hand. Only to have her target disappear.

She swung around, searching. She found him behind her and advanced on him again, the red haze of hate filling her vision.

"Stop!" Gideon held up a bloody hand, and suddenly she couldn't move.

She was seething. "Coward! You can't hold me like this forever. You might as well kill me now, because I won't stop until you're dead!"

He stepped to the right, snatched a towel off the counter, and pressed it to his arm. "I'm not going to kill you." Closing the distance between them, he stepped in so close she could smell the scent of his soap. "But know this. I will only take so much of this *bullshit* from you, Lauren."

Something in her heart stuttered at the sound of that name. She shoved it down and glared at him. "My name is *Stacia*."

He eased back some and sighed. "No. It's not. Your name is Lauren Donnelly."

"Liar!"

His silver-laced green eyes drilled into hers. "That is one thing I will never do. I won't lie to you. Ever."

Gideon walked past her to the sink. He dropped the rag and stripped out of his ruined shirt to inspect his wound.

At the first glimpse of all that taut male skin, Stacia turned her head away and reached for her constant companion, anger. "So what now? If you're not going to kill me, what's your plan? If you won't lie to me, then tell me—what am I doing here?"

When he didn't answer, she brought her head back around so she could see him. She watched him as he cleaned the cut. Once the blood was washed away, she was shocked to see that it was healing right before her eyes. Soon, even the faint red line was gone, and his skin was left unblemished.

Gideon turned and leaned his hips back against the countertop. He crossed his muscled arms over his bare chest and eyed her steadily. "I said I won't *lie* to you, but that doesn't mean I have to answer every question. And what you're doing here will have to wait for another time. You're obviously not ready to hear anything I have to say."

He watched her for another moment and then, suddenly, she was free. "Just so you know, this place is protected by very powerful spells. It's locked down, soundproofed, and hidden from sight until I say otherwise."

Outmaneuvered for the moment, Stacia huffed out an aggravated breath and stomped off toward the room where she'd awoken.

2

Gideon watched her red hair swing out behind her as she marched out. He sighed and reminded himself again that it wasn't going to be easy to undo twenty years' worth of conditioning and programming.

When he went back to the table to start putting things away, he noticed Stacia's dinner still sitting there untouched. Taking a chance, he used his teleportation power and sent it to her bedroom, hoping she would eat.

Seconds later, he heard a loud crash and the sounds of breaking glass. Given her hostility, he wasn't at all surprised by her reaction. She obviously didn't want the food. Or the clothes he'd gotten for her, seeing as how she was still in the pajamas she'd been wearing when he'd taken her from the warehouse.

Shaking his head, Gideon went back to cleaning up the mess left in the wake of Stacia's temper.

Once finished, he went to his own bedroom to get into some clean clothes. Between the food dumped in his lap and the blood trailing from his arm, his pants were ruined. Dressed again, he headed for the living room where he sank into the large leather sofa. He reached out and picked up the remote to the seventy-inch flat screen across the room.

When he'd outfitted the place, he'd wanted all the comforts. They were going to be here for a while, and Gideon had no intention of depriving himself of stock car racing for that long.

Growing up in the south, it'd been a staple wherever he'd gone. A quick glance at the clock told him he could still catch the last half hour of practice.

As he settled in and watched a pack of cars circle the mile-and-a-half track, he wondered again what the best way to break two decades of brainwashing might be.

Until he could figure out a way to defuse her, she was a heat-seeking missile. And he was her primary target. If he expected to live long enough to redirect her aim, he needed to stay one step ahead of her.

To that end, he'd maintained a soft link with her mind since their arrival. It was through that connection that he'd caught her reaction to the name Lauren. She'd shut it down pretty damned fast, but he'd still felt it.

Somewhere hidden and repressed, she knew who she was. He just had to find it, and give it enough courage to resurface. Which wasn't going to be easy, since little Lauren had been beaten down and tortured into submission a long time ago, leaving only the hard, stubborn, and hate-filled Stacia in her place.

Gideon knew there would be many more scenes like the one today before she started to believe. He prayed to whatever entity listening that he would have the strength and patience to make it through without choking the life out of her first.

Knowing what she'd been through, he thought back over his own childhood. It hadn't been great, but it had definitely been better than hers. In her short twenty-four years, she'd lived a lifetime of suffering. He hadn't had it too bad by comparison.

When he'd left the crash site that night, his goal had been to find help for his family. But Fate apparently had other plans.

~~~

He eventually found a road. In the pitch black of night, he
~~~

used his senses to search for anyone who could help. But there was nothing. At two years old, he hadn't yet grown into his full power, and what he did have was limited.

Fear and loneliness threatened to overcome him, but as the eldest, it was his job to look out for the younger ones. Hadn't his father told him exactly that after Marissa was born? So instead of breaking down, he walked on the gravel shoulder until he couldn't walk anymore.

Finding a spot on the side of the road, he curled up and went to sleep. When he woke, he was in the back seat of a car. He looked up to see a woman sitting next to him.

When she noticed he was awake, she smiled at him. "Hi, sweetie. You're going to be fine. We're taking you home."

"Help Ria," he told her.

"Yes, honey, we'll help," she soothed. She had a bottle of water in her hand. "Now you just drink this and rest."

He was very thirsty, so he drank it. But soon his head started to feel fuzzy. All of a sudden, he was really tired and couldn't keep his eyes open. He slipped into slumber, sure he'd be back with his family before long.

~~~

Gideon had come to the conclusion that she'd drugged him with something. And had kept him that way long enough for her and the man she'd been with to leave the state and head south.

When he'd finally come out from under the sedative, they were at a house somewhere. He'd demanded to see his mom and dad, but the woman had told him they were gone. She'd said he was theirs now, and he was to call them Momma and Daddy.

Gideon smiled at the holy terror fit he'd thrown at that news. He'd directed every bit of the power he'd possessed at
~~~

them, sending them stumbling backward until they'd tripped over each other and fallen. Anything that wasn't too heavy had lifted and flown through the air. He'd brought lightning and thunder raining down on them. The whole house had shaken with the force of his anger.

It was as if the wrath of God had descended upon them. The man and woman had scrambled to their feet and run from the house. From him.

Gideon hadn't wasted any time finding his own way out and ran. But since he'd had no idea where he was, he didn't know where to go.

The choice had been taken from him not long afterwards when a police officer had found him. After that, it was a blur of doctors and a succession of strangers while they'd tried to locate his family. When none were found, they'd placed him into the foster care system in the great state of South Carolina.

During that time, his powers had ceased to work. So not only had he lost his family, but his only form of protection had disappeared as well.

Because of this, he had been a distant and troubled kid. As a result of his behavior, none of the foster homes had worked out. Eventually, he'd always ended up back in a group home. By the time he turned eight, they didn't even bother trying to place him anymore.

Over the next ten years, he'd followed the rules and had kept his head down. Remembering how he'd been lost in the first place, he'd known there would come a time when he'd need to fight. So he'd read books and watched videos on every different kind of fighting style he could find. As soon as he could travel to the library on his own, he'd consumed everything he could get his hands on about magic. Being a hereditary witch, he'd figured if—no, *when*—his powers came back, he'd need some knowledge of that world.

It had taken thirty years, but they'd finally returned. With a vengeance.

After everything he'd learned, Gideon thought he'd have a pretty good grasp on what to expect from his heritage. But when power after power and ability after ability emerged, he hadn't been prepared. It had taken him precious time to master all the new gifts.

One of the first to show up had been premonitions. He'd been bombarded with what had been and what was coming. Though most had just filled in the blanks in his mind, one particular vision of his sister had required immediate attention.

It had foretold of Marissa's death if she'd continued pursuing her chosen path. He'd had to stop her from seeking him out, from finding him before he was ready. With no choice but to take action, he'd tested out his newly-surfaced astral projection ability.

Except he hadn't taken into account what the time was, and when he'd found her, it had been the dead of night. She'd been sleeping and was more than a little alarmed to wake up and find him standing at the foot of her bed. But she'd recovered quickly, and he'd been able to warn her off.

Danger had still found her, but not the deadly kind he'd seen originally. Instead, she'd been kidnapped by Roanik in an attempt to draw Gideon out. Jack, Aiden, and Amber had taken care of that and had saved her, defeating Roanik and leaving him powerless in the process.

Gideon hated knowing he was the reason his family suffered. Having the kind of power he did drew a lot of unwanted attention. There would always be people—or groups—that desired it for themselves. The coven was one such group. Thirty years ago, they'd set out to destroy his family in their bid for dominance.

Their plan had been thwarted by two things they hadn't counted on, though. A brave nanny who, at great personal sacrifice, had spirited the children away under the cover of darkness. And a grandmother who'd had enough courage to bind their powers and hide them from detection. Even though it meant they were lost to the family as well.

When she'd died in her sleep thirty years later, the spells she'd cast had broken. That's what had drawn the coven out of the shadows and back onto the hunt once again.

Gideon had known he would need to have mastered all of his magic before he faced them. So as he'd slowly made his way north from South Carolina to Michigan, he'd practiced and honed his abilities.

Along the way, he'd used astral projection to help out his family when he could. But until he'd felt sure he could take down the group of men that wanted his magic, he'd had to stay under the radar.

The time for that confrontation was almost here. He just needed to resurrect Lauren and bring her over to their side. He didn't know all the reasons why yet, but his success in that would directly affect the outcome of the final battle.

His mind had come full circle and, once again, the woman down the hall filled his thoughts.

~~~

Stacia prowled the length of windows, just as she'd done for the last few hours. Distracted, she would send one of the river-rocks hurling into the glass. It was done more out of frustration than the hope that one of the panes would actually give way.

Her mind raced as she examined their conversation. Why had he called her that name? And why had it made her heart clench? She was Stacia Mylos. Her father was Santino Mylos; her mother had been Beth, and her brother, Robby. The only thing her father had ever allowed her to keep was a framed picture of them. It was beyond precious to her.

She reached the end of the windows and turned to retrace
~~~

her steps. Why was Gideon trying to confuse her? Why tell her these lies?

To turn me against my father and uncle, of course.

Well, she thought bitterly, that wasn't going to happen. Her father was all she had left. Yeah, he'd been hard on her, but he'd just wanted to make sure she would be ready when the time came to avenge the wrongs against her family.

She gave up on the glass, leaving the rocks scattered over the floor, along with the remains of the lamp, the clothes from the closet, and the food Gideon had sent to her earlier. Seeing the dismembered hamburger strewn with broken glass made her wish she hadn't thrown it at the wall. Her head was starting to ache from hunger.

Enough of being the martyr. Starving herself wouldn't get her anywhere. She needed to keep her thinking sharp and her abilities strong if she were going to beat him. She was trying to figure out the best way to get what she needed when a tray suddenly appeared in the middle of the bed.

On top of it sat a note.

This should reassure you that nothing is poisoned. I know you have to be starving by now.

Stacia crumpled the paper and looked down at the offerings. There was an unopened can of soda, a bottle of water with the ring still intact, two sealed cans of fruit, and a plastic fork, still in the cellophane package.

Fine, she'd take it. She snatched up the peaches and popped the top. She ripped the wrapper off the fork with her teeth and dug into the sweet, juicy fruit.

She barely tasted the first can, she ate it in such a hurry. The second went down a little slower, and she alternated taking sips of the soda as she weighed her options.

If everything she'd been taught about Gideon Marquand were true, a straight-up power-against-power battle would get her nowhere. That's why Uncle had been having her gather so much magic.

But she may not need it in the end. There was something Stacia had noticed during their brief struggle. Even though he'd had any number of opportunities, he hadn't retaliated— neither when she'd thrown the knives at him, nor when she'd cut him.

His power was evident, and the quick flash of resentment she'd seen had been real and formidable. He could have taken her out at any time. But yet, he'd done nothing to her.

Why? And how could she use that to her advantage?

Stacia needed to get a better idea of what she was dealing with if she were going to come up with an effective plan. The layout of the house would tell her how many possible points of exit there were. She would have to test the spell work he'd done—find out if there were any weak spots. Maybe she could counter it somehow.

She also wanted a better idea of what the surrounding landscape looked like. When she made it out, it would be helpful to know if there were trees to get lost in. Or if she'd have to race across an open field.

To complete this recon though, she was going to have to leave this room. And that meant dealing with Gideon. She could pretend to make nice. Let him think those dreams had done their job and softened her towards him. Would he believe that, or would it be better to disregard him altogether?

She was more comfortable with the thought of ignoring him. She didn't really know how to interact with people. Growing up, she hadn't been allowed any friends. Her whole life had been dedicated to training. Which had been fine, because that was all she'd ever known.

The bright, smiling face of a pretty woman with blonde hair flashed into her mind. Stacia pushed it away. She didn't know who that was, but she refused to let herself wonder about it. That kind of thing made her weak. Made her lose focus. And that was not tolerated.

Head back in the game, Stacia strode to the door and pulled it open. She'd proceed with the fact-finding mission she'd assigned herself and get the hell out of here. She'd come back when she had more power. Gideon would not survive their second encounter.

She still wasn't sure how to play it with Gideon, but she'd deal with that when she saw him.

Coming to the end of the hall, she turned to the right. She was standing in the living room. The whole front wall was windows, as it was in her room. To the right of them was a door leading outside. Crossing to it, she grasped the handle and twisted. It swung quietly inward. After a quick glance over her shoulder, Stacia took a step over the threshold.

And ran straight into an invisible wall.

She felt along the edges of the doorframe, looking for any gaps or vulnerable spots. None. It was completely sealed. Stacia stepped back and shut the door.

The dining room and kitchen were behind her. A quick check told her they were also locked up tight. She could open the windows or doors to let the breeze come in, but nothing solid passed through.

While she was at the back of the house, she studied the grounds from that vantage point.

Like the front, there was an open, grassy area. But unlike the beach side, after the yard there was a line of trees. It was hard to tell how far the woods went on, but if she could make it that far, she had a chance.

She just had to find a way through the boundary spells.

Footsteps from the hall alerted her that Gideon was coming. Turning quickly, she yanked open the fridge and stood as if looking for something. No sense in letting him know what she was planning. When she actually took notice of what she was seeing, she gaped. She'd never seen so much food in all her life.

Covering her reaction swiftly, she snatched out a can of soda and slammed the door closed.

"How long do you intend to keep me here?" She glared at him.

Gideon stepped in close, reached past her, and grasped the handle on the refrigerator, inadvertently brushing against her. Stacia leapt back from the shock of the contact.

He, on the other hand, didn't react in any way. He just casually grabbed a bottle of beer, twisted off the cap, and chucked it in the garbage.

Embarrassment at her reaction made Stacia livid. "Well?" she demanded. "How long?"

He took a slow drink before answering. "As long as it takes."

"Cryptic much?" she muttered.

Her words brought out a genuine grin. Stacia felt a flutter in the vicinity of her stomach at the sight. She ignored it.

"Something funny?" She made sure her tone was rigid.

He took another pull of the brew and then grinned. "I've been hearing that a lot lately."

"Does it piss them off as much as it does me?"

He nodded. "Oh, I'm pretty sure it does."

"So what exactly are we waiting for?" she tried again, hoping to get a straight answer.

"It's not a what, it's a who."

"Okay, then—*who* are we waiting for?"

"I think I'll let you figure that out." He stepped around her.

She couldn't believe he was just going to leave her standing there.

His dismissal notched up her annoyance another level. "Hey, jackass. If I don't start getting some answers, I'm going to tear this place down around your ears. Don't think I won't."

"I'm sure you would." He turned to face her and casually took another sip. As he lowered the bottle, he leaned in. "But then you'd never find out the truth," he taunted.

He was close enough that she caught his unique scent. It was like the outdoors—woodsy, fresh—and all man. As the subtle fragrance teased her senses, Stacia fought to keep her face impassive. She drew on what had sustained her through many dark times…her need for retribution.

"Who's truth? *Yours?*" Stacia's hatred for her adversary took over as the comforting heat of fury settled in again. "Why would I listen to anything you, or anyone else, has to say? I know the only truth that matters."

She shoved against his chest with her magic. When he backed up a step, she advanced one.

"Your family is responsible for the death of mine." Another push. "I've spent my entire life preparing for this day. If that greedy, green-eyed bitch hadn't stolen from me, I'd have enough magic right now to destroy you." She threw another blast of power towards him.

Only this time, Gideon leaned his body into it and countered it with some of his own. "I hate to break it to you, babe, but the only reason your *uncle* set you on me is because he only wants one thing—Marquand magic. And he never would have let you kill me. Not before he got what he wanted, anyway. Every power that has ever flowed through the Marquand line runs through my veins." Gideon held both arms out wide. "One-stop magical shopping. A power-hungry bastard's wet dream."

He used the beer bottle to point at her. "You're not even the first to try. You're just the latest in a long line. A group known as 'the coven' has you beat. They've tried twice already. Thirty years ago, they ordered an attack on us. He was ultimately beaten back, but not before my baby sister, cousin, and I were lost. And just recently, they sent the same man to kidnap my sister in an attempt to lure me out. Luckily, she wasn't hurt. But my family reduced him to a quivering mass *of nothing.*"

Stacia took the way he accentuated the last two words as a warning that the same fate could await her if she weren't careful.

Animosity, and something else Stacia couldn't read, sparked in his eyes. "So if anyone has the right to revenge, it would be me. You, on the other hand, have been lied to and manipulated into believing something which isn't true. You're not even related to either of those men. So don't talk to me about avenging families until you know all the facts. Facts, Lauren, which your so-called uncle has kept from you. Or twisted to his own advantage."

"*Don't call me that*," she demanded a little wildly before reining it back in. "My name is Stacia, and nothing of what you said is true. *None of it.*"

Every time he said that name, a small part of her recoiled, but she refused to heed the niggling tendrils of doubt that were finding their way into her thoughts. Stacia held herself rigid and stoic. No matter what she was feeling, she refused to give Gideon the satisfaction. She wouldn't let him see any weakness in her. His accusations would find no place to root. She held her head high as she stormed off to her room to think and to plan.

3

Gideon had to strengthen his resolve numerous times as days turned to weeks, and weeks to months. They'd been there over two months now, and still she fought him and refused to listen to anything he had to say. She'd tried building walls up around her mind to keep him out, but Gideon had still been able to read her thoughts easily. Which had saved his ass more than once, since her attempts on his life continued and had become more and more inventive.

At one point, she'd disconnected the gas lines from the stove and dryer, filling the cabin with extremely noxious fumes. He'd caught her before she could blow them both to hell, but even that hadn't been the end. She'd tried again and again, and each time she failed, she'd retreat to her room to regroup and formulate a new plan. He and his home had taken some pretty major hits from her.

Fuck. Gideon scrubbed his hands over his face and went to stand in front of the windows overlooking the lake.

There *had* to be some way of bringing her back. So far, nothing he'd tried had worked. Maybe it was time to ask for help.

He took a quick mental peek in on Lauren. She was standing in much the same way he was—looking out over the water, thinking. Planning her next attack, no doubt.

She didn't appear to be on the verge of nuclear meltdown, so

Gideon closed his eyes. He brought to mind someone he hadn't seen in over thirty years. He felt the now-familiar rush of his consciousness leaving his body and racing across the cosmos. When he stopped, he was standing in the shadows of a darkly-paneled office. The man he was looking for sat behind a large wooden desk.

Gideon took the opportunity to study him. They'd missed out on so much. But if all went as Gideon had seen, they wouldn't miss much more.

He stepped out of the darkness and drew the attention of his father.

There was an instant of alarm on the other man's face before recognition struck. *"Gideon?"*

"Hey, Dad," Gideon said, stepping fully into the light.

As Ben stood and came around the desk, he took in the sight of his fully-grown son. Gideon tried to see himself through his eyes.

At over six feet tall, he met his father at eye-level. Gideon's own dark blonde hair was a couple of shades lighter than Ben's, and he could see from whom he'd gotten his wide shoulders and narrow waist. Gideon's facial features were an almost exact replica of his father's, but softened just a bit here and there. A contribution from his mother, he would guess.

And, of course, the Marquand green eyes...though Gideon's had an extra little something he hadn't noticed in any other family member. Once his powers had fully emerged, his already icy-green eyes had begun to swirl with silver.

It was a very strange effect. One he'd started to cover with a glamour, because people would stare in shock at the mercury-like movement in his irises.

"God, it's good to see you, son." Ben stopped just short of embracing him. Gideon recognized the yearning in his father's gaze to touch and hold his long-lost child. But since it still wasn't safe enough for a true reunion, his image standing here now would have to be enough.

"I'm sorry I haven't come to see you before now." He paused, hands finding the front pockets of his jeans. "I thought it best to stay away as much as possible."

"That's fine," Ben assured him. "We understand. We're all just glad you were able to come when you have." His father moved to the couch and sat on the arm. "Does you being here mean someone's in danger?"

"No." Gideon felt a little embarrassed now. "I need some advice."

By the shocked expression on his father's face, that obviously wasn't what he'd expected to hear.

"Advice about what?"

"Did Marissa tell you about what she saw that night?" Gideon asked, instead of jumping right in.

"Yes, your sister filled us in on what happened at the warehouse," Ben confirmed. "She said that you went there, in person, and took Stacia away. She also shared the news of who Stacia really is. Lindsay was in shock for a while, but she's finally come to terms with the fact that her late-husband's sister is still alive."

"You're going to have to get used to calling her Lauren," Gideon smiled to himself, "though she still wants to rip my head off every time I do. I'm hoping that by using her real name, it'll help her to remember the time before."

"Does she?" his father asked.

"I'm pretty sure she does. I've been keeping a light link with her, mainly to make sure she can't sneak up on me and slit my throat," Gideon explained. "And it's through that connection that I can feel her recognition of her given name. Something is definitely still in there, but she won't acknowledge it. She's fighting it to the bitter end. These last few weeks have been pushing my limits on patience. But I won't give up. There has to be a way of getting through to her; I just haven't found it yet."

"What about her mother?" Ben asked. "When Quinn went into Stacia's dreams, he saw that she has a place she goes to...a sanctuary. From what he described, if she dreams of torture or any other brutality, she immediately reverts back to that memory."

Gideon was intrigued now. This could be what he'd been looking for. "What's her refuge?"

"Quinn estimated her age at two or three. She's sitting on the floor of what must have been her bedroom. She's brushing the hair of a doll when her mother comes in all smiles, and light, and love. Her safe haven is a memory she has of Margaret."

Gideon thought this might be the key he needed. Maybe he could recreate a few items from that dream and see if they helped to jog her memories of her true identity.

"Do you honestly think you can turn her around?" Ben asked him, interrupting his thoughts. "She's been through hell—and then some—since she was three years old. Can that kind of damage be reversed?"

Gideon recalled the visions he'd had of their future. "There has to be. I just need to find the right way to bring her back."

He released a breath and prepared to give voice to another concern. "How do I help her through this without hurting her any further, Dad?" He paced while he talked. "No matter *how* I explain the past, it's going to shatter her world. How do I tell her that her own father faked her death and gave her to those vicious bastards as payment? And that we think he also killed her older brother? How do I tell her that the only family she's ever known are just the sadistic wardens of the prison she's been trapped in for the last twenty years?"

"I don't know that you *can* explain all those things without hurting her," Ben told him. "But I'm confident you'll find the right words when the time comes. You'll know when she'll be most open to those truths. And you'll know best how to comfort her."

His father rose and came to stand in front of him. "Just follow your heart, son. And remember—it's not all bad. She still has a mother who loves her very much and grieves for her every day. She has a sister-in-law and a new niece."

"Yeah, I'll be sure to tell her. For all the good it'll do." Gideon's connection to Lauren alerted him. "Dad, I have to get back. Lauren's up to something."

"Alright, son. Come back when you can. I know your mother would love to see you."

"I'd love to see her too, and I will. Soon. This can't go on for much longer." At least he hoped not.

He opened his eyes and knew instantly what had set off his inner alarms. She'd found a way to set fire to the place.

Smoke was rolling out from the hallway. Gideon took off running to find the source of it. The first room he came to was the one he'd designed as a small library and office. The curtains on the far side of the room were fully engulfed, the flames licking at the ceiling.

Before any more damage could be done, he exerted his will over the fire. The destructive beast fought against him, but Gideon pushed more of his own stifling power into it. He forced it down until it was completely extinguished, and once he was sure it wouldn't reignite, Gideon returned to the hall and raced to the next room.

She'd done the same in the full bath. Fire danced up the window treatments. He took control, and soon all that was left were the blackened remnants.

His own room was next, and he hated to see the extent of the damage she'd done there. Opening the door, Gideon felt the heat slap him in the face. Lauren—no, this was all Stacia's doing—must have started here. His bed and the wall behind it were completely destroyed.

Gideon was concentrating on putting out the fire when he

heard her dart past him down the hall.

Son of a bitch. He couldn't turn his back on this blaze; it would take off again too easily. It took him another precious few seconds to get it out. Once he had, he swung around to the door directly across the hall; it was hers. And although he didn't expect her to torch her own things, he paused there briefly just to confirm. Finding everything normal inside, he spun and bolted for the living room.

She'd already succeeded in igniting the end of the couch. Before she could get away from him and continue her vicious rampage, Gideon grabbed her from behind and lifted her high off her feet, wrenching the lighter from her hand and pitching it across the room. "Stop! You've caused enough trouble, damn it!"

She kicked and wrestled against him, fighting to break his hold. Suddenly, she rammed her head backward and into his face.

Blood instantly gushed from his nose, and he swore loudly as tiny lights burst in front of his eyes. His grip loosened, and she twisted out of his arms.

He had just enough time to duck the punch aimed at breaking the rest of his nose. Gideon pulled his head back and dodged the blow, then made a lunge for her. He tried to catch her around the middle, but she sidestepped deftly away from him, just out of reach.

She didn't go far, though. Stacia waded right back in, bent on his total annihilation. He blocked her kicks and evaded her punches the best he could, doing only what was needed to prevent further injury.

Smoke from the burning sofa was filling the room. He needed to neutralize her before the fire got any more out of hand.

He deliberately took a shot to the ribs. It brought her close enough that he could finally get his arms around her, pinning hers down at her sides. Her head was well below his face this time, so she couldn't try that move again. His nose still throbbed, and blood continued to flow freely down his chin and into her hair.

He held her until she ceased struggling. Turning his attention to the flames, Gideon had them under control in seconds, but he didn't extinguish the blaze completely. He was pissed off just enough to want to show her exactly who she was dealing with.

He manipulated the fire into a column until it was a mini funnel, floating and spiraling in the air. Slowly he brought it closer to where he still held her. "You like to play with fire?" he whispered menacingly close to her ear. "Then let's fucking *play*."

Gideon fed the tornado, making it grow and lengthen and swirl until the inferno completely engulfed them both. He let just enough of the heat through to make his point, allowing the temperature around them to intensify until it became almost unbearable. The air seared his lungs, and a tinge of burning hair wafted over him as a few flyaways fell victim to the oppressive heat.

Stacia held out longer than he'd thought she would, but eventually she gave in. "All right! You can stop now!" she yielded, shrinking into him to avoid getting scorched. "I get it—I'm no match!"

Gideon snuffed it out and then spun her around to face him. He glared down at her. "What the hell were you hoping to accomplish by that?"

Stacia shoved against him, and he let her go. She reached up and pushed her flame-colored hair out of her face and gave him a dirty look.

He conjured a towel and wiped at the blood from his nose. "You know what? Never mind. I think I know. You thought if it got bad enough in here, I'd have to release the spells on the house, and then you could get out."

"It's been months. Do you think you can keep me locked in here forever?" she asked, incredulous.

"The spells are in place to *protect* you, damn it!" Gideon threw the bloody towel onto the ruined couch. "You have no idea how many people are out there hunting me, and now you. Until we're ready to take them on, I'd rather not have them at my doorstep."

"*You* may need to hide out in here, but *I* don't," she taunted, her eyes flashing in anger. "My father is out there right now, looking for me."

"If he is, it's not for the reason you think."

"Oh yeah?" She crossed her arms over her chest. "What other reason would he have?"

"Because you know too much." Gideon's shoulders slumped under the weight of everything he was battling against. "They've put years of training into you. One of them even took you in—pretended to be your *father*. They can't take a chance that you'll remember or discover the truth. Their plan failed. You're a loose end now. One who could reveal too many of their secrets."

Her denial was immediate, and she shook her head. "No. There's no way my father would turn against me. I'm all he has."

"That's just it. *You were never his*." Gideon hated to see how hard she was fighting to remain loyal to those assholes. "You were a means to an end, Lauren."

She was silent for so long, he thought he'd finally gotten through to her. But instead, she transformed before his eyes. Her arms dropped to her sides. She pulled herself up and squared her shoulders. Her eyes turned cold, and she looked at him with disdain.

"I'm curious. Just how far are you prepared to go with these lies?"

"They're not lies," Gideon countered.

"Okay. So let's have your version of the truth. Hit me." She raised her arms and waved her hands in towards herself in a 'bring it' gesture. "Lay it all out for me."

"We're not doing this now," Gideon told her. "You're still not ready."

She laughed, but it was devoid of humor. "Is that all we're waiting for?" Stacia rolled her head around, did a few exaggerated stretches, and made a show of pushing her hair back out of her face again. She reminded him of a boxer getting ready for a match. "Okay, I'm ready. Let's do this."

She thought she was so tough...that she could take on the world. Little did she know the world had already fucked her over.

And now it was his job to try to set things right.

"Come on. You know you want to tell me," she cajoled. "Drop the bomb. The whole truth, and nothing but the truth."

Gideon looked at her thoughtfully. Maybe it would be easier with her in this kind of mood—cocky, sarcastic, sure of herself. Even if she laughed it off right now, it would be in her mind, festering and making her wonder.

When he didn't answer, she pushed harder.

"How am I supposed to start accepting your rendition, if you won't tell me what it is?" She took a step closer. "Spill it," she taunted, her hazel eyes glinting up at him. "I dare you. Make me believe."

Gideon relented. "All right." He walked over to the sofa and, with a thought, repaired the end that had been damaged by the fire. "Have a seat." He circled the room to turn on a couple of lamps and open the windows. He gave the air a little push to help clear out the smoke. "I'll tell you a story."

She rubbed her hands together as she crossed the room to sit down. "Oh boy, a story! I can't wait. Do I need popcorn?"

Gideon couldn't sit. He had to move as he laid out Lauren's life and death...and the birth of Stacia.

"Bear with me. It's better to start at the beginning. So we'll go back a little more than twenty years ago." He paused and took a breath. "A scumbag by the name of Carl Donnelly made a deal with even bigger scumbags to gain more power and prestige than he ever could have gotten on his own. The price for this gift was his three-year-old daughter."

Gideon kept a careful eye on her to see if anything he was saying caused a reaction. "He had no problem with that because, as he saw it, she was nothing. She was useless. She hadn't inherited any of his magic, so what good was she? What he didn't know, though, was that she *had*. Her mother, Margaret, had been hiding that fact from him because of his obsession with creating an unstoppable dynasty. He'd already been working with their son, Steven, and was trying to mold him in his own image."

The cocky smirk was gone, but she gave nothing else away. Gideon continued.

"Seeing what he was doing to their son, Margaret vowed that she wouldn't let the same destiny befall her baby girl. So she kept the secret. On that fateful day when payment came due, Carl took his only daughter and gave her to the men he owed. He faked the little girl's death, and told her mother that she'd fallen into a ravine and was killed. Afterward, he wiped out every piece of evidence pertaining to her existence. In effect, he made it so she'd never been born."

His words were getting to her. Some of the color had drained from her face, and her calm expression looked forced. The next part of his tale wasn't going to be easy, for either of them.

"For years after that, it became a battle of endurance for her. At some point, that frightened child shut herself away, and another was born in her place. One who could withstand the horror and abuse. *She* grew, became strong, and soon the scared little girl was locked away...forgotten. The tougher, harder one did what she needed to do to survive. And, eventually, she started to believe the lies professed to her by those closest to her. Those who had *made* her."

Gideon came closer and sat on the couch near her. He wanted to see if what he said next hit home. And so he watched her.

"That small, terrified girl is still in there, though. And when the other sleeps, when she dreams of pain and suffering, the young one is there to protect her. She takes her to a safe place inside her mind. A last memory, held and cherished. A treasured image of a mother's unconditional love. They return to a time when it was nothing but dolls with long hair to brush, and the smiling face of a pretty blonde woman."

There it was. Just the slightest widening of her eyes before she turned it off and the hazel went cold again.

"Wow. That was some story." Stacia slowly stood. "And you did a good job with the telling of it. Very tragic, very compelling." She walked away a couple of steps before turning back. "But if that's all you have, you may as well undo the spells and let me go now. Because it wasn't enough."

The tremor in her hands, and the way she kept swallowing back unwanted emotions, told a different truth. "There's a little more to the story—some secondary characters to bring in—but we can delay that for another time. It's getting late. "

"Well, I'll just wait with baited breath for the next installment, then."

Gideon let her go. This was the first time she'd listened to everything he'd had to say, and it would be a lot for her to process, no matter how hard she fought it.

4

There was no way in *hell* she was sticking around for Gideon's next outrageous lie.

Stacia stripped out of her clothes and stepped into the hot shower.

Her neck and shoulders were knotted up and sore. And it had absolutely nothing to do with what Gideon had told her. She was just tense because of the situation and their scuffle.

As if she would ever believe Santino Mylos wasn't her father. It was ludicrous. Where did he come up with this shit? Why would her father and uncle have lied to her? Her childhood hadn't been easy, but that was understandable after what had happened. Her father went to a really dark place after his wife and son had been killed.

He was distant with her and pushed her to excel, sure. But that was only to prepare her for when she would avenge their family. He'd demanded her undivided attention on training and learning to use her powers, so that no one would be able to get the drop on her like they had her mother and brother.

She looked down at the marks on her arms and body. Each represented a time when she'd not given one hundred percent. When she'd asked the wrong question, or when she'd balked at the requests made of her.

It wasn't torture, as Gideon had described. She hadn't been tormented or abused. She'd been given the motivation she'd needed to keep the mission number one.

But what about the blonde woman? She'd seen her more than once in her mind. Where had she come from? And how did Gideon know about her?

Shit. Of course he knew about her. Gideon must have planted her there. She knew for a fact that he was able to get into her head. It would be nothing for him to go in, plant the images he wanted her to see, and then sit back while she assumed they were her own. He'd done it with the dreams of them together, so why not the blonde woman, too?

Well, that was done, *right now*. Stacia closed her eyes and re-doubled the barriers she'd put around her mind. She made them thick and indestructible.

Confident of her success, Stacia scrubbed her skin clean. She refused to let Gideon's fabrication take anchor. She knew it for what it was—a *lie*. He was just trying to put a wedge between her and her father. Make her doubt. Turn her against him. Sway her from her mission.

That wasn't going to happen.

A few minutes later, she stood naked in front of her closet. Rummaging around, she grabbed the first pair of black pants she saw, and then searched until she found a matching shirt.

Her multiple attempts to take him out hadn't worked, but she was done playing now. She would find a way out of here. Tonight. Even if she had to tear the fucking walls down to do it.

Donning a pair of shoes, she turned off the lights and went to stand at the windows. She'd wait until she knew he was sleeping. Three a.m. should ensure that. She'd make her move then.

A quick glance at the clock told her she had a few hours to kill. Hours she would use to prepare.

Stacia strode into the bathroom and started going through every drawer and cabinet. She looked for anything she could use as a weapon. Five minutes later, she had nothing. Hopefully the bedroom would yield something.

While going through the dresser, she noticed the artwork hanging above her. It had a silver metal frame. Perfect.

Reaching up, she carefully lifted it off the wall. She turned and laid it face-down on the bed where she proceeded to take it apart. Her powers would have been faster, but she needed this done silently, and with precision.

Once she had the picture and glass separate from the rest, she went into the bathroom to grab a washcloth. Rag in hand, she picked up the casing and wrapped the cloth around one side. She placed the other end on the floor and stepped on it. With her hands protected by the padding, she pulled upward. It came apart with a snap, leaving the forty-five-degree corner cut that would make the ideal knife.

Once he was dead, she could move on to her next target. His mother.

Stacia settled in to wait.

~~~

Gideon had felt it when Lauren blocked him out of her mind completely. He could have forced his way back in but decided against it.

Now that he couldn't tap into her thoughts, he figured it best to take some precautions. Before fixing the damage from her latest escape attempt and going to bed, he put a spell on his bedroom door that would alert him if it opened.

Which ended up being a smart move. Sometime in the middle of the night, an alarm went off in his brain. He'd barely rolled to his back when she was on him. There was just enough moonlight coming through the windows for him to see her raised arm. She had some type of weapon in her hand.

Flat on his back, Gideon was at a disadvantage. He may outweigh her by a hundred pounds, but in this position, her
~~~

own body weight aided her attack and gave her leverage. He grabbed her wrists and held them out away from his body. Gideon had a moment when he thought he'd have to use his powers to subdue her. In comparison to her prior attempts, this was turning out to be the closest she'd come to doing him actual injury.

But as intent as she was to do him bodily harm, Gideon held his strength and abilities in check. He refused to be the cause of any physical pain she suffered. He was so centered on keeping her hands away from his vital organs, he neglected to factor in the rest of her.

She was small and agile, and that aided in her ability to bring her knee up and strike a blow to his nuts that stole his breath.

Mother fucker!

Through sheer force of will, Gideon's grip remained tight. They struggled briefly until he was able to shift his weight and roll. Now she was pinned beneath him on the bed.

He pushed her arms up over her head and held them there. When he had her secure, he turned the lights on with a thought. Now that he could see clearly, Gideon looked to see what she'd found to kill him.

It was some kind of metal stake. A makeshift hilt made from one of the washcloths from her bathroom. It was then he saw the blood staining the yellow cotton red.

During their tussle, her grip had slid, and now she was holding the sharp metal bare-handed. It was cutting into her palm.

Gideon shifted his hands so he restrained both of hers in one of his. He tried to pry the blade from her grasp, but her fingers closed tighter. The flow of blood increased.

"Stop! You're hurting yourself. Let go of it!" Gideon met her angry glare with one of his own.

She drew in a sudden breath, and her struggles ceased. Her

gaze was glued to his.

Gideon realized she was seeing his eyes for the first time without the glamour. It was second nature for him to employ it during the day, but while sleeping, he didn't bother. Gideon recited the spell in his head. Between one breath and the next, his eyes were back to being light green. Hopefully, she would think what she'd seen had been a trick of the light.

Taking advantage of her moment of shock, he wrested the weapon away from her and dropped it to the floor beside the bed. Once her hand was empty, he slid his palm along hers and then curled their fingers together.

Gideon ignored her renewed struggles and brought the healing heat of his magic to her wound. She stilled, and her lids flared slightly when she felt his power concentrated on the laceration.

Even when he knew the cut was gone, he kept their hands entwined. Now that the worst was over, their positions were bringing to mind things better left alone. Like the way her silky red hair spread out across his pillow, or the feeling of her body stretched out under his. Or the way her skin was flushed and her breathing labored. Gideon started to wish it had been something other than a fight that had brought about these responses.

He really needed to let her go.

His mind knew it was the right thing to do. But his body was too aware of all her soft parts pressed against him.

Clad only in dark blue boxer-briefs, not much acted as a barrier between them. Or hid the affect she was having on his body.

When Gideon's focus dropped to her parted lips, he knew he had to back off. Cool down.

It had been a long time since Gideon had been out with a woman, let alone had one in such an intimate position. The knowledge that she was meant to be his made holding back that much more difficult. His body wanted her now, but in his heart he knew he had a long way to go before she was ready.

Slowly, he slid one long leg off the side of the bed. When his bare foot touched the floor, he lifted his bulk away from her. As soon as she was free, she bolted off the opposite side. She stood glaring at him.

"Aren't you getting tired of this?" he asked her, reaching for some semblance of calm.

She gave a derisive laugh. "*Never*. Your family has to pay. A son for a son. A mother for a mother. I won't stop until you're both dead. And you can cool it with all the mind tricks; they won't work on me anymore. I won't be fooled again."

"What mind tricks?" Gideon's brows drew together. He didn't know what she was talking about.

"That blonde woman you buried in my memories," she accused, "so I'd believe your lies about my mother being alive. And then there are the dreams of you and me. You really pulled out all the stops there. But now I know they were all made up by you, and planted in my subconscious for your own benefit."

"To what end?" he asked her. This was the second time she'd mentioned dreams. Gideon wondered what they entailed.

"To make me trust you," she shot out. "To back up whatever you said."

"Lauren, I swore I'd never lie to you, and I haven't. I didn't do anything to your memories." Gideon kept his gaze steadily on her so she could read the truth in his words. "The woman you see *is* your mother. From a time before you were taken from her."

Gideon saw it as a step forward that she didn't immediately correct his use of her name. Maybe somewhere in there, she was starting to accept. Under the mad, he could clearly see confusion. He wanted to go to her, but stayed where he was for fear that she'd dash out of the room. "As far as your dreams, I've done nothing to manipulate your mind. But I think I know why you've been having them."

He gestured to the closet. "Let me put some clothes on, and we can discuss it."

"No. I won't let you into my head again." She walked to the door, and just before crossing the threshold, she turned back. "This isn't over."

God damn it. She was one hard-headed female. Gideon ran his hands up over his face and to the back of his neck. He closed his eyes and dropped his head forward, trying to figure out what to do next.

His thoughts were cut short when he opened his eyes and saw the bloody rag and metal spike still lying beside his bed. He bent down and picked it up. Running it through his hands, he took a good look.

It was a couple of moments before he finally recognized it. It was a portion of the frame from the landscape in her room. What he held was only one side of it, though. There were still three more for her to choose from. With his mind's eye, he searched and found the remains of it lying on her bed and quickly disposed of it.

Gideon sat down with his back against the headboard and thought over the situation. Something drastic needed to be done. He wasn't going to strip the whole house of furnishings on the off-chance she'd use one to hurt him. He had to find a way to shock her out of this rut she was in.

But how?

He'd hoped reminding her of her mother would induce more memories. But all he'd done was convince her those recollections were false. That he'd planted them there to confuse her.

If he could just prove to her that her mother was really alive, maybe she would reconsider the rest.

Gideon rose and headed to the bathroom for a shower. He'd use the next few hours to fine-tune his plan.

At seven a.m. Gideon stood at his bedroom window and

prepared to make a short trip to gather some information. He decided to announce his presence before popping in. He could arrive at an inopportune time, and then he'd have to dig his eyeballs out and scrub his memory.

Gideon closed his eyes and reached out. *"Aiden?"*

He felt his cousin's surprise. *"Gideon?"*

"Yeah, there's something I need to talk to you about. Is this a good time?"

"Sure. I'm just changing Hannah's diaper."

Gideon sent his astral self through the ether, materializing in Hannah's nursery.

Aiden pulled the second tab around the baby's belly before redressing her. Gideon walked closer to the changing table and looked down at the little blue-eyed beauty.

"Hi, Uncle G," Hannah greeted telepathically.

"Hey, sweet girl," he returned out loud. "Giving your poppa a hard time?"

She smiled, and he heard her giggle in his mind. *"No."*

"Why not? You need to keep him on his toes."

"Hey," Aiden interjected. "Don't give her any ideas."

Gideon laughed at Aiden's warning. "She won't need my help, believe me."

Aiden picked his daughter up. "Great." He turned to face Gideon. "So what did you need to talk about?"

Gideon got right to the point. "I need to arrange a meeting between Margaret and Lauren. But I don't know the best way to do that. I know Margaret still thinks she's dead, so I didn't want to just show up and scare her to death."

"Actually, she knows Lauren's alive," Aiden informed him. "After that night in the warehouse, Lindsay and I went back and forth about whether or not to tell her. Jack thought we should wait—see if you were able to bring her back. But the more we discussed it, the more we thought she had the right to know. We told her a few weeks ago."

Aiden's green eyes showed his torment. "She was almost physically sick when we explained what Lauren had gone through. We warned her that it was going to be rough, that she wasn't the sweet little girl she remembered. She didn't care. She just wants her baby home. Which I can understand completely now."

"At this rate, it'll be a while before she's ready for that," Gideon confided. "She still refuses to believe anything I say. That's why I thought if I could prove her mother was alive, then just maybe she'd come to understand that everything else I've been telling her is true, too."

"I can call Margaret," Aiden offered. "Tell her that you'll be coming to see her and explain why."

"That would be great." Gideon latched on to a flicker of hope that this might actually work. "Tell her we'll be there as soon as I can bring Lauren around to the idea. It might take some time, though. Lauren is one stubborn woman. Oh, and ask her to gather any pictures or mementos she might still have. I think that could help."

"Not a problem. I'll call her now."

"Thanks, man." Gideon reveled in having the support and help of his family. Growing up, he'd had none of that, and he'd longed for it.

When Gideon opened his eyes, he took a deep breath and prepared to go face his killer witch.

5

After her quick but intense battle with Gideon, Stacia went back to her room but found she was too wound up. The way their encounter had ended had been too reminiscent of those dreams she'd had of them. And now, as a result, she felt jittery and too warm. To burn off some of her energy, she decided to take her frustrations out on her own body.

She went to the tall chest of drawers and took out a pair of yoga pants and a tank top, and then walked into the bathroom for the hair tie she'd left on the counter. After a quick change of clothes and a hastily-done ponytail, she was ready.

Back in the main part of the room, she dropped to the floor and started with ten sets of ten crunches. Then switched positions and did the same with push-ups. Since she didn't have a pull-up bar, she used the wall to do a handstand before lowering and raising her body.

A couple circuits of that, and she was hot, sweaty, and calmer than she'd been an hour before. She stepped into the shower and let the steamy heat seep into her abused muscles.

By the time she was dressed and her hair dry, another hour had passed. Her stomach told her it was time to eat.

Stacia threw her door open and headed for the kitchen. She didn't bother to hide her comings and goings anymore. What was the point? She'd also availed herself of whatever she'd wanted. Since he was holding her here, she should be entitled to it. Reaching into the cupboard, she grabbed a box of cereal. They were all good. She'd tried every one of them. But the one she went back to most were the fruity little O's.

Until she'd come here, she'd never seen or heard of any of the sugary-sweet concoctions. Growing up, breakfast had consisted of whatever she could find, and it had always been something bland and "nutritionally beneficial." At least, that's what they'd told her. She dumped the cereal and milk into a bowl and leaned against the counter and ate.

There were only a few colorful circles left bobbing around in her milk when she heard Gideon approaching. She set the bowl in the kitchen sink and turned to face him. Not sure of what his mood would be, she chose to meet the storm head-on.

He stopped on the opposite side of the counter and placed both palms flat on the surface, his cool green eyes intent. Seeing them now, she could almost forget what she'd seen in them earlier. The swirling silver had given her a start. She'd never known anyone with eyes like that.

She looked for any hint of the liquid mercury now, but he had it completely hidden.

Before she could wonder about it anymore, he spoke. "I get why you think you have to do this. You made a promise—a vow—to right a terrible wrong."

Stacia had grown leery of his always-calm demeanor. It didn't make sense that he never lost his temper. Not once had he gotten angry or looked to retaliate for anything she'd done. She'd attacked him so many times. Why wasn't he furious? She just didn't understand him. She stayed silent now, watchful.

"I appreciate that you stand by your word," he continued. "Loyalty like that is hard to come by. But in this case, you've given your allegiance to the wrong cause. You've been lied to and betrayed by the very ones to whom you've sworn your devotion."

"Why? What would they have to gain by lying to me?" Stacia

didn't know why she was even entertaining his deceit. "My mom and brother are dead. Don't you think someone should be held accountable?"

"Your brother, Steven, *is* dead, and I'm sorry for that. From what I understand, he was a great guy. But my family had nothing to do with it. He was killed in a car accident, one we *think* was orchestrated by his own father. *Your* father, Carl Donnelly."

He was consistent, she'd give him that. "My brother's name was Robby. My father is Santi—"

"No, hun." Gideon's voice softened. "Your brother was Steven Donnelly. Your father was Carl Donnelly, and your mother is Margaret Donnelly."

His tenderly-spoken words hit her harder than his anger would have, but she shook her head in denial. "No. My mother was Beth Mylos, and she was killed by the Marquands."

Gideon came around the counter towards her. When he tried to take her hands in his, she pulled away in annoyance. "Don't touch me!" Why did she feel like crying? She never cried. "I'm not going to listen to your lies any longer." She pushed her way past him and started out of the room.

She made it to the entrance of the hall when he called out to her. "I can prove to you your mother is alive."

Her gut instinct was to turn back at his words. But instead, she straightened her spine and marched out, slamming her door behind her.

Tears she refused to let fall burned behind her eyes. Why was he doing this to her? Why was he dangling the one thing she'd always wanted in front of her?

She stood looking out at the beauty of the water lapping at the shore as her mind spun.

What if—*No*, she wouldn't let his lies get to her. He was just trying to stop her from killing him. That's all it was.

But he said he could prove it, a part of her mind argued.

Stacia was reeling and didn't know what to believe anymore. Gideon had sworn never to lie to her. And not once had she ever read any deceit in his face or eyes.

Swinging around, she went into the bathroom and took a good hard look at herself in the mirror. Petite, slender build, deep red shoulder-length hair, hazel eyes. *Was* she Lauren Donnelly? Even though her father had dark hair and eyes, she'd always thought she'd gotten her coloring from her mother. From Beth. The only picture she had of her was black and white, but Stacia had always just assumed her mother's hair had been red like hers. The one time she'd asked her father about it, he'd shut her down with a stern reprimand about the uselessness of living in the past. She'd never asked again.

Had she been fooled? Brainwashed?

She didn't want to believe it. If it were true, it meant her whole life had been a lie. A brutal betrayal. One she'd completely bought into and thrived on. How could she have done that?

Just then, Gideon's words came back to her. *"At some point, that frightened child shut herself away, and another was born. One who could withstand the horror and abuse."* Is that what Stacia was? The beast created to protect Lauren?

She just didn't know, and her reflection wasn't giving up any answers. Frustrated, she turned and left the bathroom.

~~~

Two days later, she was no closer to figuring it out.

She'd completely separated herself from Gideon and his tempting offer. She'd ignored the repeated knocks on her door until he'd eventually just stopped trying.

She'd taken to sleeping for most of the day, eating and living by night. That way, she knew she wouldn't run into him.

But she'd grown tired of her self-imposed seclusion. And she'd finally decided she owed it to herself to see what this
~~~

proof was that Gideon claimed he had.

The mid-afternoon sun was shining bright when she opened her door and went in search of him.

He was sitting on the couch when she emerged from the hall. The television was on, but his attention was focused outside. When he heard her approach, he swung his head back around. She stopped a few feet away from him.

"I'm not saying I believe you, but I think I want to see your proof."

He turned the television off and rose slowly to his feet. "All right."

He said nothing of her two-day exile. "So, where is it?"

"It's not here. We'll have to go there."

"You're going to take down the spells?"

"No. I'll astral-project us there." He closed the distance between them. "But you'll need to hold my hands."

She hesitated briefly, and then ran her palms down the outside of her thighs before resting them in his.

"Let me make sure everything's ready first."

At her nod, he closed his eyes. Only moments passed when he opened them again.

"It's all set. There's just one thing I ask of you before we go. No matter what you think of me or this situation, do not hurt this woman. She's lived the last twenty years believing you to be dead. She's only recently discovered that you're alive, and now she wants nothing more than to have you back in her life. She loves you, so don't trample on that."

Stacia was a little taken aback at his request. "You know her that well?"

"No, I've never met her. I just know that you and she have lived through hell at the hands of merciless men. You both deserve to be cared for and protected now. Can you promise me you won't harm her in any way?"

Was any man truly this selfless? This gallant? Surely none

she'd ever met. She'd just have to wait and see if he really was what he seemed. "Yeah. Okay."

"Good. Ready?" he asked her.

Not trusting her voice, she nodded.

She had a brief moment of disorientation before they were standing in a different living room. Stacia looked up at Gideon. He smiled tenderly down at her before raising his gaze to focus on something over her shoulder.

She was almost afraid to turn and look. She could hear the jerky, nervous breaths of the person behind her.

Gideon's hands were still wrapped around hers. She didn't know if they needed to maintain contact, but it didn't matter; he was her anchor in more ways than one right now. She took a breath and released one of his hands. While keeping a tight grip on the other, she gradually made the turn, coming face-to-face with her past.

Stacia felt the direct hit to her heart when the blonde woman from her dreams stood before her.

"Oh God, *Lauren*." Margaret's hands trembled their way to cover her heart. "I can't believe it's you. I was so afraid to hope—terrified they'd been wrong. Oh baby, I've missed you so much."

Stacia knew this woman was supposed to be her mother? *But how*? There was no resemblance to be seen.

She remembered Gideon's warning and chose her words carefully. "Not that I doubt you believe me to be your daughter, but what makes you so sure? You have blonde hair; mine is red. You're clearly taller than I am. Your eyes are blue, where mine are hazel. Was your husband a leprechaun? That's the only thing that would account for my coloring and size."

Gideon's hand tightened on hers, telling her she hadn't chosen carefully enough.

Something she'd said must have been close to that line he'd told her not to cross. But thinking back on it, Stacia didn't know where she'd stumbled. To make up for whatever it may have been, she apologized.

"I'm sorry."

But instead of being upset at her words, Margaret let out a laugh. "Don't be. And no, your father was not a leprechaun. He was actually a big brute of a man. But I can show you where you got your looks and build from, if you'll allow me."

"Sure."

Margaret went to the fireplace and took something down from the mantel. As she approached, Stacia was curious in spite of herself. It looked like a small book of some kind.

Gideon must have explained that they wouldn't be able to touch anything here, because Margaret opened it, took out a loose photo, and held it up so she could see it.

It was an old black and white shot of a young girl. A girl that looked remarkably like Stacia. But unlike the picture of Beth Mylos, the flame that lit this woman's hair radiated off the paper.

"Who is that?" she choked out as emotion clogged her throat.

"My great-grandmother," Margaret answered fondly. "She was probably around twenty in this picture. You were the first in three generations to favor her."

Before Stacia could fully take in what she was seeing, Margaret turned to the first page of the book and angled it to show her.

"This one was taken right here in this room. It was shortly after we brought you home from the hospital. That's Steven there, holding you. He was eight when you were born. See?" Margaret lovingly ran her finger over the infant's head in the photo. "Your hair was red, right from the start."

Stacia could only nod. The love this woman had for the children captured in that moment in time was palpable.

The rest of the photos Margaret leafed through covered the first three years of Lauren's life. Rolling over, crawling, standing, walking. Every milestone she'd reached had been documented.

Reaching the final page of the album, Margaret cradled it to her chest. "These are all I had left of you. After you died—*were taken*," she corrected. "Carl took everything and destroyed it. The only reason I still have these is because I'd been putting together this album of you. I'd already pulled these out of the main boxes of photos. They were tucked in an envelope in the drawer of my desk. He didn't know he'd missed them."

Stacia didn't know what to say to her. "I'm sorry." Gideon must have felt some of her distress. He started rubbing small circles on her hand with his thumb.

All at once, it was too much. Stacia needed to go, before she crumbled as her world had just done. She spun around and pinned Gideon with pleading eyes.

He cupped her face with his free hand and shifted his gaze to Margaret. "We have to go now, but we'll be back."

"Oh. Okay." There was disappointment in her voice and a slight pause before Margaret spoke again. "I understand. We both have a lot to process right now, and as much as I want to take you into my arms, I know I'll have to wait. But please just remember one thing for me—I've never stopped loving you, Lulu."

Stacia gasped just as Gideon started the return trip back to their bodies. When she became fully aware of herself again, he was there holding her.

"What happened?" he asked her. "There at the end?"

"That name—Lulu. I remember it," she confided.

"Come on, let's sit down," he suggested, already leading her to the couch. "Do you want some water or anything?"

Her throat felt like it was on fire. "Yeah, water would be good."

An icy bottle suddenly appeared in his hand. She was a little startled at the suddenness, but at this point she didn't really care where it came from. Stacia reached for it and twisted off the cap. She swallowed three or four mouthfuls before the dryness subsided.

She put the lid back on but didn't take her eyes off the clear liquid. "I hope I didn't hurt Margaret's feelings by leaving so abruptly. It just got to be too much all of a sudden. I had to get out of there."

"She understood. I connected with her telepathically and explained," he admitted.

"Good." Stacia finally lifted her eyes to his. "Now will you help *me* to understand? Will you tell me again what happened to me?"

"You're sure?"

"Yes."

He studied her for a long moment before starting the story of her life once more.

She sat silently and listened to every detail.

"Sounds like I traded one lowlife father for another."

"Yeah, and unfortunately, your brother really is gone. He did leave a part of himself behind, though. You have a niece; her name is Hannah. She's a few months old now. She's at Marquand Manor with her mother, Lindsay."

That surprised her. "Why are they at your parent's house?"

"Well, you and your mother weren't the only ones Carl tormented." He went on to explain the sequence of events which had led Lindsay to Aiden.

"I know I've only met her once, but Margaret doesn't seem the type that could take someone's life," Stacia speculated. "I just don't see that in her."

"Knowing Carl's history and what he did, can you blame her?"

She shook her head. "No. No, I can't." She pushed off the couch and went to the windows. A war was raging in her head. "I think you deserve to know that a big part of me still wants to deny what you're saying. Even in the face of all you've told and shown me, I still feel the urge—no, the *need*—to complete my mission and kill you."

Stacia wrapped her arms around her middle. "What does that say about me? And how deeply they've corrupted me? I can't even accept a good thing when it's handed to me."

She heard movement behind her, and Gideon joined her at the window. He laid his hands on her shoulders. "Those are Stacia's thoughts. We just need to coax Lauren back out, so we can start to merge them."

"You make it sound like I have a split personality." She laughed humorlessly. There was really nothing funny about any of this. Her whole life was collapsing around her.

"In a way, you do." Gideon rubbed and kneaded her knotted muscles. "Lauren never could have handled what Stacia did. You needed her, and her ruthlessness, to protect what was inside."

"And I was...*am* ruthless." She was surprised that his touch gave her some measure of comfort. She'd never been offered any kind of compassion before. "How do I come back from that? It's still in there; I can feel it. It's pushing at me."

"It won't be a sudden change." He slid his hands down her arms, and then wrapped her in his warm embrace. "And it won't be easy. But I have it on good authority you'll come out of this just fine."

She turned in the circle of his arms. "Oh yeah? Whose?"

He smiled down at her. "The universe."

"The universe told you I'd beat this." She looked at him, doubtful. And try as she might to adapt to the feeling of his arms around her, in the end, being held that close was just too much. She backed up and put some space between them. "And how did it do that?"

"I can show you, if you'll let me." He'd picked up on her unease. "I'll have to touch you, though."

She'd learned long ago that being near enough to touch could result in getting hurt. She didn't want to leave herself that vulnerable to him. But if what he showed her proved she'd make it through the hell that her life had become, she wanted to see it.

Making her decision, she stepped within reach.

Gideon slowly brought his hands up to cradle her head. "Close your eyes," he whispered.

She held his gaze, trying to read if he'd betray her, but saw nothing except calm reassurance. Finally she did as he'd asked. A moment later, she was seeing scenes and images of herself and Gideon. Life and love. Kids and grandkids.

When the flashes stopped, Stacia opened her eyes and stared up into his. "Was that...?"

"Our future," he finished. "As soon as my powers showed back up, I started seeing that. Maybe The Powers That Be used your dreams as a way of letting you in on the secret."

Stacia didn't know what to think. Part of her screamed to end this now. To end him. His guard was down. Now would be the perfect time. *Do it. Do it now!*

But then there was another part that *so* wanted the future he'd just shown her. A family to love and be loved by. She'd locked those wants and needs away a long time ago, when she'd thought they'd have no place in her life. And here he was, offering them to her now.

Did she dare to place her trust in him and reach for what she'd seen? To believe she was Lauren Donnelly?

Somewhere in her mind, she heard a child's voice. *Yes. Do it. Believe.*

Decision made, she looked deep into Gideon's eyes. "So, in this life we have together, I won't always have the urge to kill you?"

"Oh, I think you probably will—just not for the same reasons as now," Gideon grinned. "I am a man, after all. And I've heard we can be pretty frustrating at times."

She returned his smile but really didn't understand. She didn't know anything about men. Her life had been so regimented, she hadn't been allowed interaction with anyone. At the time, she'd thought it had been for her protection, but now she knew that had not been the case.

She had a lot to learn if she and Gideon were going to have that family she saw.

Family. *Oh shit.*

"What's wrong?" Gideon read her sudden apprehension.

Lauren stepped back out of his arms. "That future won't happen. It can't."

"Why not?" His brows came together.

"Who are we kidding? Your family isn't going to accept me." There was an unfamiliar pain in her chest at the thought. "Why would they? I'm the one who robbed Amber—and countless others—of their magic. I'm the monster who oversaw the torture and imprisonment of an innocent man. I'm the one who tried to kill you, multiple times."

She brought her hand up and rubbed at the ache. "They'll never get past that."

"Hey." He approached her carefully and took hold of her hand. "They'll accept you. Do you want to know why?"

Lauren still didn't believe it was possible but nodded.

"Because we're meant to be together." Before she could decipher his intentions, he pulled her in close, lowered his head, and captured her mouth with his.

She had a moment of panic before finally giving in to the kiss. She'd only been kissed like this in her dreams, and had often wondered how the real thing would compare. There was no question. His kiss in real life far surpassed any imagined one.

When his tongue traced the line of her lips, she opened instinctively, giving him full access. She was tentative at first, but soon started to explore and experiment. He must have approved, because he groaned into her mouth and pulled her in tighter.

Long before she wanted it to end, Gideon raised his head and took a step back. His breathing was as erratic as hers.

"Wow," he said in awe. "Guess I should have seen that coming."

Lauren was still dazed and breathless. "What?"

"Just how fiery and passionate you are." He picked up a lock of her red hair and ran it through his fingers. "You do come by it naturally."

Lauren's brain cells were starting to come back online, and she remembered what they'd been talking about. "So, you think just because of this," she waved her finger in the air between them, "they'll forget everything I've done?"

"I didn't say forget. I said they would accept." He held her gaze. "There are a few people whose forgiveness you'll have to earn, though. You probably don't know this yet, but Amber and Quinn are together. And that's where you'll have to work the hardest. They know what happened to you, but there's a lot of bad blood between the three of you."

Her actions against them had been barbaric, especially to Quinn. So if she truly wanted a chance at this new life, she'd have to do her part in making up for what she'd done.

She looked up at Gideon. "Okay. So where do we go from here?"

Gideon took a deep breath. "To be honest, I don't know."

"What? The most powerful witch in two centuries doesn't know something?" she teased.

Gideon grinned good-naturedly and motioned her back to the couch. Once they were seated, he resumed. "I only know what The Powers That Be show me. The rest of the time, I'm as clueless as everyone else. But what I do know is that you play an integral role in my family defeating the coven once and for all."

"Me?" Lauren hadn't anticipated his response. "How could I possibly help?"

"I'm not sure yet, but wherever my visions come from made it clear that if I tried to go up against the coven without you, my family would be devastated by the losses we would suffer. I had to find and help you first. That would be the only way we'd make it out alive."

"I have no idea what that could possibly be." She racked her brain trying to remember if she'd ever heard anything about this group of men. "The only time I've ever heard the word 'coven' was in relation to your family. My fath—" She stopped and took a breath. "Santino didn't really confide in me. It was all about the training."

Gideon was silent as he thought it over. "I think it may be time for all of us to come together, combine all our knowledge. It's going to take some planning, though. Between the coven, Mylos, and this uncle character, we have too many people out there looking for us."

Lauren's heart pounded in her chest. The prospect of being hunted didn't intimidate her nearly as much as the idea of a reunion with all the Marquands. "You want to have a family meeting. With everyone."

Gideon reached out and took her hand in his. "I know the thought of seeing them again has you worried. But I don't think there's any other option at this point. I've been keeping tabs on what they've discovered, which is how I was able to find you, but that's not enough anymore. This confrontation with the coven is coming sooner than we think. We need all the information we can get. And we need to figure out what it is you know."

Lauren still wasn't sure this was a good idea. The last time they'd all been together, she'd been trying to kill them. It didn't matter that she'd thought she'd been punishing those who had killed her family. Attacking someone like that wasn't something that would be easy to forgive or forget, no matter what Gideon said.

Lauren hated the thought of going in there blind, but she had no other choice. She just hoped there would be no bloodshed when she was put into the same room as Amber and Quinn. She started listening again when Gideon began to work through the details.

"I think it will be better if we go there," he told her. "It's time. We need to finish this."

6

They decided to leave the following morning. Gideon conjured a suitcase and travel bag for her to pack the clothes and toiletries from her room.

He knew she was extremely nervous about seeing his family, but he couldn't delay this any longer. The time had come. This was the next step they needed to take before battling the coven.

While she was packing, Gideon had preparations of his own to make. If he wanted to keep the house hidden from his enemies, it would need to be protected while they were gone. He'd have to reinforce the cloaking spell, and for that he needed a few things.

Going into the library, he stopped in front of the left-hand bookcase. Reaching up, Gideon pressed a button on the side wall of the top shelf. On silent runners, the whole cabinet slid sideways, revealing a hidden chamber. All of his magical stock was in this room. Books, ingredients, tools, jars, herbs. Everything he'd gathered over the last thirty years.

Collecting what he needed, he turned to the work bench and started grinding and mixing.

"Holy hell," Lauren exclaimed from the doorway a short time later. "You've got quite the setup in here."

Gideon looked up and smiled. He glanced around the room and saw it from her perspective. "Yeah. I guess I do."

She stepped in. "I can see why you kept this a secret. What

I wouldn't have given to get my hands on some of this a couple of days ago. There's still a part of me that wants to do that, you know," she admitted. "My inner Stacia still wants the upper hand. She's thinking about all the potions she could make to take you out."

Gideon heard the truth in her words. "Well, it's a good thing she's not in control anymore." He caught her eye. "If she had been, you never would have known this was here."

"Yeah, I kind of figured that." Lauren looked down at the work top. "How can you be sure she won't take over again? All of this is really new and still a pretty big temptation for her. Lauren's resurrection happened only a couple of hours ago."

"That may be," he agreed, finishing up his work. "But in her own way, Lauren is every bit as strong as Stacia."

"But what if she rears her ugly head while we're at your family's home? What if something triggers those more...base instincts? I don't think you realize what Stacia—what *I*—am capable of."

"I think I, more than anyone, know what you can do." He walked around the table to take her hands in his. "But I also know why you thought you had to do those things." Gideon grasped the sleeve of her shirt and started to push it up. Lauren caught it and pulled it back down before her scars could show.

His brows snapped together at her reaction. "Lauren?"

"Now that I know exactly what these mean, I can't bear to look at them." She wrapped her arms around her middle. "I just accepted what they did to me. I thought I deserved it because I wasn't being a good student, a good daughter."

Gideon lifted her chin with his finger. "You didn't deserve anything those bastards did to you. None of it was ever your fault. You did what you had to do to survive."

She tipped her head out of his reach and walked around the table, running her hands over the items he'd pulled out.

"Quinn never quit fighting," she said in almost a whisper,

avoiding his gaze. "No matter what we did to him. A lot of it was before my time, but I was told he fought from the moment he was brought in. He never stopped. He was able to escape, because he never gave in."

Gideon turned and placed his hands flat on the work surface. He took a solid hold on his temper and forced out a tone of calm. His anger was the last thing she needed right now.

"Quinn wasn't three years old when they took him. He wasn't a frightened little girl who had just been ripped from her mother's arms. No one...not one person on this fucking earth could have done any better than you did. You survived."

Gideon decided a distraction was needed. "Do you want to help me finish this, and then we can get some dinner?"

Some of the tension in her shoulders relaxed. "What are you doing?"

He reached out and picked up the mixture he'd put together. "I was going to reinforce the cloaking spell I put on the cabin. I like this place, and I want it to still be here when I get back. To do that, I need to keep it out of sight from my enemies."

"Yeah. Just tell me what to do."

~~~

Half an hour later, they were standing in the kitchen deciding on something to eat.

"Is there something you've got a taste for?" Gideon asked her.

The first thing that popped into Lauren's mind was that burger he'd made the first day she'd been there. The smell of it had haunted her since.

"Would you mind doing those burgers again? They smelled amazing." She grinned sheepishly at him. "I've regretted wasting that first one from the moment I pitched it at the wall."

Gideon laughed and went to the refrigerator. "You should
~~~

have said something. I would have made you another."

"Up until a few hours ago, I wouldn't have asked you to spit on me if I were on fire. It was the principle of the thing."

"Yeah. Okay." He pulled out some ground beef, an onion, lettuce, tomato, and cheese. He set the onion and tomato on the counter and grinned at her. "Can I trust you with a knife long enough to slice these up?"

"I'll try to control myself," Lauren teased and selected a blade from the block. The knife brought to mind something she'd been wondering about. "I've wanted to ask...the instant-healing thing. Is that a part of you being this Super Witch?"

Gideon added salt and pepper and a few other things to the meat. "Yeah. Though I wish I'd had it growing up. Would have saved me a couple of summers spent in a cast."

"Uh-oh, what happened?" she asked. Slicing vegetables was new to her. Usually when she had a knife in her hand, it was to cut something else.

"Just kid stuff." He started to form the beef into patties. "There was this one boy in one of the group homes I lived in. He and I wanted to see how far up this tree we could get. Well, needless to say, he won because about halfway up, I lost my grip and fell to the ground. Busted my arm."

He set the two burgers aside to get the grill pan going. "Six weeks of no swimming, and no ball games."

Finished, Lauren set the knife down and looked over at Gideon. "You grew up in a group home?"

"A few, yeah."

"I guess I never thought about where you'd been all those years." She remembered he'd only been two the night they'd disappeared. They had that in common, being taken from loved ones at such an early age. "What happened to you after that night the coven attacked?"

Through the rest of the dinner preparations, Gideon explained what his early life had been like.

"And you remember everything that happened that night?" Lauren stopped setting the table to look at him.

"Everything," Gideon confirmed, bringing the food over. "From the sounds of the attack, to the fear of our nanny as she whisked us out of there."

"That must have been a heavy burden for you."

"It prepared me." Gideon sat and she followed suit. "I was able to take that time to learn about magic and how to protect myself. I wasn't at the same disadvantage as Marissa and Aiden had been. They were completely blindsided when their powers came back."

"Did you ever try to find them, to warn them about what was coming?"

"I did. But by the time I was old enough to start searching, so much time had gone by that there was no way for me to find them. Until my powers returned, I hadn't even known if they'd made it through that night. Maria was in bad shape, Marissa was only a few weeks old, and Aiden was hurt and locked in his car seat. After I was taken away by that couple, I never knew what happened to them."

"What *did* happen?"

"Maria eventually woke up, but she was hurt severely. Head injury. She had just enough left in her to leave Aiden and Marissa where they would be taken care of. She dropped him off at the nearest hospital because of his wound, and my sister was left on the steps of a church. She was raised in an orphanage there."

"I never knew any of that," she admitted. "They only said that once the old—" Lauren winced. "Sorry. That once your grandmother died, the spells she'd used to hide you from us would be lifted. Once she was gone, you'd be vulnerable, and we could finally take our revenge."

"When she died, we were left exposed. But I had enough knowledge to get myself out of sight, which kept me out of reach of you and your...for lack of a better word...uncle."

"It was my mission to find you and kill you. That's why they had me gathering all that power." Lauren picked up her hamburger and took a big bite. All other thoughts left her brain. "Oh my God, this is so good." She spent a few bites just savoring it. "How did you learn to cook like this?"

"Trial and error." He smiled at her obvious enjoyment. "It was either learn or starve. And if I was going to learn, it had better taste good when I was done."

The rest of the meal passed with casual conversation. Lauren was relaxed and more at ease than she'd been in a while.

"Since you cooked, I'll clean up," she told Gideon.

"Thank you. That will give me time to pack up what I want to take tomorrow."

Lauren cleared the table and drew a sink full of hot, soapy water. She plunged her hands down into it and just enjoyed the mundane act of washing dishes. Periodically, she would look out the window over the sink and take in the beauty of the property Gideon had chosen.

She couldn't remember ever being able to take pleasure in the simple things. Up until Gideon had pulled her out of that warehouse, her life had been highly disciplined and strictly controlled.

She looked down at the chef's knife in her hand. Most of her days had been devoted to training hand-to-hand with weapons much like this one. She'd spent many hours with a blade at the ready, sparring with her trainers. If she were cut, it only meant she needed to try harder and be more diligent.

Well, not anymore. Lauren turned her thoughts to the future Gideon had shown her. She was lost to all but that when a sound behind her caught her off-guard. Even before the command from her brain was given, she spun quickly and threw the knife in one smooth motion.

By the time she realized what she'd done, it was too late.

Her target had been acquired, and the weapon flew true.

The only thing that saved Gideon was his fast reflexes and his innate power. As he'd done before, the blade stopped mid-air, right in front of him. Reaching up, he plucked it from where it was suspended. He studied it for a moment and then brought it back to her.

"You missed a little chunk of onion." He pointed to the side of it. "Right here."

Lauren realized just how hard it was going to be to change. She took it back wordlessly and dropped it in the sink. She couldn't look at him.

"Hey." Gideon grasped her arm. "Did you think all of that would just go away instantly? Twenty years' worth of conditioning is going to be hard to counter."

She swung her gaze up to his. "I could have killed you." The thought of a knife sticking out of his chest used to bring her pleasure. Now it made her sick.

Gideon grinned at her. "You haven't yet, and how many times have you tried now?"

"This isn't funny." But the humor in his eyes relieved some of the tension she was feeling.

"My personal favorite was the hunk of picture frame." He pulled her fully into his arms. "Nice ingenuity there."

It was getting easier to accept the feeling of his arms around her. "I thought so." Lauren's thoughts turned serious again. She looked up into his eyes. "What if something like this happens with your family? What if one of them startles me, and my instincts take over? I'm sure not all of them can halt a blade in midair like you can."

Gideon reached up and brushed her hair off her shoulder. "Most of my family does a pretty good job of protecting themselves. But if it would ease your fears, we can put some precautions in place until you feel better in control of Stacia's more…violent tendencies."

Lauren hated that this whole other side of her was so volatile and such a potential danger to others. It would probably be better if she didn't go. That was the only way she knew for sure she wouldn't hurt anyone.

"I know what's floating around in that pretty head," Gideon interrupted. "We both know you need to be there. There's something buried in your subconscious that will help us to defeat the coven."

"I still don't know what that is," she reminded him. "And neither do you."

Gideon smiled. "We'll figure it out."

Lauren took a deep breath and rested her head against his chest. She listened to the steady beat of his heart while she made her decision.

She closed her eyes and steeled herself, strengthening her resolve. "Okay," she breathed out, "I'll do it."

Ready or not, Marquands, here I come.

7

That night after Lauren went to bed, Gideon thought it better to warn his family of their arrival in the morning.

Standing at his bedroom window, Gideon closed his eyes and sent his astral form to the one person he knew would be most affected by Stacia walking into their midst tomorrow.

Quinn Harrison. The man held captive, tortured, and left to die by her order.

As luck would have it, Gideon found Quinn in the car, alone. He popped into the passenger seat.

Quinn swore and swerved over the center line of the road, the blare of horn from the oncoming car loud in their ears.

Once the vehicle was righted, Quinn looked over at him. Gideon saw the recognition immediately. "Gideon, damn it. Now I understand why Jack wants to shoot you every time you do that. A little warning next time?"

Gideon grinned. "Hey, he's marrying my sister. If I can't torment him, who can?"

"I take it there was something you wanted to talk to me about?" Quinn gave him a quick glance before returning his focus to the road.

"Yeah. There is." Now that he was here, Gideon didn't really know where to start. How was he supposed to ask the person who'd been used and made to suffer, to accept the person who'd done the damage?

"Let me save you some trouble," Quinn offered. "I take it this has something to do with Stacia. Sorry, *Lauren*," he corrected. "Marissa told us what she saw when she'd touched her. I've been trying to separate them in my head, but it isn't easy."

"I understand." Gideon did, completely. "I just wanted to give you a heads-up. She and I will be coming to the manor in the morning. She's dreading it, but we need her."

Quinn just drove, not saying anything.

"She hates what she was made to do to you," Gideon told him.

"It wasn't real fun on my end, either."

"I could never ask you to forgive what was done, but I think she needs you."

That brought Quinn out of his brooding silence. "Why the hell would she need *me*?"

"Once she learned the truth," Gideon tried to explain, "once she realized what had been done to her, she started feeling ashamed that she hadn't fought harder in the beginning. Seeing as how she was also taken, she holds herself up to your standard. She knows how you battled them every step of the way. You fought until the day you escaped."

Gideon glanced down at the raised ridges on Quinn's forearm. "She looks at her scars as a mark of weakness now…because she didn't resist as you did."

"She was three fucking years old," Quinn gritted out. "Of course she couldn't hold out against them. I was twenty, and even I had days I barely made it through."

"I've told her that. She pretends like she believes me, but I've seen how she's started covering her arms and chest now. I think it would go a long way towards helping her come to terms with it if she could sit and talk with you."

Gideon went on before Quinn could respond. "I haven't said anything to her about this, and I won't push. But I'd like you to think about it."

He sat and waited for Quinn to make his decision. When the car slowed, Gideon noticed they were nearing Marquand Manor.

Quinn pulled around to the side where the garage doors were and put the car in park. He shut it off and turned to face Gideon.

"Yeah, I'll think about it."

"There's one more thing," Gideon told him. "Some of Stacia's more brutal responses still rear their heads once in a while. She's afraid something will happen, that she'll inadvertently hurt someone. It's a valid concern, seeing as how she chucked a knife at me when I startled her earlier tonight."

"So what can I do?"

"Just prepare the family. All those killing instincts that were drilled into her are still there. She's doing a good job of suppressing them, but like I said, in certain situations they could take hold. She wouldn't mean it; it's just how she's been trained to react."

"Yeah, I'll warn them. What time do you think you'll be in?"

"Look for us around ten a.m."

Gideon made the journey back to his body. Once there, he stripped and got into bed. Tomorrow would be an emotion-filled day for him and Lauren both. This would be the first time he'd set foot in his family home since he was rushed out of it when he was two. Like Margaret, his parents were also anxiously awaiting the day he'd return.

That day had finally come. His entire family would be reunited and whole for the first time in thirty years.

<center>~~~</center>

Gideon had been driving for about half an hour when Lauren recognized some landmarks from the maps she used to research the Marquands. "Right under everyone's noses," she acknowledged. "Sneaky."

The cabin was only about an hour away from where Gideon had found her. He'd liked the remoteness of this particular section of Burt Lake in northern Michigan, yet he was still close enough to the action to step in if he'd had to.

When he'd seen the piece of property, he'd known it was perfect. He'd bought it under the name the state of South Carolina had given him. A name no one who was looking for him would recognize. He wasn't overly concerned anyone would find it, but on the off-chance someone did, he and Lauren had reinforced the protection spells before they'd left.

"I wasn't really trying to be sneaky. I just wanted to be close in case anyone needed me. And I knew I had to be within driving distance to come for you when the time was right." He grinned over at her.

Lauren turned sideways as far as her seatbelt would let her. "How did no one find you there? I know we did everything we could to locate you. I'm assuming your family did the same when your sister and cousin came home without you."

"Yeah, they kept looking, even when I told them not to."

"So how did you stay so far under everyone's radar?"

"When that couple picked me up and took me out of state, it effectively wiped out any existence of me. By the time I was swallowed up by the welfare system of South Carolina, I had a different name."

Her brows came together. "Why? You said you remembered everything. Why didn't you just tell them your name?"

"I was two," he reminded her. "My family had been attacked. I'd been taken on the run, involved in a car crash, kidnapped, drugged repeatedly, and was abandoned by my kidnappers. By the time that police officer found me, I was traumatized. When my powers and my last level of defense disappeared, it was just too much for me to handle. I shut down; I refused to answer any questions. I wasn't the most cooperative little guy for a while."

Gideon looked over at her. "So between being out of state and having a completely new identity, it wasn't all that difficult to remain anonymous. I purchased that property using the name of record I was given when I was two."

Lauren took all that in. "Wow. You had quite an upbringing, didn't you?"

"Yup." Some of the frustration Gideon had always felt at being the cause of his family's distress slipped through. "All because of the power running through my veins."

"Gideon?" The soft tone of her question told him she'd picked up on his change of mood.

He said nothing.

"You can talk to me." She surprised him by reaching out and touching his arm. This was the first time she'd initiated physical contact, besides her attempts to kill him. "It's only fair. All my problems have been dumped in your lap."

Gideon took her offer of comfort and gave voice to his biggest regret. "Sometimes it just gets to me, knowing I'm the cause of all the troubles plaguing my family."

"How can you say that?" she asked. "You're not responsible for any of what happened."

"Aren't I?" He cast a quick look at her. "The coven attacked thirty years ago because of me. My sister and cousin became collateral damage in that mess. All these years later, and they're still trying. Marissa was recently kidnapped in an attempt to flush me out of hiding."

Gideon paused before finishing. "Amber lost her powers. And, ultimately, you and Quinn were both taken and tortured for the sole purpose of stealing my magic. Everyone around me has suffered, and for what? Because others wanted what I have. So how is it I'm not the one to blame?"

"You didn't ask for all that power, Gideon." Her tone told him she was angry on his behalf. "None of that was your fault. You were a victim in this, just as much as anyone else." She

six two. Her blue eyes shimmered with unshed tears as she waited for her son to finally return to her.

"You go," Lauren coaxed. "I'll wait here and give you guys some time."

Gideon turned to argue, but she cut him off.

"They need a few minutes alone with you. And you with them." He knew she was thinking of the reunion she would eventually have with her own mother, now that she knew the truth. "Go."

He touched her hand. "Thank you."

When he pushed his door open, his mother broke away from his father and started forward. They came together a few feet from the steps. She took his face in her hands and held him.

"Gideon," her voice trembled. "My sweet baby boy." The tears she'd been holding back trickled down her face in a silent show of relief and happiness. "You're really here." She moved her hands over his shoulders and around his neck, pulling him in close to her.

"I've missed you so much," she whispered to him.

Gideon bent and wrapped his arms around her waist. "I'm home, Mom."

He felt his father's large hand come to rest on his back. Gideon released Mia and turned to greet his father.

Ben smiled and wrapped him in a fierce hug. Gideon held on just as tight.

"Welcome home, son."

"Thanks, Dad."

His mother's hand came to rest on his arm. He stepped back and met her concerned gaze. "You've been okay? The time you've been gone? Was it..." Her words trailed off. Gideon knew she was asking how he'd grown up but was afraid to find out if it had been horrible.

"I was fine," he assured her. "I was well-cared for. I ended up out of state and grew up in a group home."

"Out of state?" There was surprise in his father's voice. "You were only two—how did that happen?"

"The night of the attack, after Maria had the wreck, I went looking for help. I fell asleep on the side of the road, and that's where this couple found me. She gave me a drink of water that made me feel funny, and I fell asleep. But instead of taking me to the police, they decided just to keep me. When I woke up, they told me they were my new parents. I threw a magical temper tantrum and they took off, scared out of their wits. After that, a cop found me, and I ended up in the foster care system."

Mia's hand went to her mouth. "My God. Did she drug you?" Her blue eyes went cold with rage. "Who was she? What was her name?"

Gideon smiled. "I never knew their names. I wasn't with them that long. And when I brought the wrath of God down on them, they didn't want to know me any longer." He faced her fully and took both of her hands. "I was fine. I promise."

"I hate that you had to go through all that." Another tear slipped out.

"Growing up the way I did gave me time to prepare," Gideon explained to her. "Since I remembered everything that had happened, I knew I would need to ready myself for what was coming. In a far-off state, with a different name, I was able to remain anonymous to train and learn."

"A different name?" Mia asked, stunned.

"Yeah. By the time the cop found me, I wasn't talking much, so they gave me a name. I grew up as Nathan Calhoun."

"That's why we could never find any trace of you," his father said. "As soon as those people picked you up, Gideon Marquand ceased to exist."

"Exactly," Gideon confirmed. "But it's time for me to step back into the light. And now that we have the last piece of the puzzle, we can put a stop to the coven once and for all."

Mia's focus shifted over his shoulder to the woman waiting in the car. "Is that her?"

There was censure in her tone.

"Yes." Gideon looked down at his mother. "Are we going to have a problem?"

"I know what she's been through," his mother told him, "and it breaks my heart that someone would have to endure that. But she's done a lot of damage to this family. You included."

Gideon started to remind Mia that none of that was Lauren's fault when she continued.

"With that being said, we're prepared to give her the benefit of the doubt. So why don't you bring her over here, so we can meet her?"

The tension that had briefly tightened Gideon's gut relaxed. He swung around and started back to where Lauren patiently waited. He opened her door, and when she was clear, closed it behind her. "My parents want to meet you."

He saw the anxiety flare in her eyes when she looked up at him, but she quickly got it under control. "It looks like it went pretty well between you three."

"Yeah, it did." He liked that she was concerned about him. "Remember, just breathe."

She inhaled deeply and released it before nodding that she was ready. Gideon guided her back to where his parents stood and made the introductions.

Lauren surprised him by stepping forward and addressing his mother. "Mrs. Marquand, I know you have no reason to like me, let alone trust me. But I wanted to tell you how very sorry I am for the part I've played in hurting your son and family."

Something flashed in his mom's eyes. Respect, maybe. "Please, call me Mia. I understand my son thinks you have some knowledge that will help us to finally be free of this dark shadow that's been hanging over us for years."

"I still don't know what it could be," Lauren told her honestly.

"I'd never heard of them until Gideon filled me in."

"Well, if Gideon says there's something," Mia stated confidently, "we'll find it."

Ben spoke up then. "Why don't we take this inside? Everyone is waiting in the library."

Lauren shot Gideon a quick glance and then nodded. It wasn't an expression one would call relaxed or happy.

He took her hand in his and gave it a squeeze. He kept hold of it even as they entered the room where his entire family waited.

8

Having grown up studying these people, Lauren took in the group gathered here. The man and woman seated at the table had to be the other Marquand twin, Conner, and his wife, Becca. The looks on their faces said they were reserving judgment on her.

Another couple sat on one of the couches. She had the exact same hair color as Gideon, that perfect middle point between their father's dark and their mother's light. This was his sister, Marissa, and the man next to her was her fiancé, Jack.

On the sofa across from them was a handsome man with jet-black hair and green eyes. This could only be Aiden. Seated with him was a petite woman with long blonde hair, the one who could only be her sister-in-law, Lindsay.

Lauren was so focused on people's faces to judge their intent towards her, she almost missed the fact that Lindsay was holding a baby. When she saw that little blonde head resting in the crook of Lindsay's elbow, Lauren's breath caught. This was her brother's daughter. Her blood.

The baby's eyes fluttered open, and Lauren could swear they zeroed in on her.

"Aunt Lauren."

Lauren gasped, drawing Gideon's attention. "What is it?"

"The baby, she…" Lauren was shocked that one so small had that kind of power and control.

Gideon smiled and swung his gaze to the child in Lindsay's arms. "She's a very strong telepath. She and I have had a few little chats."

"But she's so small," she murmured.

"That doesn't seem to be a factor for her," Gideon shared.

Lauren wanted to find out more about this little person who was her niece, but she knew now wasn't the time. Her gaze tracked to the last pair in the room. To the woman with the long black tresses and striking beauty, and the Native American man with deep blue eyes and scars that matched her own. These were the two she'd dreaded encountering most. Amber and Quinn. What she had done to them in the name of misplaced loyalty was unthinkable.

She wasn't quite sure what to say to them, and she was still trying to decide when Quinn rose and walked towards her. Lauren felt her muscles tighten in preparation for whatever he had planned. She instinctively put her defenses up.

Whatever Gideon had done to her had worked. She was able to draw on her training and skills, but she wasn't overwhelmed by Stacia's darkness. She could control it.

Quinn was now standing right in front of her, towering over her. She looked up, met his fierce gaze, and silently dared him to try something.

"Breathe," she heard Gideon in her head. *"No one is going to attack you. Give him a chance before you sic Stacia on him."*

She heard the humor in Gideon's tone, but that was easier said than done. She wouldn't blame Quinn if he wanted retribution for what had been done to him. Or Amber either, for that matter.

Lauren stood calmly and waited.

"We're all willing to give you a chance," Quinn surprised her by saying. "You and I have been through something not many could have endured. For that reason alone, we're going to wait and see how this goes." Quinn's dark blue eyes went cold. "But know this. If we see anything that suggests you're playing us, or planning to betray us in any way, remember that there are a number of witches in this house who can, and *will*, stop you. Permanently."

Lauren was more taken aback by the generosity of this group than by the threat Quinn had issued. The warning she understood. The other she did not. She'd been hoping for it, but she hadn't let herself count on it.

"I understand. Thank you for giving me this time to prove who I really am."

During the exchange, Amber had yet to say anything, and her expression was indecipherable. Lauren cast quick glances her way and wondered if the dark-haired witch agreed with their decision.

Before she could find out, Gideon's father was calling everyone's attention. He and his wife had taken a seat at the table with his brother. "Let's all sit. We might as well start compiling the information we have. Maybe whatever it is that Lauren knows will come to light."

She followed Gideon's lead and sat in one of two matching chairs. "Like I've said from the start, I don't know how much help I'll be able to give."

"Why don't we take it back to the night of the first attack?" Conner recommended. "Work our way forward. Gather together everything we know about the coven and Roanik. Maybe something will click."

Something already had as Lauren felt a jolt of recognition. Roanik. She'd heard that name before.

"You said this...this *Roanik* attacked you again, not too long ago?" Lauren's throat had gone dry. What were the chances?

"Yes. When our powers were unbound," Gideon supplied. "I was already out of sight by that point, but he sent some goons after my sister and cousin." He turned and looked at her. "I've told you all this already."

"But you never said his *name*," she pointed out.

Lauren remembered Uncle had become uncontrollably enraged over something a few months or so ago. He'd ranted of incompetence and ineptitude. That's when she'd heard him say the name Roanik.

It couldn't be a coincidence. No two people could have a name like that. And if Uncle was tied to the man who had attacked Gideon and his family, did that mean he was involved with this coven they were hunting?

Was that the connection they were looking for? Was that why she was here?

Gideon picked up on her introspection. "Lauren? What is it?"

She turned to him. "Something happened a few months ago. Uncle was beyond furious because someone had failed him. It was him. It was Roanik he was yelling about."

"Roanik worked for the man you call Uncle?" Aiden's leafy-green gazed drilled into hers as he sat forward in his seat.

Lauren nodded. "Yes."

Jack began rifling through the papers on the desk. Everyone else in the room was silent. Lauren knew something huge had just happened.

"Lauren," Jack started when he found the document he'd been searching for, "I'm going to read off some names. I want you to tell me if they're familiar to you."

"Okay," she agreed.

"Jared Howard, Davis Sutter, Alexander Mattison, Warren Newland, and Theo Zeeman."

With every name Jack listed, Lauren's heart beat a little heavier. All of those men had had a hand in her training over the last twenty years. They each carried power of some kind, and they all reported to her uncle.

"I know them." Lauren kept her eyes trained on Jack as her pulse raced. "I know all of those men. At one time or another, each was my trainer and teacher."

A shockwave rolled through the room.

Jack leaned forward. "And I'm guessing that none of them is your infamous uncle."

Lauren shook her head.

"Son of a bitch!" Aiden swore. "With Mylos, that's seven men. What are the odds that another group of seven is out to cause us trouble?"

"Next to none, I'd bet. So, the men who pulled Roanik's strings," Marissa spoke with unease in her voice, "are the same ones responsible for Lauren and Quinn's abductions. *Everything* that's happened to us, right from the beginning, can be tied back to these men. The coven has been right there, lurking in the shadows, the entire time."

"Wait a minute." Amber spoke for the first time. "The man I saw in Quinn's dream looked to be in his fifties. Unless he was an extremely early bloomer, I just don't think he was the one who gave Roanik his orders thirty years ago."

"That might not have any bearing," Jack countered. "Look at Roanik himself. He was much older than he appeared. He used all that power he stole to maintain his younger appearance."

"Uncle doesn't have any magic." Lauren was a little unnerved by how quickly every eye in the room snapped to her.

"What?" Jack asked incredulously. "Are you sure?"

"Yes," Lauren assured him. "The other six do, but not him. He *has* aged through the years, so I don't think he's doing anything special to extend his life." She paused, remembering something that had always seemed odd to her. "And I'm not sure he would, even if given the option."

"Why do you say that?" Gideon asked.

"He has...I don't know," Lauren tried to find the right words, "almost an underlying hatred for anyone with magical talent. I could see it when he'd look at us."

"Why would a man who carries such disdain for magic," Quinn put forth, "lead a group of men who possess it?"

"For what they can do for him, I'd imagine," Mia said. "We all know he's a pretty ruthless individual. I would think for him, the ends would certainly justify the means."

"And as Lindsay can attest," Aiden added, "the best way to fight magic is with magic."

"If he's not extending his own life by supernatural means," Marissa ventured, "it would be impossible for him to have been the leader when grandfather was killed. And it's a stretch that he would have been there when Roanik attacked thirty years ago. He must not have taken over until after that night."

Marissa looked over at her father and uncle. "There's a really long span of time between when your father died and when we were lost. Were there any other incidents during those years?"

"We dodged a few bullets," her father told her. "But nothing in comparison to Roanik's assault the night you were lost."

"That's when they tried for Gideon," Marissa said.

"Somehow, they discovered I was coming into the kind of power no one had seen in hundreds of years." Gideon's tone carried a hint of guilt. "I know for a fact that Roanik's orders that night were to take me alive by any means necessary."

Lauren knew this was his biggest burden and reached out to offer him comfort.

Out of the corner of her eye, she saw Amber shift in her seat. Lauren looked over and noticed something in her eyes change. Not sure of what it meant, Lauren disregarded it and brought her attention back to the conversation.

"Gideon, none of what happened was your fault." Marissa smiled softly at her brother. "The fault lies at the feet of the ones consumed with greed."

A tender look passed between Gideon and his sister. Lauren squeezed his hand to reiterate that she agreed with Marissa's sentiment.

"So the arrival of Super Witch here," Jack grinned, and Lauren sensed a lightening of Gideon's mood, "changed their plans. Instead of destroying the power like they tried to do by killing your grandfather, they wanted to *acquire* it. Three decades later, and they're back to wanting to wipe you all out of existence. I think Rissa's right. Sometime since that night, a new regime took over, led by someone who hates anyone who carries power."

"I think we need to ask ourselves," Conner interjected, "whether his focus on us is random, or is it something more personal?" Conner looked at his twin. "Maybe he has a vendetta against us in particular?"

"I guess it's always a possibility, but I can't think of any reason why that would be," Ben shrugged.

"Lauren," Jack came back to her, "do you know his real name? Anything about him?"

"He never revealed anything personal about himself; our days were just training and business as usual. And no, I've only ever known him as Uncle, although the other men always referred to him as Dominus."

"Is that his name, or is that just a title?" Aiden asked.

"It's Latin," Ben answered. "It means Ruler or Lord. Basically, they're acknowledging him as their leader."

"Okay," Jack said, pulling their focus back, "before we speculate any further, we need a game plan. First, we have to find the identity of this joker. Once we have that, we can figure out what he has against this family." He looked over at the two older couples. "If this *is* an act of revenge, somewhere along the way, he thinks the Marquands slighted him. Whether that's factual or imagined remains to be seen. But you guys need to start thinking back. If you remember anything, no matter how small, let me know."

"If this *slight* is all in his mind," Ben reasoned, "we'll never be able to figure it out."

"I know," Jack agreed. "Just give it some thought."

"We'll get right on that," Mia acknowledged. "But for now,

why don't we take a break? It's well past lunch, and Gideon and Lauren haven't even had a chance to unpack. I'll show them to their rooms, and then we can all get a bite to eat before we delve into this more."

"I think that's a good idea," Jack agreed. "We've learned a lot already, but there's still a ton we don't know." He sent a quick grin to Aiden. "And I know Aiden has to be withering away over there. He hasn't eaten in a couple of hours. That has to be a record."

Aiden smiled at Jack's ribbing. "Hey, I expend a lot of energy. I need to keep the tank full."

"None of us need to know what you do in your free time," Quinn teased as the others laughed.

Lauren watched the byplay and saw that the three younger couples had formed a strong and lasting bond. She had no doubt Gideon would fit right back in seamlessly. She wondered if she would ever find friendship like that.

She glanced at the many scars on Quinn's forearms. He wore a short-sleeved t-shirt, not bothering to cover them in any way. She knew there were many more under his shirt and wondered how he'd become so comfortable with them.

Looking down, she made sure the cotton of her own shirt covered her arms completely. She doubted she would ever be able to look at the marks and not feel ashamed at what she'd let them do to her.

Movement around the room jerked her out of her thoughts. When Gideon stood, she rose with him. He placed his hand at the small of her back, allowing her to precede him through the door. They fell in behind his mother as she led them out and up the main staircase.

"After that night you were lost," Mia said as she reached the landing and turned left down a long hallway, "we had to rebuild. We took the opportunity to make some changes. When we had the designs drawn up, we basically split the manor in half. Sophia took the upper floor of the center section, leaving each wing to her boys and their families. With this setup, even though we all live under the same roof, we have the privacy we would in our own homes."

She continued to explain. "The family sections started out with four bedrooms each, but that's grown to seven, because all of the rooms we'd designed for you kids had a Jack-and-Jill bathroom adjoining your playroom. Through the years, as Becca and I would update your rooms, we eventually changed the playrooms into additional bedrooms."

A little over midway down the corridor, she stopped in front of a dark oak door. "We never gave up that all of you would come home to us." She looked up at her son with love shimmering in her eyes. "And now, finally, you have."

She reached up and kissed his cheek. "Well, I guess I'd better show you your room then." Mia smiled and blinked back unshed tears. She reached out and turned the knob. It swung inward on silent hinges. "I already had your bags brought up. And like I said, there's another room that adjoins this one, if Lauren wants it. If you need anything else, let me know. I'll leave you two to get settled. Come down to the dining room when you're ready." She grinned. "Just follow the noise. The bigger this family gets, the louder it becomes. I love it. I've waited years for loud and crazy meals."

With that, Lauren and Gideon were left standing in the doorway of his bedroom.

"After you." Gideon held out a hand to usher her in.

As soon as she stepped over the threshold, Lauren saw both of their bags sitting on the floor. Looking around at the decidedly masculine tone of the decor, she wondered if her own mother had kept a room decorated for her. Probably not. She'd thought her child was dead all of these years, so why would she have preserved it for her? Lauren pushed away the hurt that wanted to squeeze her heart.

Thoughts of her mother made her long for another visit. She considered asking Gideon if he would take her there again. She felt stronger now and ready for a real visit. But with the coven hovering over their heads, that might not be possible.

Which brought to mind how alone and vulnerable Margaret was out there all by herself. Would Uncle or the others do anything to harm her mother? They hadn't in all these years, but Lauren hadn't known who she was then. Now that she did, she couldn't help but worry they might try to use her mother as leverage to get to her.

Panic started to rise in her chest that something might happen to Margaret before she could reunite with her again properly. She swung around to Gideon.

"I need to ask a favor," Lauren said in a rush. "Can we bring Margaret here? I'm worried that Uncle will try to hurt her because of me. Now that I know she's out there, he may try to use her against me."

"Of course," Gideon swiftly agreed. "I should have thought of that before now."

Lauren hesitated. "Do you think she'll come?"

Gideon cupped her face in his hands. "Yes, she'll come. She'll do it because *you're* here."

Lauren reached up and held his hands in hers. The urge to push him away was fading. It was getting easier to make these shows of affection. She looked up into his eyes and lost herself in the crisp, luminous green.

"Can I ask another favor?"

"Anything." He smiled down at her.

"I want to see your eyes."

His easy grin slipped a little. Would he deny knowing what she was talking about?

Just when she thought he would refuse her, the silver liquid emerged to swirl in his irises. She'd seen it briefly once before, and it had stolen her breath.

Lauren slowly raised one hand to his face. She traced his brow with her fingertip and around the ridge of his cheekbone, completely encircling the magnificent sight.

"Stunning," she murmured.

She was caught off-guard when he pulled her close and took her mouth with his. He demanded a response, and when she gave it to him, he deepened the contact even more. Her hands slid down, gripped his upper arms, and held on as he sent her world spinning.

9

Gideon knew he needed to withdraw before he completely overwhelmed her. She wasn't ready for all he had to give her yet. But at the moment, his brain didn't have command of his body.

Her request, heightened by her reaction, had his blood flowing hot and heavy. Most people who'd seen his eyes in their natural state had recoiled or stared at him in disgust. To keep from drawing too much attention to himself, he'd started using the glamour to hide the unusual display.

But Lauren had done neither of those things. When she'd looked up at him in wonder, he'd not been able to temper his need. Her absolute acceptance of something which set him apart from others was a heady thing.

Gideon finally found some control. He separated their mouths but rested his forehead against hers. Eyes closed, he took a deep breath and dropped his hands to rest at her waist. They stood panting for another moment before he pulled back to take in her beauty. Her skin was flush with passion, and her eyes were lit with heat.

Lauren took a shuddering breath. "I...um...wow." She stepped back out of his arms and ran her hands through her fiery hair.

Gideon had to fight to keep his face straight. She was utterly rattled. "Are you okay?"

"Yeah, sure." She pressed one hand to her forehead. "Wow," she repeated. "That was some kiss." Lauren brought her gaze back to his.

Gideon took a step towards her with a wicked gleam in his eyes. "That's only the beginning."

She retreated another step. "Only the…" He heard her mutter something under her breath; he swore it sounded like "yikes."

Gideon dropped his head forward and glued his eyes to the floor. It took a minute to wipe the ear-splitting grin from his face.

"We should probably unpack and get back downstairs," Gideon said, giving her a reason to retreat, once he had his mirth concealed.

"Yeah, okay."

While Lauren took her bag into the other room, Gideon unpacked what he'd brought. He was putting his last t-shirt in the drawer when she came back through the connecting door.

"I'm ready when you are."

Gideon nodded, and together they set out to retrace the route they'd taken with his mother.

"I'm guessing it has something to do with your powers? Why your eyes are that way?" Lauren asked as they walked down the hall.

He nodded. "They changed as soon as I fully regained all of my abilities. I knew you'd seen them that night. But when you didn't say anything, I figured I got the spell back up in time, that maybe you'd think it was a trick of the light or something."

"At first I did," Lauren admitted. "But the more I replayed what had happened, I knew what I'd seen was real."

Gideon thought he knew the answer, but he wanted to hear her say it. "They really don't bother you?"

"Not at all," she assured him. "But I think I understand why you use the glamour."

"Yeah, people started looking at me like I was possessed or something," he told her at the top of the stairs. "It was just easier to hide them."

"I haven't failed to notice you've hidden them again. Aren't you going to let your family see them?"

"Probably, at some point. We just have more important things to think about right now."

She stopped midway down the stairs and turned to him. He read the sincerity in her gaze. "Gideon, don't ever feel like you have to change them because of me."

Gideon leaned in and kissed her softly. "Thank you." They slowly pulled apart. "We'd better get moving. Jack was right; there's still *a lot* of information we need to dig up on the coven and its leader."

And just as his mom had said, when they got to the bottom of the stairs, they could hear the rest of the family.

He looked down at Lauren and smiled. "I'm going to take a wild guess and say you've never attended a large gathering like this for a meal."

"No, why?"

"It might be a little overwhelming at first," he warned. "Living in a group home, I've had more than a few—as my mother put it—loud and crazy meals. I just wanted to give you a heads-up before we go in."

"It's just lunch with your family," she said dismissively. "How crazy could it get?"

Famous last words, Gideon thought as he ushered her through the doorway and into chaos.

As he'd expected, multiple conversations were going on, everyone talking over the person next to them. It dimmed a little when the others noticed they'd joined them, but once seated, the volume picked right back up. Gideon turned to see Lauren's eyes widen in amazement as she tried to follow the snippets of discussion going on around her.

Gideon was barely seated when a bowl floated past them to land in his dad's outstretched hand. Beside him, Lauren nearly spit water over the table.

"Benjamin!" Mia scolded. "You could just *ask* for the dish to be passed, without having to use your powers."

"Why?" he countered with a smile. "This is faster than trying to get someone's attention."

Laughing, Gideon leaned in close to her ear. "How crazy could it get, huh?"

She looked up at him and grinned easily. "Lesson learned."

Eventually, inevitably, talk around the table turned to the coven. "So how do we figure out who this asshole is?" Aiden asked the table in general.

No one had to ask who he meant. But no one had an immediate answer, either.

"The only thing we *can* do," Jack said into the silence. "We handle it the same way we've done everything thus far. We compile as much information on these guys as we can." He turned to Lauren. "And that's where you come in. We need to go through everything you know about these men. The more we know, the easier it will be to find them and, ultimately, their leader."

Before the discussion went any further, Gideon had something to address. "If we could hold off on that for a minute, we might have another problem." All eyes turned to him. "Lauren's worried the coven might go after her mother in an attempt to control her. She asked if it was alright to bring Margaret up here."

Across the table, Lindsay gasped. "Do you really think they'd target her?" she directed at her sister-in-law.

"Knowing what I do now, I wouldn't put it past them," Lauren told her. "And Margaret's all alone and defenseless against magic."

"We'll have her brought up immediately," Ben promised.

"They won't touch her. We all love Margaret, and she'll be safe here."

Gideon saw some of the tension in Lauren's shoulders ease. "Thank you." She turned and pinned Jack with her gaze. "And I'll do anything I can to help. I'll tell you everything I know."

With lunch finished, they moved the conversation into the library to begin building files on each member of the coven.

~~~

Lauren didn't realize how much she didn't know until she tried to list out what she did.

Each man had power, but she wasn't really sure to what extent. She didn't know where they resided, because they'd always come to her. They never told her anything of a personal nature, and they always came one at a time, never allowing her to see them interact with each other.

She *was* able to provide them with a drawing of the scum who'd taken her away from her family. "Uncle" was now a full-color rendering for everyone to scrutinize.

Amber held the picture in her hand and studied it.

"What is it?" Quinn asked her.

"I thought he looked vaguely familiar when I saw him in your dream," she told him. "I still do, but I just don't understand why."

"You think you know him?" Jack inquired.

Amber shook her head. "No. There's just something about him. Around the eyes, maybe. They remind me of someone. It's driving me nuts."

While everyone was talking, Lauren took a moment to visit the restroom. Exiting the library, she crossed the hall. A few minutes later, she was on her way back when someone else came out of the library.

She looked up to see Amber standing against the doors she'd
~~~

closed behind her.

Oh, here we go.

Lauren knew this meeting had been inevitable; she'd only hoped to have had more time to figure out what to say.

"Lauren, I'd like to talk with you."

"All right." Taking a deep breath, Lauren tried to stay calm.

"The rest of my family may have been willing to give you the benefit of the doubt, but I wasn't. I needed to see for myself before I made up my mind."

"I understand."

Amber advanced slowly towards her. "I've been watching you throughout the day."

"Yes, I've noticed." Lauren had caught her scrutiny more than a few times.

"Do you want to know what I saw?" Amber crossed her arms and tilted her head slightly in question.

Lauren tried to remember what she'd been doing on those instances when Amber had been observing her. "Okay. Sure."

"I saw someone who goes all gooey over a baby. Someone who genuinely hurts for Gideon when he hurts. And I saw someone who cares about a woman she barely knows."

Amber dropped her arms to her sides. "I see a woman who is in a battle for her life. I think a few of us here can relate to having something inside of us that we can't control—something that has the potential to inflict serious damage on someone we care about. We've all had to find an inner strength to make it out whole. And so will you."

Amber paused and then added, "We'll respect your boundaries. But if you ever get tired of keeping it bottled up and want to blow off some steam, let me know." Amber grinned for the first time. "Maybe we could spar a little down in the gym."

Lauren felt another level of tension drain away. She hadn't been sure how this first encounter with Amber would go.

"I'd like that. For a long time, my whole life revolved around training. As surprising as it is to hear myself say it, I kind of miss it."

"We have an entire gym set up here. So whenever you're ready, come get me. I could use a good match." Amber gave her a sly look. "My brother refuses to work out with me. He knows I can kick his ass. And it would be nice to face off against someone other than Quinn."

Some of the stress returned at the mention of his name. Lauren hesitated, pulling at the sleeves of her shirt. "Can I ask you something?"

Amber's eyes dropped, noting the movement. "Sure."

"How did Quinn get comfortable with the marks? He's wearing a short-sleeved shirt," she said in wonder. "Knowing what caused them, I don't think I could ever do that—be that *open* about them."

Amber took a breath. "That's something you and Quinn will have to discuss, but I'll tell you this. The way he's dealt with everything that's happened to him amazes me. What would have broken other men only made him stronger."

"I broke." Lauren hadn't meant for the words to slip out and was humiliated when they did. She made a move to walk around Amber. "We'd better get ba—"

Amber took a step to the side, blocking her path to the safety of the library. "Lauren, you and Quinn may bear some of the same scars, but that's where the similarity in your situations ends. He was a street-smart punk with a 'go-fuck-yourself' attitude when they took him. You were a traumatized three-year-old little girl who'd just been ripped from the arms of her mother. No one is blaming you for not being able to withstand that kind of torment as a toddler."

Lauren was still embarrassed and wouldn't look at her until Amber softly touched her arm.

"Hey. You need to remember the most important part of this

whole mess. You're here. Both of you made it out alive. You may have used different methods to do that, but *you did it*."

Lauren didn't know what to say.

"Talk to Quinn," Amber told her. "I think it'll help."

Before Lauren could find any words, the library doors opened again, and Gideon strode out. "I wondered where you'd gone."

"I'll get back in there," Amber said. "I want to look at that drawing again. It's killing me that he looks so familiar and I can't place him."

Lauren watched as the doors closed behind Amber.

Gideon stepped up to her and ran his hand through her hair. "Everything okay?"

She wrapped her arms around his waist and buried her face in his chest, inhaling his soap-and-man scent before gazing up. "Yeah. That went better than I thought it would. After the way she was watching me all day, I thought for sure she'd light into me the first chance she got. But she didn't."

She looked over at the door Amber had disappeared through. "She also suggested I talk with Quinn."

"I think that's a good idea," Gideon agreed. "I really believe he can help you."

"I'll consider it," she offered.

"That's all I can ask." Gideon kissed her lightly.

"We'd better get back in there," she said. "I get the feeling Jack is quite the taskmaster."

And he proved that true over the next several hours. He took them through everything they knew, over and over, making sure no detail, no matter how small, was missed.

When she finally fell into bed, Lauren thought she'd sleep like the dead.

But as soon as her eyes closed, she was thrown into a nightmare of abuse, torture, and pain. She fought to get free of it, but nothing worked. She screamed and cried for a mother who never came as the young Lauren endured treatment no child should ever suffer.

Lauren wrapped her arms around her head and shrunk back into a corner of her dream.

"Aunt Lauren?"

She ignored the voice calling to her.

"Aunt Lulu?"

Lauren slowly raised her head. *"Hannah? Baby, what are you doing here? You can't be here—they'll hurt you, too. You have to leave. They can't know you're here."*

"We're trying to help you, but you have to stop now."

"Stop? Stop what?"

"You're using your magic to block your bedroom doors. You have to open them."

"No! They'll come back. I can't let them hurt me again."

"Those bad men aren't here anymore, Aunt Lulu. You have to let go of the doors, so Gideon can come in and help you. You have everyone and everything blocked out."

"If that's true, how are you here?"

"I'm little, silly. Even scared, your brain knows I won't hurt you."

Lauren heard and felt the laughter in her niece's voice. And just that little bit of humor amid the terror was enough to break through her fear to recall her magic and release the doors.

She opened her eyes at the same moment Gideon finally burst into her room. Lauren barely had time to sit up before he was there, taking her into his arms.

"Don't ever do that again," he growled. "Don't ever lock me out like that."

Lauren didn't know if the shaking she felt was him or her. But she held on either way. "I didn't know I was doing it. I'm sorry."

Just then, she noticed the group of people standing in her room. She struggled out of Gideon's hold. "What are you all doing here?"

"Every witch in the house heard your screams in their heads," Marissa told her.

"Yeah," Jack added, a little disgruntled. "And they thought even the non-witch members of the family needed to be awake, too. Thanks for that, by the way." He softened the rebuke with a warm smile.

Lauren felt awful for having woken the whole house. "I'm so sorry." She sat up against the headboard. Gideon turned and slid in next to her, never breaking contact. "I didn't realize..."

"It's okay," Mia consoled. "We're just glad you're all right now." She turned to the others. "Come on, let's all get back to bed."

The others started filing out, and soon the room was cleared but for her and Gideon. They sat side-by-side on her bed.

Lauren pulled her knees up, wrapped her arms around them, and dropped her head to rest on top, curling herself into a tight ball in protection.

Gideon's hand came up and rubbed her back. "Hey. You're not in this alone anymore. Let me help you." He was silent for a moment. "Or would you rather I go get Quinn, since we both know the origin of this particular nightmare? Would it be easier to talk to him about this?"

Lauren forced her arms to open and her legs to unfold. She turned and leaned into Gideon's warmth. "I think everyone in the house knows what caused that dream. I feel terrible about waking everyone up. I'm not telepathic. How did I even do all that?"

Gideon tucked an arm around her shoulders and pulled her in close. "I think you were in such a heightened state of distress, your powers just took over in order to protect you. When I first heard you scream, I ran to the door, but I couldn't get it open. I pounded on it, trying to wake you up, but it did no good."

Lauren glanced down at his free hand resting in his lap and noticed the swollen, bruised, and bloodied knuckles. She sat up and grabbed his hand. "Gideon! Oh, look what you did."

He lifted it to inspect the damage. "It's fine. It's already healing."

She didn't know where the urge came from, but right here, right now, it felt right. She lifted his hand to her lips and kissed each knuckle in turn.

"Lauren," Gideon murmured.

Still holding his hand in hers, she tucked it against her chest. Resting her head against his shoulder, she lifted her face and looked up at him. "Kiss me. Make me forget."

Gideon lowered his head to hers and took her mouth in a way she was beginning to crave. She met him need for need, and as the kiss deepened and grew more demanding she soon wanted more. Her body felt tight and suddenly ached for something she didn't know how to ask for.

The hand she still clutched in hers flexed. That slight movement against her breast had sensation zinging through her body. She slid his palm over her cotton-covered peak and shuddered.

Gideon pulled back, his breath warm on her face. "You're trying to kill me again, aren't you? This is just a new tactic."

Lauren didn't know what he was talking about, and she was too lost in feeling to care. She repeated the move, but this time his hand closed around her breast and gently squeezed.

Her breath stopped in her lungs. When he rolled her nipple between his fingers, Lauren gasped at the resulting pull in her lower body. She clamped her legs together, trying to ease the ache.

Gideon kissed her again, and then said in a husky voice, "Oh God, baby. We need to slow down." His actions contradicted his words as he continued to wring gasps of pleasure from her.

"Gideon, what's happening? I need..." She trailed off, not sure how to finish the sentence.

"I know, baby."

His mouth came back to hers, and his hand resumed its torturous play. She was drowning in the wonder of this new journey.

She had a moment of uncertainty when his hand left her breast and slowly slid down her body. When his searching fingers found the waistband of her panties, she instinctively squeezed her legs together.

"No, baby," he breathed against her mouth. "Open for me."

His lips descended on hers again, and she relaxed under his touch.

Lauren held her breath as he cupped her mound. The heel of his hand pushed and rubbed against her, until he slowly withdrew to slip underneath the thin layer of flimsy fabric. When his palm pressed against the juncture of her thighs once more, a finger split the folds and dipped gently inside. The dual assault had her hips tilting up to demand more.

She was still reeling when he eased out of her. Lauren craved his touch now, and when it returned and slid into her again, she gasped. He'd done something different. Her body felt full, stretched as he probed farther before retreating, only to slide deeper the next time. Little mewling sounds escaped from her throat as her hips rose to meet his thrusts.

Over and over he pushed into her until Lauren thought she would cry out from the tension tightening her body. She didn't know how much longer she could stand it. She knew something was just beyond her reach; she just didn't know how to get there. Until Gideon moved his thumb and pressed on the little nub hidden within her.

Stars burst behind Lauren's eyelids. Her breath caught in her lungs, and she swore her heart stopped as she was thrown headlong into the deep end of passion. The muscles of her inner walls spasmed and released in wave after wave of pleasure.

She was still floating when Gideon laid down beside her and pulled her close into his side. Her head was resting on his shoulder, her hand covering his wildly-beating heart.

"Gideon?"

"Shh, try to get some sleep."

As Lauren lay there, she couldn't help but notice the state his body was in. A sheen of sweat covered his bare chest and stomach, the bulge beneath the tight cotton of his shorts reminding her of one other time she'd seen him this way.

The night of her last attack. After he'd disarmed her, he'd laid on her, and she'd felt his body change, harden, as he stared down at her. His body had looked then as it did now. Something in the back of her mind told her he'd denied himself the same pleasure he'd just given her.

She raised her head to look at the man lying beside her. His other arm was raised above and tucked under his head. His eyes were closed.

"Gideon, why didn't you..."

When he opened his eyes and looked at her, she was surprised by the heat still lingering in the depths of his gaze.

"I didn't mean for that kiss to lead to so much. But once it had, I couldn't just leave you like that."

He closed his eyes again and took a deep breath.

"But what about you?"

"I'll survive." He gave a pained laugh. "Maybe."

Lauren laid her head back on his chest and thought about what he'd said. "Why didn't you want the kiss to go that far?"

Gideon rolled to his side and faced her. "I didn't want things between us to go there before you were ready. In spite of how tough your life has been, you've been pretty sheltered. Choices have always been taken away from you. I wasn't going to do the same by pushing you into something too fast."

His words touched her. "Thank you." She leaned in and kissed him softly. "And now that I know what it's all about," she grinned at him, "I'll definitely choose that again."

He hugged her to him, tucking her head beneath his chin.

"Go to sleep. You've had enough excitement for one night."

She smiled and burrowed into his warmth.

10

Gideon lay awake a long time after Lauren's breathing evened out and deepened, his thoughts returning to the moment he'd been awakened by her screams. The fear and pain he'd heard caused a gut-wrenching need to get to her. He'd flown across the floor in seconds and jerked at the doorknob, only to discover it was held tight. His way was barred.

He glanced down at his hand, completely healed now. The skin on his knuckles had been ripped and torn from beating against the solid wood panel. He remembered calling out to her, both out loud and mind-to-mind. But his telepathic abilities hadn't broken through her barriers any better than his hands had gotten through the door. Gideon had been to the point of throwing every destructive force he had at the wood, when he'd heard Hannah's little voice reaching out to Lauren.

As hard as it was, Gideon had held off and waited. It was about that time he'd sensed the rest of the family descending on Lauren's room.

He'd monitored Hannah's end of the short conversation and hadn't failed to notice she hadn't referred to him as Uncle G as she usually did. The smart little witch somehow knew that just hearing the word "uncle" might cause Lauren more pain.

Hannah had finally gotten through to her, and the door had given way. He was through it in an instant. When he'd seen Lauren, his heart had settled in his chest again instead of riding in his throat.

He'd crossed the room in a few strides, sat down next to her, and gathered her up. So great had his focus been on the woman in his arms, he'd barely noticed when his family had eventually left.

As far as what had happened after that, Gideon wanted to believe adrenaline and heightened emotions had been the cause. But he knew that wasn't true. With every kiss, every touch, he wanted her more and more. And now that he'd seen how she responded to him, and what she looked like in the throes of passion, he knew he'd have to have more of her.

He looked down to where she was curled up next to him, sleeping peacefully. They'd talked about choices. If he had his, she'd be tucked into him like this for the rest of their lives.

~~~

Gideon was dragging ass the next morning and needed caffeine, desperately. He'd watched over Lauren for the remainder of the night, determined to bring her back if her mind took her away again.

He was in the dining room, drinking his second cup of coffee, when Jack came in.

"Morning," Gideon said in greeting.

Jack crossed to the carafe and poured a cup. "How's Lauren?"

"She's good," Gideon told him. "She slept the rest of the night with no further issue."

His sister's fiancé studied him over the rim of his steaming brew. "It doesn't look like you got much."

"No," Gideon admitted. "I wanted to make sure there was no repeat of that nightmare."

"Did she talk about it at all?" Jack rounded the table, pulled out a chair, and sat down across from him.

"No, but we all know what it was about."
~~~

"Yeah, we do." Jack's gaze dropped to the liquid in his mug. "You know, I envy the magic of this family sometimes," he admitted before returning his focus to Gideon, "but not last night. From what Marissa described, Lauren's mental screams sounded like she was being skinned alive."

Jack paused, and Gideon could see he was trying to give voice to something beyond thought. "They didn't actually do that to her, did they?"

"No." He left it at that. It would be up to Lauren to decide how much she wanted them to know about her ordeal.

Jack steered the conversation to less-sensitive ground. "Margaret should be here this morning."

"That's good."

"Aiden told us you'd taken her to see her mother. How did that go?"

"It did the job," Gideon went on to explain. "Up to that point, Lauren wouldn't believe anything I told her. *Especially* that her mother was alive."

"I have to admit, I wasn't sure how well that would work," Jack confided. "Lauren doesn't look much like Margaret. Or any of them, for that matter. What convinced her?"

"Margaret had pictures of her great-grandmother ready. Lauren is her, recreated. Plus some shots of the first three years of her life. It's hard to dismiss that hair."

Jack sat forward, resting his arms on the table. He cupped both hands around his mug. "Shit. I still can't believe what a convoluted mess this is. And how long it's been going on. Whoever this fucker is, he set all this in motion the moment he took over the coven."

Before Gideon could answer, Aiden and Quinn came in. Quinn grabbed some coffee while Aiden headed straight for the buffet.

"Serious talk, huh? Well, let me get fortified first," Aiden said over his shoulder as he grabbed a plate. "We had a hard time getting Hannah back down after all the excitement. My brain is toast."

All three men watched as he heaped food high. When Gideon caught Jack's eye, they both grinned and shook their heads.

Aiden strolled back to the table and took the seat next to Gideon.

"Dude, where the hell do you put all that?" Jack asked Aiden.

Amber's brother forked in a big bite of scrambled eggs and grinned. "Just special that way."

"Yeah, you're special, all right," Quinn added as he sipped his coffee.

"I prefer to think of myself as unique." Aiden bit off the end of a piece of bacon. "And speaking of," Aiden turned to Gideon, "Mr. Super Witch. Now that you're actually here, we have a few bones to pick. What's the deal with popping in and spouting all the cryptic shit? Straight answers would have been nice once in a while. Why all the puzzles?"

Gideon laughed. "Hey, don't blame me. I only passed along what was told to me. I have no control over what The Powers That Be tell me. You're just lucky my astral power showed up shortly after my precog, or you'd still be stumbling around."

"Oh, I think we would have found our way," Jack protested. "And speaking of popping in, couldn't you have given a little warning beforehand?"

"No, I really couldn't," Gideon goaded with a smile. "It was just too much fun watching you go for your gun."

"Yeah, well—I still might shoot you." The glint of humor in Jack's eyes completely cancelled out the warning in his voice.

Between bites, Aiden brought the conversation back around. "So, back to our current problem. What do we do about the coven?"

After the night they'd all had, the brief levity had felt good. But Gideon let that slide away now and looked at each man in turn. "There's only one option. We finish them here and now.

They're done destroying lives. We find this asshole leader, and we take him out. If his followers come at us, we take them out, too. Their evil has touched too many and caused unspeakable damage. That stops now."

"How do we find them?" Quinn asked, his tone telling Gideon he was completely on board.

"We work together," Gideon told him. "We use Jack's investigative genius and Aiden's computer skills. We use premonitions, spells, dream-walking, along with any other tools available to us, whether it's normal or paranormal."

"I was giving this some thought last night after Lauren's nightmare," Jack started. "I think our best shot at finding these guys lies within Lauren herself. She may know something or remember something she's not aware of." He turned his gaze to Quinn. "Kind of like when you and Rissa worked together."

"Yeah," Quinn nodded in confirmation. "I had my doubts at first, but she was able to pick up on some pretty valuable information that I wasn't aware I'd witnessed."

Gideon knew how Marissa had used her visions to tap into Quinn's mind. It had shown her things they wouldn't have known otherwise. It could work. With one condition. "If anyone is going to be fishing around inside Lauren's head, it's going to be me."

"No question," Jack acknowledged and waited.

Her conscious mind hadn't recalled anything, but with his help, maybe her subconscious would. Gideon hated the thought of making her relive any of the time she'd spent with those barbarians, but it was the best way of uncovering more information. This wasn't going to be simple or easy, for either of them, and that was assuming he could even talk her into it.

"I'll ask her about it," he agreed, rising from his seat.

Gideon left the others and retraced his steps back to the family wing, his mind searching for a way to broach the subject with her.

Halfway down the hall, he started to hear the music. As he neared Lauren's door, it got louder. He reached out and twisted the doorknob.

She was in the middle of doing some rapid-fire push-ups. Her hair was pulled back into a bundle on the back of her head, and judging by the sweat dripping from her nose, she'd been at it for a while.

He watched her and wondered how anyone so small and delicate could be so fierce and strong. What she'd gone through should have broken her. And now he had to ask her to experience that abuse and torment again.

How could he approach someone with that kind of request? How did he ask her to go back there? He just hoped he could find the right words.

"Are you going to stand there all day and watch me?" Lauren asked, still pumping away.

"Sorry, I should have told you. There's a fully-equipped gym downstairs."

She pushed herself up and stood, picking up the water bottle from the floor as she went.

"I'd heard that," she said on a laugh before taking a long drink.

Gideon advanced into the room, closing the door behind him.

Lauren sat on the edge of the bed. She watched him while she wiped the sweat from her face and neck with a small towel. "Uh-oh. This can't be good."

He leaned a hip against a low dresser and tucked his hands into his pockets. "Jack, Aiden, Quinn, and I were talking this morning. Jack suggested a possible way to discover some clues on the members of the coven. It's worked before with Quinn, and they thought it might in this case as well."

"I can tell by your tone I'm not going to like this. So just hit me with it. What's the plan?" Her voice sounded even and steady, but the way her hands worked the towel gave away her nerves.

"We think we can learn more about them through your memories, things only your subconscious knows."

Everything about her stilled—her hands, her breathing, and Gideon could swear her heart stopped.

"No." Her voice was flat and final. "No one is traipsing through my memories."

Gideon thought he knew the root of her fears. He crossed the room in long strides and knelt down in front of her. "It would only be me," he assured her. "I would never ask you to open up like that to anyone else."

"It doesn't matter, because I'm not doing it." She pushed off the bed and away from him. "You'll just have to find another way."

Gideon stood but stayed where he was next to the bed while she fidgeted around the room. "We could do that, but doing it this way might mean finding them before they can hurt anyone else." He gentled his voice. "Lauren, it's all right. I know what they did to you."

She whirled around to face him, her eyes flashing heated sparks. "No, you don't. You may think you do, but you don't. You weren't there. I was." She slapped her hand against her chest. "I was there. For *twenty years*. And I will not relive a single moment of that for anyone's pleasure."

Gideon's formidable temper instantly spiked, but he held it with staunch restraint. "You think I ask this of you for my own *pleasure*? That I could possibly witness that and *enjoy* it? That I would put you through that kind of hell on earth again for *kicks*?"

She met his anger with plenty of her own. "Why not? If it'll get you what you want, what's the problem? The ends justify the means, right? My whole life has been about people sacrificing me for their own personal gain."

"Don't you dare compare me to those sadistic mother

She stopped and sent her thoughts back to him. *"No. I'm just a realist. She's not going to want to know me. Not after she learns what I've done, and what I let them do to me. I'm glad she's here, safe, but I think it would be better if we leave it like it is. And besides, she's got Hannah."*

"Yes, she does," Gideon agreed. *"She also has Lindsay and Aiden, and everyone else in this house. But none of them are her daughter."*

His tone was taking on a hard edge. *"A daughter she's loved and grieved for, for the last twenty years. One who she knows has been abused and hurt. She wants nothing more than to hold and protect you, because that privilege was taken away from her so very long ago."*

Lauren wiped away a tear that had fallen at Gideon's words. She was so confused. She didn't know what to do. Did she take a chance and let Margaret in? What if she rejected her? She wasn't the sweet, innocent little girl that Margaret remembered.

"Aunt Lauren." She gasped when Hannah's little voice came to her. *"We all love you. And Nana Maggie really misses you. She's upset that you were hurt. But she's sad that you might blame her."*

Lauren's brows furrowed in surprise. *"Blame her for what, sweetie?"* she asked her niece.

"For letting Carl take you away and give you to the bad men."

"Oh, God," Lauren whispered, utterly shaken that Margaret could ever believe that.

"Hey, cutie?" Gideon directed at Hannah. *"Can Aunt Lauren and I have a minute?"*

"Sure, Uncle G. Love you, Aunt Lu."

"Love you too, sweet girl." Lauren was glad this conversation was taking place in her head, because she didn't know if her voice would work past the tightness in her throat.

"Gideon?"

"I'm here, baby. What do you need from me?"

"Will you come out here?"

Between one breath and the next, he came striding through the door and over to where she stood. She turned her tear-streaked face up to his and drank in the sight of him.

"Is everyone in there?"

He reached up and wiped the moisture from her cheeks. "It's only Aiden and Lindsay with Hannah visiting with Margaret right now. But I can clear them out if you'd rather."

It did ease some of her anxiety to know the whole family wasn't there to witness her meltdown. "No. They're fine."

"You can do this," he assured her.

She took a minute to compose herself and nodded. "Okay. But stay close." They walked hand-in-hand into the room where her mother waited.

Margaret was sitting on the couch with Hannah in her arms. When she saw them enter, she stood and quickly transferred Hannah back to her mother. She started towards Lauren and stopped, unsure.

"Go to her," Gideon nudged in her mind.

Lauren crossed the last few feet that separated them. She saw fear, worry, sorrow, and pain reflected in the older woman's eyes. She knew some of the same would be evident in her own.

"Hi, Mom," Lauren murmured.

Margaret reached out and gently cupped her cheek, touching her for the first time. "My baby. My beautiful, beautiful baby."

Lauren couldn't ever remember feeling a mother's loving caress. She tilted her face into it now and soaked it in.

"If you think you can handle it, she would dearly love to hug you," Gideon whispered. *"She's afraid of pushing you too far and making you uncomfortable."*

She looked up into Margaret's watery blue eyes. "Would it be okay if I hugged you?"

Surprise and desperate need filled her mother's gaze. She

smiled and nodded. "I would love that."

Lauren hadn't expected to have an issue with the physical contact, as she and Gideon had been rapidly progressing in that arena. So she was surprised to find she was having a difficult time maintaining the embrace with her mother. She began to feel trapped, and the need to fight her way out nearly overpowered her.

One more reason to hate the vicious men who'd raised her.

She prayed Gideon was still holding their connection open as she called out to him.

"Gideon, I thought I could do this, but I can't. I don't want to upset her by freaking out."

"Hold on, baby."

He moved into her direct line of sight. As soon as her eyes met his, she marveled at what he had done. She'd told him his eyes calmed her, and now she was gazing into the swirling pools of silver and green. The panic she'd been feeling settled, and she was able to return Margaret's loving squeeze.

Margaret finally released her, and they all chose a seat. Conversation stayed pretty casual, and a short while later Aiden and Lindsay excused themselves, taking Hannah with them. By that point, Lauren had her feet back under her and didn't feel so ready to bolt.

"I have a confession," Margaret said from where she sat across from her and Gideon. "I was trying to think of some way to come up here without it feeling like I was stalking you." She smiled self-consciously. "I was already halfway packed when Ben called me."

Lauren grinned in return. "I'm glad you were able to come. And I hope you don't mind hanging out here for a little while. I would hate it if they tried to hurt you to get back at me. I'm not sure that would happen, but I didn't want to take the chance."

"I'm just happy to see you," her mother reassured her. "I can get reacquainted with my daughter and spend some time with my granddaughter. Believe me, it won't be a hardship."

Margaret's demeanor turned pensive. She looked down at her hands lying in her lap. "I'm sorry for letting Carl walk out of the house with you that day." When her blue eyes returned to Lauren, they were clouded with torment. "Why didn't I realize he had something planned? He'd never given you a thought before that. It was my job to protect you, and I failed, miserably. Why didn't I demand to see your body? There was never a funeral. I should have known. I should have looked for you. I just let him take my baby, no questions asked. I'll try to make up for that until the day I draw my last breath."

Lauren couldn't bear to have this woman blame herself. She leaned forward in her seat and held Margaret's gaze in her own. "There was no way you could have known what he was going to do. As far as looking for me, why would you have? He told you I was dead. Why would you question that? Neither one of us was to blame for what happened. We couldn't have done things any differently." Lauren remembered Amber's and Gideon's words. "And you know what? We survived. That's all that matters."

"I still hate that you had to suffer so badly. But you're right," she said as she tried to shake off some of her guilt. "We did make it. We're here now, together, so we'll concentrate on that. We'll move forward and build our relationship from here." She paused, and her voice lowered. "And maybe at some point, you can talk to me about what happened to you."

Lauren felt she owed this woman the truth. "I hope one day I can, but I may never get there. Quinn has offered to help me, since we went through some of the same things, but I just don't know yet."

"I'll accept anything you give me," Margaret told her. "I'm just so relieved you're alive and here with me now. And when those vile men are finally dealt with, we'll be able to put it all behind us." She turned her attention to Gideon. "How close are you to finding them? The sooner the threat of them is gone from my daughter's life, the better."

"We're working on it," Gideon told her. "We're all anxious to finish this."

He didn't give anything away, but Lauren knew her refusal to let him search her memories was going to slow the hunt significantly. But every time she thought about Gideon seeing what she'd been through, her stomach lurched, and a feeling of dread swamped her.

To know that she'd taken it as her due, that she'd allowed them to do those things to her, was a humiliation too great to reveal to anyone.

She wouldn't be able to stand it if she ever saw pity in his eyes when he looked at her.

Despite what she'd said in anger, she knew Gideon would never hurt her. She knew he'd do whatever he could to protect her from the pain of those moments. But she just couldn't take that chance.

Lauren became aware that they were waiting for her response. "I'm sorry, what?"

Gideon studied her carefully before repeating what he'd said. "I'm going to go meet with the others and get some plans started. You and your mom take as long as you'd like. I'll be in the library if you need anything."

Lauren watched him leave. When she brought her eyes back around to her mother, she was giving her a speculative look.

"What?"

"I feel like I stepped in something I shouldn't have," Margaret said. "When I mentioned the coven, a tension came over you and Gideon. Is everything okay?"

Lauren's first instinct was to deny but decided to take a chance with this mother/daughter relationship.

"Gideon thinks we can find the coven faster if I let him search through my memories. He believes my subconscious may remember, or may have picked up on, more than my conscious mind. He said they've done it before, and it worked."

"If it was successful the first time, why not try it again?"

Lauren paused, trying to think of what to tell her. It turned out she didn't need to.

"Ah, I think I understand," Margaret said. "You don't want him to see *exactly* what they did to you."

Lauren nodded ruefully.

Margaret took Lauren into her arms. This time there was none of the panicked desperation to get away. Lauren was able to accept the love freely given.

Her mother pulled back but still held her hands. "Is he pressuring you to do this?"

"No. I kind of freaked when he asked me, and he said we'd find another way."

"So that's what you'll do."

Lauren rose and paced a couple of feet away. "But what if someone else is hurt because I'm too afraid to do this? By refusing to try, I could be putting others in jeopardy."

"Laying yourself bare for someone is a daunting task," Margaret told her. "But I think you need to ask yourself if keeping your secret is worth the risk."

Lauren went to the window and looked out over the front lawn. Could she let him see her greatest humiliation?

Margaret came to stand behind her. "He's important to you, isn't he?"

"I'm not really sure what it is between us," Lauren told her truthfully. "He's been really careful about not pushing me. But he's shown me things...future things. Us, in years to come. Children, grandchildren. A whole life."

Margaret was silent for a moment. "These things he's showing you—are they just possibilities, or are they fact?"

Lauren turned to face her mother. "The power he wields is mind-boggling. I've come to the realization that I never stood a chance against him, even with all the power we'd stolen. Knowing that, I'm fairly certain whatever he's shown me in his visions is inevitable."

"How do you feel about that?"

Lauren thought about it for a minute before she spoke. "My entire life, I was taught one thing—revenge. The quest for it was my only goal. I never looked past that. The next thing I know, I've woken up, locked in a house with the very man it was my duty to kill. And he's telling me things I don't want to hear, let alone *believe*."

"I'm sure that was hard on you, and I'm sorry you had to go through the pain of learning you'd been lied to."

With a need to move, Lauren took a couple of steps away. "Within the span of a few days, my life flipped a hundred and eighty degrees. And then, while I'm still trying to catch up with that, Gideon shows me what my world *could* be like if I let it all go."

Margaret stayed where she was by the window but turned to follow Lauren's progress around the room. "Do you want that future for yourself?"

"I see it through the images he showed me, but I don't know how I can get there," Lauren admitted as she sat back down on the couch. "That hate-filled, vengeance-bound woman is still inside me. And kids," she gave a humorless laugh and looked up at her mother, "the thought of kids scares the crap out of me. What do I know about babies?"

Margaret went to sit next to her. She looked her straight in the eye. "You've said a lot about why you shouldn't have that future, but you still haven't answered my question. Do you *want* the future Gideon showed you?"

"Yes," Lauren finally whispered desperately.

Margaret took her hands in hers. "Then you do everything within your power to make that possible."

When Lauren didn't say anything, Margaret reached out

and ran her hand down her fiery tresses. "Go talk to Gideon. It sounds as if you and he have a lot to discuss. I'm going to go get settled in, but if you ever need to talk, I'll be here. I love you."

"Thank you," she answered back.

Lauren stayed where she was until she knew what she had to do. Once her decision was made, she went in search of Gideon.

12

Gideon and the others were deep into the hunt when he felt Lauren's presence outside the closed doors of the library. He lifted his head as she came in.

Her clear hazel eyes were sharp, her red hair swaying as she moved. She strode to the middle of the room and stopped. "I still don't like the thought of anyone prying into my mind," she said before turning and looking straight at Gideon, "but I want a chance at the future you showed me."

He felt a weight lift he hadn't been aware of bearing. He didn't realize until that moment how much he wanted those visions to come true. With her.

She swung her gaze to Jack. "And in order for that to happen, the coven has to go. So I'll allow Gideon, and Gideon only, to search for the clues you need."

"There was never any question that he'd be the one," Jack told her. "I don't know what changed your mind, but I'll just say I'm glad you did, and thank you. I know it won't be easy for either of you, and if this weren't so important, we never would have asked."

"When do you want to do this?" She sounded steady, but Gideon could see the slight tremors in her hands.

"The sooner, the better," Jack informed her.

Gideon was already gaining his feet. "I need to talk to Lauren alone for a minute."

"Okay," Jack agreed.

He waited until they were in the hall before he spoke. "I won't ask you if you're sure, because I can see that you are. I'll just ask that you trust me to protect you while we're doing this."

"I do trust you," she told him. "Or I wouldn't have agreed."

"Good, because I've given it some thought, and I want to project what I'm seeing to the others." He was ready for her objection. "Minus what's none of their business. I think the more eyes we have in this, the better chance we'll have of finding something. Especially Jack. He's a trained PI, and he'll notice things the rest of us would miss."

Gideon waited for her to think it through.

"You really think you can sort through and hold back certain things?"

"Yes," he stated simply.

She was silent for another few moments. "I can see your point." She hesitated briefly. "But how are you going to know what I want to stay private?"

"I'll be inside your mind. When we come to something you'd rather not share, just tell me."

Lauren took a deep breath and released it. "Okay."

"There's just one more thing." Gideon reached out and took her into his arms. He brought her in close and found her mouth with his. When he released her, he looked into the depths of her eyes. "You are the strongest, bravest woman I have ever met. In spite of everything you've gone through, you've managed to hold onto your heart. I guess that's something to thank Stacia for. She protected the best part of you."

She lifted her hand and trailed it over his face. He knew what she wanted and let his eyes become her touchstone.

He bent and kissed her again. They were both breathing heavily when he stopped.

"You've got some special skills, Gideon Marquand." She

grinned up at him. "I didn't think anything would be able to take my mind off of what's coming next. But between your mouth and your magical, swirling eyes, I don't have a thought in my head right now."

"You think my eyes do it for you," he teased. "Try this."

He slowly slid his hand around and down her flat stomach until he reached the area between her hip bones. Sending a little power down through his arm and into his palm, he sent a pulse straight into her core.

Lauren erupted into a climax that would have brought her to her knees if Gideon hadn't been holding her tight.

"Oh my," she said when she had her breath back. "You...just by...*wow*."

He ignored the demand of his own body and leaned down to whisper in her ear. "I've got a lot to show you."

Her pupils dilated at his words, and she gave him a sly, sultry look. "That's twice now this has been one-sided." She separated their bodies and looked pointedly at the bulge behind his fly. "We'll have to see about evening that up."

The urge to throw her over his shoulder and make a run for his bedroom nearly overwhelmed him. Gideon breathed through it, knowing they were expected back any minute.

"If everyone weren't waiting for us, I'd give you the chance right now."

She leaned up on her toes and kissed him softly. "Thank you."

He wrapped his arms around her middle. "For what?"

"For making what we're about to do a little easier."

"Just remember—if it gets too bad," he grinned at her, "me and my magical, swirling eyes are here for you."

He was glad she was still smiling when they returned to the library. He'd hated to see the fear clutching at her.

Jack glanced up from where he sat at the desk. Marissa, Lindsay, and Amber were all seated on the couch going through spell books. Quinn and Aiden were still up on the second floor gathering even more journals.

"Hey guys," Gideon addressed the two up above, "can you come down here?"

They set aside what they had in their hands and descended the spiral staircase. "What's going on?" Aiden asked.

Gideon kept his hand on Lauren's back. He needed that contact as much as she did. "I had an idea, but I wanted to discuss it with Lauren first to get her approval before I mentioned it. I believe the more eyes we have looking at this, the more information we'll gather. So I want to link you all in when I read through her mind. But given what she's endured, there will be certain things she wants to keep private, so if one of those pop up, I'll block you all from seeing it." He looked down at her. "This way, she retains some privacy, and we still have multiple people being able to search out the smaller details."

"You can do that? Feed the rest of us what you're seeing?" Jack gaped.

Gideon nodded.

"This could work." He rose and stepped out from behind the desk. "And you're right; with all of us seeing what you are, someone is bound to pick up on something to tell us who, and where, these guys are."

Lindsay leaned forward in her seat. "What do you need us to do?"

"Not much, really," Gideon told her. "Just watch and pay attention to everything."

"Are we going to be locked in the vision with you?" Marissa asked. "Or will we still be conscious and able to move?"

"It'll play out like a movie in your heads. If you can multitask, you should be fine." Gideon cast her a questioning glance. "Why?"

"I'm thinking we should all be ready with a notepad and pen to write down what we see, so that nothing gets left out or forgotten. Then afterwards, we can compare notes."

"That's a really good idea." Gideon smiled at his sister.

The next few minutes were spent shifting chairs around and gathering supplies. Once everyone was seated, Gideon looked across at Lauren and took her hands in his. "Here we go. Remember—just say the word, and the feed stops."

She took a deep breath and nodded.

Gideon closed his eyes and sank into Lauren's past.

He followed the stream back all the way to the beginning, to the day she stood on the side of a dirt road with her father and another man. Gideon took one look and knew this was the one they'd been looking for. He was the younger version of Uncle.

With no sign from Lauren, he linked the others in and began the journey that would take them through the worst years of Lauren's life.

Everyone watched as Carl Donnelly, the father who should have loved and protected her, placed her into the hands of a stranger. They heard as Carl bent down and spoke to her, "If you ever want to come home again, you will go with him, and you will do everything he tells you."

Her little head bobbed up and down, even as tears rolled down her cheeks.

Bastard, Gideon thought as she was led into another car and driven off.

Over the next four hours, they viewed one scene after another, each one worse than the last. On Lauren's order, Gideon disrupted the link almost a dozen times. As he alone viewed these memories, Gideon began to pick up on a pattern. The scenes where she took the pain and punishment as her due, when she thought herself lacking in some way for not doing what they'd asked, were what brought her the most shame. And those were what she wanted hidden from the others.

She was still holding herself against the standard Quinn had set. In her mind, she hadn't fought hard enough, or held out as long as she should have.

What she didn't realize, though, was that even in those situations, she was still fighting. Gideon had seen it in her eyes. He would have to set her straight on a few things when he got her alone. She may think she buckled and took what they dished out, but he knew for a fact that wasn't the case.

After the last and most recent memory dissolved away, Gideon eased out of her mind. He glanced over at everyone else and saw that they all looked tired from the experience, but they were writing feverishly to account for what they saw.

He brought his gaze back to Lauren and squeezed the hands he still held in his own. "You okay?"

"Yeah." She looked over to where the rest of his family sat. "You'd think they were going to have a quiz or something."

Gideon laughed softly. He was glad she was trying to keep a sense of humor through what was most likely a traumatic ordeal. "I just hope something in those notes will tell us what we need to know."

"Me, too," she agreed. "Thank you for keeping my embarrassment to a minimum."

"You had nothing to be embarrassed about."

"We both know that's not true," she told him, her eyes clouding with shame.

He let the subject drop. This wasn't where he wanted to have that conversation. He was about to get the main discussion underway when there was a knock on the door.

Gideon rose and crossed to the large double doors. When he swung them inward, he found his mother and aunt. Together they pushed a two-tiered rolling cart loaded with pizza, soda, plates, and napkins.

"We knew you all would need some food by now," Mia told him. "So we had Peter put this together." They guided the cart into the room and over near the couch.

"Mmm, that smells so good." Amber rose and went to grab

a slice.

"My favorite," Aiden added, coming over to peruse the offerings.

"What isn't?" Jack asked, giving him a teasing shove.

Aiden grinned, picked up a slice, and took a huge bite.

Gideon was actually glad for the distraction, just as he knew the others were as well. He could feel the waves of grief and sympathy rolling off of them. Normally, he could block all that out, but today they weren't so easy to quiet. His mind was in such turmoil, the barriers he relied upon weren't holding as firmly as usual.

Telepathy and empathy were among his countless talents. Having them meant he not only heard every thought, but he also felt each emotion that went with it. He'd learned pretty quickly to shield his mind from a world's worth of disorder and pain, or else get crushed underneath the weight of it all.

Sequestering himself away had kept him out of the coven's crosshairs, as well as given him the chance to build the walls which would allow him to live a normal—or somewhat normal—life.

Gideon watched as Lauren accepted a plate from his aunt and returned to her seat. He took a couple of steps back from everyone and worked on clearing his mind and strengthening his defenses. Experiencing everyone's reaction to what they'd seen wasn't going to help. He needed to be able to think and plan without it all pushing in on him.

"You okay?" Mia came over to stand next to him, handing him some food.

He took it and smiled at her. "Yeah, I'm good. Thank you."

"You're welcome. If we can't do anything else right now, we can at least make sure you all eat," she told him. "You have a lot of work ahead of you." She paused briefly, then turned her concern-filled blue eyes up to his green ones. "I hope you're not allowing the burden of this mess to rest solely on your shoulders." She took his free hand in both of hers. "You weren't the cause of what happened all those years ago. And you're not responsible for what's happening now."

Some of his surprise must have been evident on his face.

She gave him an indulgent smile. "I may not have raised you, my love, but I've been married to your father for a very long time, and this particular apple didn't fall very far. Even at two, that was abundantly clear. It's not hard to guess how you feel, because your father fully believes that everything that happened the night Roanik attacked was his fault. He thinks if we'd known about your powers sooner, we would have been able to protect you better. So you see? You're not the only one to assume the guilt."

Gideon didn't know what to say.

"And also like your dear old dad, I know you won't listen when I tell you that feeling that way is pointless. So I'll just tell you as I told him—you are loved completely and unconditionally. No one blames you for anything." Her face took on a determined, pointed expression, and her voice held a note of bitterness. "The ones accountable for all the pain and heartache this family has suffered are those seven men. *And no one else.*"

She leaned up and kissed his cheek, her features softening. "Now find them, sweetheart, so they can regret ever messing with the Marquands."

Gideon watched her turn and walk over to where Becca was standing. Together they collected the empty plates and then left them to do as she'd instructed.

Lauren slowly approached. "Now I'll ask you. Are you okay? That looked like a pretty serious conversation with your mom."

He smiled down at her. "Yeah, it was. But I think it helped."

She reached up and touched his face. He grinned and dropped the glamour. She returned the smile. He enjoyed the intimacy of sharing this with her. It had become something for just the two of them, a way to be closer, even among the many people filling the library.

"Hey," Aiden called, "if you two are done over there, you may remember we've got some work to do."

Gideon replaced the spell before looking over at the others. "We were all just waiting for *Sir Eats-A-Lot* to finish stuffing his face," he teased.

The easy camaraderie remained as they gathered to discover what clues they'd been able to identify.

"Okay," Jack began. "We'll take this one memory at a time, starting with the first." He consulted his notes. "I think the biggest thing that stood out to me was the coven leader's car. As they drove up, I was able to get a partial on the plate. I want to try to run that with the make and model and see what pops. It's a long shot—the car was probably registered to Nemesio, but it may still give us a lead."

Amber spoke up next. "I concentrated solely on him. I'm still trying to figure out why he looks so familiar. It was harder to see in his younger self, but there is definitely something around the eyes that strikes a chord in me. I can't disregard it until I know."

"It might be a good idea to show your parents the sketch of him," Lindsay said. "If he's familiar to you, they may see it too and have a better idea of why."

"I'll do that," Amber agreed, "once we're done here."

"Anyone else?" Jack asked. Heads around the room shook. "All right, let's move on to the next."

And that's how it went, late into the night. When they finally called a halt to the evening, they had a pretty solid list of things to check out. A snippet of a phone conversation overheard, telling someone to take something to a certain address, a quick look at a newspaper showing the date and city, an unguarded moment between Mylos and the leader when they thought little ears wouldn't understand. And of all things, one of the men ordering take-out to be delivered to his home.

All of these things would be thoroughly investigated. But later. Right now, they were all running on fumes.

As they ascended the stairs, they felt good about what they'd found. They agreed to meet up again the following morning. At the top, Aiden, Lindsay, Amber, and Quinn split off to the right, headed to their wing of the house. Gideon, Lauren, Marissa, and Jack turned left.

Midway down the hall, they stopped outside Marissa's room and said good night. Gideon and Lauren continued on.

A few more doors down, they both entered into Gideon's room. Lauren went directly to the seating area and fell down onto the couch, resting her head against the back.

"We learned more than I thought we would," she admitted on a huge yawn. "Oh, sorry." She rubbed her tired eyes. "I didn't think we'd get anything near what we did. I'm glad I decided to do it."

Gideon settled into the corner of the sofa and pulled her closer until she was reclined against him. He laid his head back and let out a weary breath.

"We'll just have to wait and see where it leads. Hopefully, something will point to a location of at least one of the seven." A jaw-cracking yawn caught him by surprise. No sleep the night before and a late night tonight meant he was beyond exhausted.

His eyes felt like someone had thrown a handful of sand into them. Gideon closed them for a minute to alleviate the scratchiness.

When he opened them again, it was obvious time had passed. He was pleased to see Lauren still stretched out across his lap, sound asleep. He conjured a blanket, and once they were both covered he sighed and closed his eyes again.

13

Lauren awoke to feather-light kisses covering her cheek and neck. She opened an eye just enough to see Gideon leaning over her, smiling.

"Morning." The low, deep breath of his voice brushed against her ear.

Her heart took a long, slow beat. "What are you doing?" Her voice was rough from sleep and what he was doing to her.

"I woke up," he kissed the lobe of her ear, "and you looked," the hollow beneath, "so peaceful and beautiful," where her neck met her shoulder, "sleeping in my arms."

"So you thought you'd wake me up?" She tried to sound put upon, but the purr that rolled out of her throat gave away her true thoughts. She slowly came to realize she wasn't in her bed. "We fell asleep on the couch."

Lauren heard and felt the hum of his affirmative answer along her neck.

Sometime during the night, they'd ended up lying back to front on the small confines of the couch. She turned in his arms to lie facing him. He took advantage and laid his lips on hers, settling in for a proper, mind-blowing kiss.

Fuzzy sleep-brain instantly cleared, to be replaced with heightened senses and heated blood pumping. Lauren felt a pull deep inside and knew it for what it was now. Arousal. She wrapped her arm around Gideon's neck and ran her hand up through his hair. She let the soft strands slide between her fingers.

His hand came around her waist and stopped in the middle of her back to bring her even closer into his heat. She tipped her hips into his, trying to ease some of the building pressure. Gideon slid his hand down over her butt and continued lower until he reached the back of her knee. He pulled her leg up and over until it rested on his hip.

When he ground his pelvis into her, Lauren gasped at the feel of him between her legs. Even though they were both still fully clothed, she was aware of the size and shape of him pressing against her.

He groaned, then rose up to look down at her. His eyes were heated, swirling silver orbs. "I want you. Now." His voice was gruff and serious. "If you're not sure about this, you'd better say something. If this goes any further, I won't be able to stop."

Lauren didn't want it to stop. She wanted everything he had to give her. "Now."

She gasped in surprise when in the next moment they were standing next to the bed. "What—" He'd teleported them across the room.

"Your first time will *not* be on a couch." He cupped both hands under her jaw and brought her in. This kiss was no less smoldering for as gentle as it was. Her hands found his chest, and her fingers curled into his shirt to hold on.

She was breathless when he straightened and dropped his hands to her waist. He slowly pulled the bottom of her shirt up. The first time she felt his hands on the bare skin of her stomach, she drew in a breath.

"It's like touching silk," he whispered.

She raised her arms, so he could sweep it up and over her head. Standing before him naked to the waist, there was a brief thought about the scars that littered her torso. Lauren pushed away the feelings of shame and embarrassment and instead concentrated on the heated way he was looking at her. She used that to bolster her courage and reached out to grasp the hem of his t-shirt. When it was gone, she lost herself in running her fingers through the light dusting of hair on his chest. His skin was soft, but under that was a solid wall of muscle.

Her nails trailed lightly down his chest and across his stomach to stop at where his jeans rode low on his hips. She brought her gaze up to his for a moment before returning her attention to the closure.

The pop of the button and the rasp of the zipper seemed loud to her ears. No other sound could be heard in the room. It was almost as if they were both holding their breath in anticipation.

Once the fly lay open, she lost her nerve. She couldn't take that next step and free him. Reading her hesitation, he bent and captured her mouth with his. He wrapped one arm around her middle, and with the other lowered them to the bed.

He spent the next few minutes wiping every thought right out of her mind. She was still reeling when he rose up and went to work on the rest of her clothes. He had everything off and was stretched out over her again before she could become self-conscious of her nudity.

He kissed and licked every square inch of her until she was writhing and begging beneath him. She knew where they were headed and wanted to share it with him.

"Gideon," she panted out. "Please."

Before her next breath, she felt the warmth of skin and the light texture of hair from his legs against her smooth ones. His pants had disappeared.

"That's an extremely convenient power to have."

Gideon grinned down at her. "Isn't it, though?"

He used his knee to make room for himself and nestled into the V of her thighs. When she felt his shaft against her for the first time, she shivered. He reached down between their bodies, and then his hips flexed. Lauren felt him press against her entrance and slip in. Her pelvis made small movements with no command from her.

"Easy," Gideon murmured. "Let's take this slow."

He put his words into motion and gently pushed into her before pulling back out. Each thrust sent him that much farther inside of her. Until he bumped against the thin barrier of her virginity.

"Look at me," he whispered softly. "Just watch my eyes."

Lauren was impatient and wanted to spur him forward, but she looked up into the silver depths. She felt him withdraw and then thrust forward with more force then he'd used before.

Lauren felt a quick snap of pain. She stiffened and tried to back away from him.

"Shhh, it's okay. That was it." He held perfectly still, allowing her body to adjust to him. He started kissing her again, planting small open-mouthed kisses along her jaw, down her throat, and across the top of her shoulder. Everywhere he could reach and still remain pinned against her.

The burn slowly receded, and Lauren's body remembered how it had felt before. The need, the want, the search for fulfillment. She tentatively tilted her hips into his, waiting for the burn to return, but it didn't.

That must have been the sign he was waiting for. He began a leisurely pace of thrust and retreat. He'd pull almost completely out before pushing back in until he was as deep as he could go.

She thought she'd go mad until, finally, he picked up the pace. His breathing was as short and shallow as hers. It wasn't too much longer when she began to feel the tightening in her lower body.

Gideon plunged deep, and she erupted into spasms of pleasure. Lauren was still lost in the throes of sensation when Gideon stiffened above her, finding his own release.

They lay breathing heavily. The weight of him on her felt incredible. And long before she was ready, he rolled off to the side. She would have protested, except that he pulled her into his arms and settled her cheek against his chest.

"You okay?" he asked gently.

"Better than, actually." She tipped her head back to grin at him. "I usually hate working out in the mornings, but that's one I wouldn't mind trying every day."

He gave her ass a pinch and made her laugh as she tried to squirm away from him. He just pulled her in and kissed her.

Her brain was going all mushy again when he let her come up for air. "Well, any time you feel like working out, just let me know."

"*Any* time?"

Gideon slid his hand down her back and pressed his reawakening member against her. "A little perk of my power. Injuries aren't the only part of me that recovers quickly."

"So we can...?"

"Oh yeah." In one fluid move, he was on top of her again and sliding deep.

~~~

An hour later, Lauren was sitting on the edge of her bed tying her shoe when Gideon came out of the bathroom. He sat down next to her.

"Before we head down, there's something I want to talk to you about."

"Okay." Whatever it was, it sounded serious. "What's the matter?"

"It's about the memories you had me hide from the others yesterday."

Lauren brought her second foot up and proceeded to tie it, so she wouldn't have to look at him. "What about them?"

"I saw something. Something I think you need to look at a little more clearly."
~~~

She rose up and stalked a few paces away. "Believe me, I see them clearly enough. I lived them. I know exactly how they go. Don't you think once was bad enough? I'd really like to just forget them now." She turned and pleaded with him. "Look. We've had an amazing morning. Why ruin it? Can't we just leave all that in the past where it belongs?"

Gideon came to where she was standing and took her hands in his. "I honestly think you need to do this. Please. Let me show you what *I* saw."

The thought of going back there again was almost more than she could stomach, but the pleading note in his tone and the sincerity in his eyes swayed her. He wasn't doing this to hurt her. He truly believed there was something more for her to see.

"All right."

"Close your eyes."

Lauren took one more moment of strength from Gideon and did as he asked. And found herself back in time to one of the moments that humiliated her most.

She didn't want to witness any part of this again, but she did it because she knew it meant a lot to him. She watched as her fifteen-year-old self stood placidly and allowed them to beat her over and over with a long, thin rod. This particular punishment was for not having bested her opponent in the sparring ring.

"Don't look at what's being done to you," she heard Gideon's voice in her head. *"Watch your face. Look at your eyes."*

Lauren blocked out everything but her younger face. With each lash, her eyes would close and her lips would tighten. A small gasp would escape between them. With the next strike, her eyes again shut, but when they opened, the observing Lauren was taken aback.

The anger and resentment in her teenage eyes was clear and bright. Now, with every swing of the rod, the rage grew, and she uttered no more sounds.

"You didn't just *take it. You were fighting,"* Gideon shared.

"I was a teenager. I was defiant."

"Just watch."

Gideon took her through each memory she'd hidden from the rest of his family. And in every one, he showed her the same thing.

"You did what you had to do to get through it. You played their game, but you never gave up. That fight was—and is—still inside of you."

He brought them back to the present. "I said it before, and I'll say it again. You have *nothing* to be ashamed of."

After seeing those memories through his eyes, it was a little easier for her to believe.

"But why don't I remember feeling any of that rage at what they did to me?"

"Probably because you knew that to make it through you had to suppress all of that. Make yourself be what they wanted. But in those moments of pain and stress, your true feelings came to the surface."

The weight of her disgrace lessened. She hadn't given in, or given up. If Gideon hadn't forced her to look more closely at herself, she would have gone on carrying that burden. She still wished that she'd been able to fight like Quinn had, but she'd done what she'd been able.

And she'd survived. Survived to reunite with her mother. Survived to meet Gideon. Survived to be a part of taking down the ones who had hurt her.

She walked into Gideon's arms, cupped his face in her hands, and leaned up to kiss him. "Thank you."

He wrapped his strong arms around her and pulled her in. "You're welcome. I hated knowing you felt that way about yourself."

"I still wish I could have done more," she went on, "but I know I did what I could."

Gideon kissed her lightly. "Have you given any more thought to talking with Quinn? I really think it would help."

She *had* been thinking about that more and more. If anyone understood the feelings she was having, he would. And she could ask him how he'd been able to accept the marks left from his encounter with evil.

"I think I might, actually."

"That's good to hear." He gave her a smacking kiss. "Now, we'd better get downstairs before Aiden eats everything."

Lauren's spirit felt lighter as they made their way down to the dining room. Not even the rain she heard coming down outside could dampen her mood. Stepping into the room, she noticed they were the last ones there. Everyone, even the parents, was seated and talking over their breakfast.

Her mother was also there and sent her a quick smile in greeting. Lauren returned it easily.

Mia saw them next. "Good morning. Grab some food; there's plenty."

"Don't tell them that," Aiden whined. "I had my eye on that last cinnamon muffin."

"Sucks to be you," Gideon said, picking up the muffin and taking an enormous bite.

"That is so wrong," Aiden groused. "I can't believe you'd do a guy like that."

Lauren had to smile at their antics as Gideon guided her to the table once their plates were full. She took the seat that would put her between her mother and Gideon.

Aiden, who was down the table and across from them, wasn't done poking at Gideon.

"So, Super Witch," Aiden goaded good-naturedly, "we've heard about all these powers you have, but we haven't really seen much of them. How about a demo?"

Gideon gave Lauren a mischievous smile and turned back to address Aiden.

"You want a demonstration of my powers, huh?"

Aiden rested his elbows on the table. "Sure. Let's see something."

Lauren had no clue what Gideon was up to until Aiden suddenly disappeared, his chair sitting empty next to an astonished Lindsay.

Jack snorted coffee out of his nose, and Marissa's eyes widened. Everyone else sat in stunned silence.

Gideon's mother, trying to hold back a laugh, scolded her son. "Gideon, bring him back."

"What?" he answered, completely unrepentant. "He said he wanted a show."

"I know, love, but still."

Aiden reappeared behind his chair, dripping wet.

The whole table lost it. Everyone rolled with laughter at the thunderstruck expression on Aiden's face. It was a cross between being pissed that Gideon had gotten the better of him, and admiration of his cousin's tremendous power.

"As badass as that was, did it have to be outside?" Aiden stood still for a moment, and a look of concentration filled his face.

Lauren started to see puffs of steam rise up off Aiden's clothes. *What the hell?*

"Someone's been practicing," Jack said. "Using your own fire power to dry your clothes. Nice. How many times did you scorch your shirt?"

Dry now, Aiden rounded his chair and sat back down. "We don't need to get into that."

The group laughed again at Aiden's dismissal.

Margaret caught her attention, and Lauren turned towards her as the rest fell into conversation. "You seem more at ease."

"I am," Lauren shared, smiling.

"I can see it in your eyes. They're brighter now." Her mother's gaze flicked to Gideon over her shoulder and then back. "I take it you and Gideon worked out your problem?"

"Yeah." Lauren turned in her chair to fully face her mom. "I *do* want that future he showed me, so I'm taking your advice. I'm doing everything I can to ensure it comes true."

Margaret smiled softly. "I hope you get everything your heart desires. You deserve to be happy and loved."

Lauren felt the backs of her eyes stinging with emotion. "Thank you." She took a breath before continuing. "You're doing okay here? Do you need anything?"

Margaret reached up and cupped her face. "I'm fine, baby; don't worry about me. You and the others have plenty on your minds at the moment. And that's where your focus needs to be. On finding those reprehensible men and putting a stop to them."

"I just hope something in what we saw yesterday points us in the right direction," Lauren told her. "That's what we're concentrating on today—digging into the clues we found in my memories."

"I know that had to be hard for you," her mother sympathized. "And I'm sorry you had to go through them again."

Lauren nodded. "It wasn't easy, but Gideon helped me to see them from a new perspective. They don't have the power to hurt me as badly anymore."

"Then it was worth it." Margaret leaned over and kissed her cheek. Straightening, she laid her napkin on the table beside her plate and grinned. "Now, I think I'll go enjoy the day spoiling my granddaughter." She looked over at Lauren again. "If you take a break, maybe you could come sit with us for a while. I know Hannah would love to spend some time with you."

"I'd like that, too." And Lauren was surprised by exactly how much she meant it.

14

Half an hour later, Gideon and the others were back in the library. Jack started things off.

"Okay, before we get to the list of things we found yesterday, there are a few questions that came to mind last night."

He turned to Lauren. "You mentioned that each member of the coven had trained you in some way. How did that work?"

Lauren stirred next to Gideon and sat up a little straighter. "Each day, one of them would come to the training facility."

"Training facility?" Jack asked.

"Yeah," Lauren told him. "It's where I lived and studied."

"You didn't stay with Santino?"

"No. He always said it was safer for me to be separate from him. I didn't understand it at the time, but it makes sense, now that I know I was just a prisoner. Anyway, each day was set aside for different regimens. Hand-to-hand was Jared Howard, Davis Sutter showed me everything about guns, Warren Newland was martial arts training. I learned knife fighting and throwing from Alexander, and Theo was sword work."

"Swords? Really?" Amber asked, awe in her voice. "You have *got* to show me that sometime."

Lauren grinned. "It was kind of fun, once I got the hang of it. Which didn't take long, believe me. When you're dodging a razor-sharp blade, you learn fast."

The off-hand comment sobered not only Gideon, but the

others as well. He wondered which of the scars she carried had resulted from those sessions. How many wounds had she sustained until she'd gotten good enough to defend herself?

Knife fighting, martial arts, hand-to-hand. Gideon would bet his ass there was no practice equipment or protective gear involved in any of that. He couldn't fathom what learning those disciplines would be like with the fear of injury or death looming with every strike.

And then to be punished on top of that if they deemed a performance unworthy was unthinkable. No wonder Stacia had been so brutal.

Jack spoke and pulled his attention back to the conversation. "What about Santino?"

"A little boxing, but mostly he worked with me on my telekinesis. His power is the only one I ever saw in use. I'd thought he was where I'd gotten it from...when I still thought he was my father, of course."

"You never saw any of the other men use magic?" Aiden asked.

"No."

"Then how do we know for sure they have any?" Aiden countered. "Maybe they're just a bunch of posers."

"For the simple fact that the leader has no magic," Amber answered. "We've already theorized that he's using them for what they can do for him. He probably hand-picked each one. I'd bet he looked for the specific gifts he thought he would need, and then brought them into the fold. Isn't that what he did with Quinn?"

"It makes sense," Marissa agreed. "We're a family of very powerful witches, so it would stand to reason that he would align himself with who he feels are the right people for the job. Even though he finds anyone with abilities abhorrent."

"That begs another question, though," Quinn interjected. "Why would they just blindly follow him? By the sound of it, between the fighting skills and the magical abilities, any one of these men could take him out. Why haven't they? Is it mind control, like they did with me?"

Lauren was already shaking her head. "No. I've seen the way they look and act around him. They're almost...I don't know... *afraid* of him."

"We already know he's vicious and sadistic," Gideon added. "But I don't think that would account for the way these guys defer to him. My guess would be that he either has something, or knows something, to keep them in line. While we're researching these guys, if we find any kind of blackmail-worthy information on them, make a note."

"Agreed," Jack stated. "We'll add that to everything else we have to find out about this joker. Now that I have a little clearer picture of how this operation works, let's get back to what we learned last night and see how it ties in with what we already know." Jack consulted his notes. "Okay, we have a phone conversation Lauren overheard, where someone is directed to move something to 'the building on Gornick.'"

"But that could be anywhere," Amber put in. "We don't know city, state, country...anything."

"I'm going with the theory that it's here in Michigan," Jack told her. "Most of what we've found on this group has been here in-state. I think we should start with the Northern half, from the Saginaw/Midland area on up. Let's hope Gornick isn't that common of a street name."

Jack rose and went to sit behind the desk at the computer. A few minutes spent tapping, and Jack was nodding. "Not too bad. There's only a couple listed: Gornick Ave in Gaylord, and Gornick Trail, which travels from Gaylord to Vanderbilt."

"How do we know what kind of building to look for?" Lindsay asked.

"They seem to have a preference for warehouses," Jack reasoned. "So let's begin our search with that."

"Amber and I will take that one," Quinn offered. "If we find anything we think fits, we'll bring everyone else in."

Jack nodded. "That'll work. All right, the next one was the newspaper. It was an edition from Cass City and showed the date of August 28, 2006."

"Could be where one of the men lived," Marissa guessed. "Or another warehouse."

Gideon pulled the image of the paper into his mind. He scanned every detail. A partial article just above the fold caught his attention. 'The Search Continues for Nine-Year-Old Derrick Abbott.'

A sick feeling took root in Gideon's chest. "Jack, go online and pull up a copy of that paper."

"You know something." Jack stated.

"Just pull it up. I hope I'm wrong." Gideon knew in his gut he was right. But he waited until Jack had found the page. "About halfway down. The article about the missing boy."

Gasps could be heard around the room as they joined Gideon's train of thought.

"No," Quinn muttered and sat forward. "Not another one." He turned concerned eyes to Amber first, then to Jack, waiting for confirmation.

Gideon knew Quinn was thinking about what he'd gone through after he'd been abducted. Had the coven taken this little boy too? Was he another casualty in this war they were waging against the Marquands?

Jack looked up from the computer. "This may not even tie in. But I think it would be a good idea to find out if this boy had power of any kind. If that's the case, we may have an MO."

"How many more?" Lindsay's voice wavered. "How many innocent children did this monster brutalize?" She looked at Aiden as tears filled her eyes. A moment of silent communication passed before she returned those eyes to Jack. "Aiden and I will take Derrick. We'll talk to his parents."

"Are you sure?" Jack asked her.

Gideon thought Lindsay was likely the most soft-hearted of the bunch. She was probably thinking of her own daughter and how she would have felt if it had been Hannah who'd been taken. She knew firsthand the terror involved when Carl had kidnapped Hannah, and she wouldn't have suffered nearly the fate as the ones the coven had stolen. As a mother who loved her child, she could relate to another who had lost hers.

She straightened her shoulders and took a deep breath. "Yes." Her voice was clear and strong with resolve.

Gideon gave voice to a worry this new development had brought to mind. "If they did take Derrick, that makes three that we know of. Theoretically, he could have countless soldiers like Quinn and Stacia at his disposal—powerful children he's tortured and trained to be killers, just waiting to be given the order." He swung his gaze to Quinn and Amber. "I'm betting when you track down the Gornick location, it's going to be another training facility like the one Lauren was raised in."

Everyone was silent as his words sank in. Jack responded first.

"If that's the case," he directed at Amber, "then you two need to be extremely careful. We know what they're capable of now. Take whatever precautions you need before going in."

Quinn and Amber both agreed with a nod.

Jack took a deep breath and released it on a curse as the weight of what the coven had done settled over him. "Fuck." He scrubbed his hands over his face and Gideon knew what he, and every other person in the room, was feeling. Disbelief, anger, and sadness.

"Okay," Jack dropped his hands to his lap, "nothing we can do about that now. Let's move on." He turned still-tormented eyes to the next item on the list. "Well, this conversation between Mylos and the leader that five-year-old Lauren heard makes more sense now. The words: 'slipped free,' 'looking for,' and 'get rid of' in conjunction with the name Melanie has to be referring to one of the kids they'd taken. She must have escaped somehow. And the order was to 'get rid of' her as soon as she was found."

Lauren spoke. "If we could find her, she may know more than I do. She may have some of the answers we need." She looked up at Gideon.

"We should be able to run a search on that," Aiden offered. "Have it look for any news stories from say…nineteen years ago and back. Tag anything that mentions the name Melanie. We might get lucky if a spread was done like the one for Derrick."

"I think Gideon and I should look for Melanie," Lauren said beside him. "If we find her, I'm hoping our similar experiences will help her to talk to us."

"I agree. And if she'll consent, maybe Gideon can do his mind-meld thing with her and find out more." Jack made a note. "All right, that leaves the takeout order. And since Marissa and I are the only ones left, we'll take that one. It's about the most straightforward of them all, as we have an actual address to check out. It's only about an hour away, so we'll just go and see who's home." Jack set his pen aside and sneered, the kind that said I-can't-wait-to-get-my-hands-on-those-assholes. Ice-cold and deadly.

A short while later Jack and Marissa left, and everyone else split off to start their own searches.

Gideon took the seat behind the desk. He was about to key in the parameters they needed to look for Melanie when Aiden walked up.

"What's the range on your teleporting?" Aiden asked.

Caught off-guard, Gideon sat back in the chair. "What? Why?"

"I was wondering if you could get me and Lindsay to Cass City. If we have to drive it, it'll be over five hours just to get there. I thought if you could beam us there, it would be a lot faster."

Once this power had manifested, Gideon had practiced with inanimate objects. He'd started out going from one room to another, then from inside to outside. After he'd gained some control and confidence, he'd even teleported himself outside. Then to push his range, he'd sent himself the two miles across Burt Lake. He'd never tried anything over that, though. And Cass City was hundreds of miles away.

The more he thought about it, though, the more intrigued he was becoming by the idea. *Think of the possibilities.* "It shouldn't be a problem, but with a distance that great, I'd want a few practice attempts first." He grinned evilly at Aiden. "Wouldn't want to lose you in the ether or something."

"Lose..." Aiden's green eyes narrowed. "Nice. Way to build confidence in your passengers."

Gideon laughed. "I think we'll be good. I've never lost anything...yet." He grinned at Aiden's expression. "Just let me try something a little more innocuous first."

Lindsay stepped forward. "I might have an idea. I have a framed picture of Hannah I've been meaning to send to my mom in Chicago. You can try that. It's even farther than you'd need to send us. I can call them, tell them what's happening, and what to expect."

"Yeah, sure," Gideon agreed. "Good idea."

He listened to Lindsay's end of the conversation. He knew she and her parents had gotten a crash course in magic when she'd fallen in love with and married Steven Donnelly, a man with power. Their experience with the world of witchcraft had taken a turn for the worse when Steven died.

In spite of all that, they didn't let the acts of one power-hungry man spoil the relationship they had with their granddaughter, who had been born wielding magic. Or with Aiden, the man their daughter had fallen in love with. They had accepted him into the family whole-heartedly.

Lindsay was disconnecting the call when he brought his thoughts back to the present.

"They're ready," she smiled. "They actually sounded pretty excited to be a part of this little experiment."

Gideon nodded. "All right, then. Let's do this."

Lindsay ran to grab the object he'd be sending over three hundred miles away. Gideon looked over at Aiden.

"You sure you trust me to do this?" Gideon asked him.

"As the one who was zapped outside in an instant, yeah, I trust you." Aiden rubbed his hands together. "And can you imagine how handy this will be? No more hour-long drives back and forth from here to Saginaw or Chicago. Lindsay's parents could see Hannah a lot more often." He paused, and an unholy gleam sparked in his eyes. "Or you could pop me and Linds to some deserted tropical island for some alone-time."

Gideon held up his hand but laughed. "Okay, too much information."

Lindsay came back before any more was said. He stood and walked around the desk. He took the eight-by-ten-inch package and held it in his hands.

"Picture your parents' house in your mind. Think of someplace I can set this down that it won't get broken or ram into anyone." Gideon waited for her response and then gently entered her mind to see the scene she'd drawn. Looked to be the dining room table. Good.

"Here we go." Gideon concentrated on the image he'd pulled from Lindsay and sent a burst of his power. As he lowered his now-empty hands, Lindsay's phone rang.

"Hello?"

Lindsay smiled up at him. "It got there in one piece. It's good." Her attention was drawn into the phone. "What? Yeah, I suppose we can try that." She dropped the mic end of the phone away from her mouth. "My mom has a gift for Hannah she wants you to bring back. She removed the picture from the table and put the gift there instead."

Gideon reached out with his mind to that same location. He found the box lying on top and brought it forth. It landed in his outstretched hands, safe and sound.

"It's here, Momma," Lindsay said. "Okay. Thank you. Bye."

Gideon handed her the wrapped present after she slipped her phone into her pocket. She studied the gift for a moment. "Just when I think I have a handle on it." She shook her head and laughed.

"Cass City, here we come," Aiden said.

"You've got some research to do first," Gideon reminded him. "On top of locating the missing boy's family, you need to find a place for your landing. Preferably someplace private."

"Oh yeah, right." Aiden swung around, and he and Lindsay headed to his computer.

Lauren, who'd hung back through the whole exercise, approached now. "Are you really going to teleport Aiden and Lindsay all the way across the state?"

"Yeah." He reached out and grasped her hand, pulling her into his body. He wrapped his arms around her waist, letting his hands rest on the top curve of her rounded butt. "And depending on where our investigation takes us, I may zap us somewhere, too." He leaned in and nuzzled her neck. "Maybe to that deserted island Aiden was talking about."

Her breathing gave an almost imperceptible catch before she spoke. "It won't be deserted if you, me, Aiden, and Lindsay are all there."

He drew back and looked into her mischievous hazel eyes. "Imp." Gideon leaned down and took her mouth with his. He slowly brought his right hand around to the front of her body and laid it on her stomach. He pulsed a little power down his hand that quickened her inner muscles and gave her a nice, mild orgasm. One that would only leave her wanting more. Whatever sound she would have made, he caught with his mouth. To anyone that bothered to notice, they looked like they were simply enjoying a long, leisurely kiss.

He gradually released her and looked down at her flushed cheeks and bright eyes.

"I can't believe you just did that here," she whispered.

"What? Kiss you?" He had to work to keep the knowing smile off his face. "I always want to kiss you."

"That was *so* wrong." Her brows came together in mock warning. "You just wait."

"Quit teasing me," he told her. "We've got work to do."

She stood speechless beside him, and he laughed.

A little while later, Gideon's mood had taken a nosedive. They'd found more information on Melanie. She'd been taken from Colorado twenty years before at the age of fifteen. And if they were judging Lauren's age right at the time of the memory, it meant the coven had had her for a year before she'd escaped. She'd be thirty-five now.

The roadblock was that she'd not been seen since her abduction. No mention was ever made that she'd returned home. She was still listed as missing.

Gideon hoped she was alive out there somewhere—that the coven hadn't caught her and eliminated her. The best way to find that out was to start with her parents and see if they knew where she was now. With any luck, she'd made it back home, and her parents had done what they could to protect and hide her.

With that in mind, he turned to Lauren. "Looks like you and I are going to Colorado."

"I figured. As soon as I saw the story, I knew that would be our next move."

Gideon took a page out of Jack's book and pulled up a satellite image of the town where Melanie's mother lived. Studying the map, he saw what looked to be a car lot. It gave him an idea. He opened a new window in the browser and searched for businesses local to where they were going.

There. Perfect. A car rental place would serve a dual purpose. It would not only hide their arrival, but allow them to have transportation once there.

Gideon looked over at his cousin. "Hey, Aiden. Find the nearest car rental, and I'll set you down near there. Even if it's still a little ways out, you'll have a way to get around."

"Yeah, smart thinking." A few keystrokes later, and Aiden had the location. He glanced at Lindsay beside him. She gave him a nod. "I think we're ready."

"When you're done," Gideon told them, "just return to the same place, give me a call, and I'll bring you home."

Aiden patted his pockets to make sure his phone and wallet were there. "Good to go."

Gideon took the image from Aiden's mind and sent them both off on their way.

Amber and Quinn walked back into the library just as Aiden and Lindsay disappeared.

"What the hell?" Quinn exclaimed. "Did he piss you off again?"

Gideon laughed. "No, I sent them to Cass City to look for Derrick's family."

"You've got that kind of range?" Quinn asked.

"Evidently. Do you want me to help you get to Gaylord?"

The Native American shook his head. "No, man. I'm good driving." Beside him, Amber muttered, "Chicken."

Quinn's blue eyes darkened and narrowed at Amber's ribbing.

Gideon fought a grin. "Well, Lauren and I are headed to Colorado. That's where Melanie's mom is. If anyone knows where she might be, it would be her."

He looked at Lauren. "You ready?"

She stepped into his arms. "Whenever you are."

15

Lauren hadn't known what to expect. How would being teleported across the country feel? In the end, it didn't feel any differently than being teleported from the couch to the bed, aside from being a lot more prepared for it this time. One moment she was standing in the Marquand library, and the next she was outside, standing beside a cinderblock wall.

Going from the air-conditioned coolness of the manor to the oppressive heat of a late Colorado summer took a minute to get used to.

Gideon placed his hand at the small of her back. "You okay?"

"Yeah," Lauren assured him. "It's just strange to know that ten seconds ago, I was in Michigan."

He smiled down at her. "Come on. Let's get out of here." He guided her around to the front, and fifteen minutes and a swipe of a credit card later they were getting into a 2013 Chevy.

Before taking off, they got familiar with the navigation system and entered in the address they had for Melanie's mother. Once it was done calculating, it told them they'd reach their destination in thirty-five minutes.

"Do you really think she knows where Melanie is?" Lauren asked when Gideon pulled out of the parking lot. "That she'd risk her own safety to hide her daughter?"

The moment Gideon's silver-green eyes stole a glance at her, Lauren knew she'd said something wrong. She thought back over her questions but couldn't see where she'd gone wrong.

"What?" she finally asked.

"Nothing," he hedged. "When you say stuff like that, or when you talked about learning to sword fight with real weapons, it just brings home the fact that no one was ever there to protect you. To stand between you and danger."

She thought that through. "And that's what you think Melanie's mom is doing?"

"Yeah. A parent's instinct to protect their child is the strongest there is," he told her evenly. "Despite the risk."

Lauren sat mute. Was it any wonder she couldn't believe there were people out there who would do that? No one had ever been willing to do it for her. Her real father had delivered her into the hands of psychopaths, and the man posing as her father had practically welcomed harm upon her. His training technique had been to hurl objects at her using his magic. She'd had to use her own to stop from being struck or impaled.

Gideon reached out and grasped her hand in his, rubbing her knuckles with his thumb. "Hey, that's over now, and you have any number of people willing to step in." He sent her a quick grin. "Not that you need it at this point. I've been on the receiving end of your anger. Let's just say I'm glad you decided to join our team.

"But to get back to what you were asking, yes—I believe her mother knows exactly where she is. The hardest part is going to be getting her to trust us enough to tell us. And I think that's where you come in. Like you said, you and Melanie have a lot in common. She may have only been there for a year, but you can bet her training had already begun."

Thinking of her own situation, Lauren's next question had as much to do with her as it did Melanie.

"We know the coven had to have looked for her. How do you think she's stayed hidden for so long? Or what if she didn't? She could have been dead this whole time. They wouldn't have been willing to leave a *loose end* like that out there. I'm sure if Quinn and I weren't smack in the middle of all the Marquands, they'd be on us, too."

His grip tightened on her hand. "Hey, we'll know soon enough if Melanie survived. And as far as the coven coming for you or Quinn—if it happens, we'll deal with it. But remember, this whole thing will be coming to a head very soon. Then they won't be out there anymore to worry about. You, Quinn, Melanie, and Derrick, and anyone else they've taken can return to your lives without having to watch over your shoulders."

They rode the rest of the way in thoughtful silence. Lauren tried to envision what her life would have been like if her father hadn't traded her into the hands of evil. She knew Margaret loved her unconditionally and would have protected her given the chance, but that hadn't been possible. And Lauren had been left on her own, with no one to stop the pain.

She stole a look at Gideon. He was doing everything within his power to do that. Where would she be now if he hadn't come for her? Probably dead. Or punished severely enough that she'd wish she were.

Would she have even met this man if she'd been raised with the family she'd been born into? Probably not. It was her death that had driven Steven out of the house. If he'd never left, he wouldn't have met Lindsay. He wouldn't have died, leaving her pregnant and on the run, where she'd met Aiden and the whole Marquand family.

In a roundabout way, Lauren had her brother to thank for Gideon being in her life now. She sighed wistfully, both out of sorrow for the loss of the brother she never really knew, and gratitude for having brought this most amazing man into her life. Maybe one of those children from the vision she saw of her future would be named Steven...

A computerized voice telling them their destination was on the left broke Lauren out of her musings.

She consulted the address one more time and started looking for the right house. "There, the brown one."

Gideon pulled into the driveway, parked, and shut off the car. They exited and walked up to the door. As he raised his hand to knock, the door swung inward, and a short, heavyset woman stood looking up at them.

"Can I help you?" she asked them.

Lauren couldn't help but notice the huge dog at the woman's side. She had her hand wrapped around the two-inch-wide leather collar, not that she'd be able to hold the beast back if it decided to charge. The animal's head was waist high on Gideon, its wiry grey coat a wild mess of fur. It had to weigh in at close to two hundred pounds. This guard would give anyone who approached this house second thoughts.

Gideon paused for a moment and then spoke. "Mrs. Boone, my name is Gideon Marquand, and this is Lauren Donnelly. If we could, we'd like to speak with you about your daughter."

"My daughter is gone," she stated bluntly. "She was kidnapped twenty years ago. Now you need to leave."

Gideon studied her. "But she's not gone, is she? We're not here to cause either of you any harm. We're looking for answers. Can we please take this inside?"

"No. I *said* you need to go," she demanded more forcefully.

The dog at her side tensed, sensing its owner's unease. A low rumble emitted from its deep chest.

"Please," he added, a wary eye on the hound. "We need your help."

Lauren thought for sure they were headed back to the car, and home to Michigan. But the older woman slowly backed into the house, pulling the dog with her. "Come on, Rufus. We'll at least hear them out."

Rufus took one more appraising look at her and Gideon and turned to walk into the living room. He positioned himself on the floor beside a small recliner-type chair. Mrs. Boone sat and motioned for them to take the couch.

"So, what is this about?"

Lauren knew this part was hers. "When I was three, I was taken by a group of men. We have reason to believe those same men are the ones who took Melanie. We also know that within a year she was able to escape them. I know what she went through for that year. I've lived it…twenty times that." Lauren slowly pulled her sleeves up.

She was watching for any sign that Melanie's mother recognized the marks. And saw it in the way her eyes widened, and her breathing stuttered just a little.

"Mrs. Boone," Gideon directed her attention to him, "does your daughter have any special powers?"

"Why would you ask that?"

"We think that's why she was targeted," Gideon told her. "We've found other children with magic who were taken. Once they have them, they're put through a brutal training regimen. They've done it to three that we know of. There may be more, but we don't know how many yet."

"They had me under their control until just recently," Lauren cut in. "We want to put them out of commission, so they can't do this to anyone else. These men are evil and cruel. They've ruined countless lives, and it's time for someone to stop them."

Lauren waited a beat. "If you'll help us, Melanie won't have to hide anymore. She won't have to live in fear every minute of every day."

They sat quietly, expectantly, giving her a moment to think.

She reached down and petted Rufus before looking up at Lauren. "You have abilities?"

"Yes. I'm telekinetic."

"Melanie can control water."

Lauren felt her heart give a kick. *Can*—not could. She was speaking in the present tense. She glanced quickly at Gideon. They'd done it.

"We would really like to talk to her," Lauren pleaded. "She was older than I was when they took her. We're hoping that maybe she heard or saw something that might give us clues as to where these men are."

Mrs. Boone's eyes narrowed. "You just said you'd been with them for twenty years. Shouldn't you know that already?"

"I was only three," Lauren explained. "I was kept separated. I wasn't allowed contact with many people, and I was never permitted to leave the facility where I lived. We're hoping that because she was fifteen at the time of her abduction, she'll remember more details."

"I'm not just going to tell you where she is," she warned. "But I'll get word to her and have her get in touch with you." Tears gathered in her eyes. "I want her home. It's killed me to have to pretend that she's still been missing all this time. But I swore to her that I'd protect her. We've used every spell and potion we could find to conceal her. We never knew if they'd come for her again."

She drilled her gaze into Gideon. "If you can promise me that my daughter will be safe and able to come home, I'll talk her into helping you."

"We won't rest until these men are finished," Gideon vowed. "They've hurt too many people, a good majority of which are my family or those I care for very much. And please tell Melanie that she need not worry about us being followed to wherever she wants to meet. I have the gift of teleportation, so there's no possible chance of someone trailing us."

Lauren reached into her pocket and pulled out a slip of paper. They'd written down all their contact information before coming in. "Please give this to Melanie and tell her to call any time."

She stood to take the paper. Rufus also lumbered to his feet. "I will. Thank you."

Lauren and Gideon followed suit, and soon they were back

in the car.

"How did you know for sure Melanie wasn't dead?" Lauren asked, once they were back on the road.

"I was monitoring her more surface thoughts. And when I asked about Melanie, she had a brief moment of panic where she wondered about her daughter's safety, and if she'd been discovered."

"Any insight as to how long it might be before she calls?" Lauren asked.

"None yet. The Powers That Be aren't being all that talkative lately. But, hopefully, not too long. I'm sure Melanie wants this over with as badly as we do."

Gideon startled her by suddenly smacking his hand against the steering wheel. "Damn it! This fucker has destroyed one family after another! How many kids has he deprived of being raised in a home by loving parents?"

Before Lauren could think of anything to say, Gideon's cell phone rang. He took it out of his pocket and snapped out, "Hello?"

Lauren listened intently.

"Yeah…Where?… How many?…We'll be right there."

He hung up and pressed on the gas. "That was Quinn. He and Amber ran into a soldier and some guards at the Gornick facility. They're holding their own but could use some help. It's six against two."

Coming up on slower traffic, Gideon swerved out and passed two cars at once before sliding back into their lane again and speeding off. Within five minutes, they roared into the parking lot of the car rental place. He parked at the end of a row of cars, as out of sight as he could manage. After shutting off the engine, he turned to her. "Ready?"

A quick nod, and he took her hand in his. They teleported directly to where Amber and Quinn were fighting.

In the next instant, Gideon had set them down behind

the coven's men, in effect trapping them between the two Marquand lines of defense. She seamlessly fell back on her training. Within seconds, she'd evaluated the scene and settled on a plan of attack.

The African American man before her was wielding fireballs. Lauren recognized the high-speed assault as the same one she'd learned. He'd also been taught by the coven. But this wasn't Derrick Abbott. By their calculations, Derrick would only be seventeen, and this man was much older. This was another soldier they had stolen and tortured into doing their bidding. And right now, he was throwing fireballs at Amber, raining down one after another. She had to dodge and roll to keep from getting hit. Lauren wondered if that was the reason Amber hadn't frozen him yet; she'd been too busy just trying to stay ahead of him.

Lauren was about to wade in when a sound from above drew her attention. She looked up to see fifteen to twenty birds of all shapes and sizes coming in hot. They dive-bombed the five guards that were taking aim at Quinn with semi-automatic assault rifles.

She didn't know where the cavalry had come from or who was controlling them, but she was glad for the assist.

Spying some logs and other debris, she started chucking them at the men's legs. Since the flying forces were concentrating on the heads, she tried to knock them off their feet.

A couple went down, and Gideon tore across the concrete lot. He used his power to fling the weapon away from the first guy he reached. Leaning down, Gideon hefted him to his feet and plowed a fist into his face.

She'd never seen this side of Gideon before. Even when she'd attacked him, he'd never shown this much anger and aggression. The frustration and rage he'd exhibited in the car had carried over to here. He was taking all of those feelings out on those who'd helped to destroy lives. When he'd finished with one, he moved on to the next, leaving unconscious men in his wake.

She couldn't blame him. She wanted to hurt them, too.

Bringing her attention back to the matter at hand, she noted the rest of the guards were busy with Quinn and the animals. Taking her chance, Lauren shifted her focus to the most prominent threat. When he drew his arm back to fire off another volley at Amber, Lauren knew she had to act. With a flick of her hand, the ball veered off-course. It struck the side of the building with a small explosion. Only a black soot mark remained.

She started across the lot when he turned and saw her. Behind him, Amber came out from where she'd taken refuge. He was now between them. Lauren readied herself for whatever happened next.

Arms flailing at the birds attacking him, one of the guards who still held his gun fired wildly. Everyone ducked at the deafening sound, not sure where the shots had landed.

Then she knew. Lauren felt the burning pain in her chest, and looked down to see blood saturating the front of her shirt.

She vaguely heard Gideon shout her name before it all went dark.

Lauren didn't know where she was. At first there was nothing. Then slowly, a shape started to emerge in front of her. It revealed itself to be a man. As he came into focus, she took notice of his blonde hair and blue eyes.

She recognized his smile from the pictures her mother had shown her. This was her brother. Steven.

He nodded and held his hand out to her. Beckoning her.

"I can't," she told him. "This isn't the future I'm supposed to have. I survive, and I live a happy life. I deserve that, damn it."

"Then fight," she heard in her head.

With one last look, Lauren turned away from her brother and fought her way back to Gideon. She called out to him over and over.

She came back to consciousness gasping Gideon's name. He and Amber and Quinn were all kneeling over her. Gideon's hands were pressed to the gunshot wound in her chest, the heat of his healing working to bring her back and repair the damage done by the stray bullet.

Lauren tried to sit up, but Quinn held her shoulders. "Just stay still until he's finished."

She did as he said and instead looked up into Gideon's tortured eyes. Lauren saw a mix of emotions she couldn't make sense of, but before she could try to decipher them, he moved his hands from her chest to her shoulders and pulled her into his embrace.

He held her so tightly she could barely breathe, but she didn't object. She knew how close she'd been to death. Why would she have seen Steven otherwise?

Gideon finally released her, and she gazed up at him.

"I nearly lost you." He ran his hands over her hair. "I almost didn't make it to you in time."

Lauren realized that one of the emotions she'd seen in his eyes had been fear. Fear of losing her. She'd never had anyone who cared for her like that—someone who actually cared whether she lived or died. Warmth bloomed in her heart.

"But you did," she reminded him with a smile. "I'm here."

"Yes, you are. And I don't plan on letting you go anytime soon."

She suddenly remembered the men they'd been fighting and looked around. "Where's the soldier? The guards? Did they get away?"

"Um, no," Quinn said from behind her.

The tone of his voice implied something had happened while she'd been out. Lauren took a closer look at their surroundings and saw the soldier sitting next to the building looking lost and confused. The guards were nowhere to be seen. "What happened?"

She looked to Gideon, but he wasn't talking. Her gaze went back to Quinn and Amber. "Is someone going to tell me what happened?"

Amber glanced up at Gideon before returning her focus to Lauren. "Gideon destroyed the guards. They just vaporized. I don't know exactly what he did to the soldier, but he suddenly just dropped like a stone, unconscious. When he came to, he had no idea where he was. His memories have been completely wiped." Amber glanced over at the man sitting propped against the wall of the warehouse. "He's been like that ever since."

Lauren couldn't believe what she'd just heard. She swung back around to face him. "Gideon?"

"After the shots rang out, I looked for you. I saw the blood. *Your* blood." His eyes dropped to the red still staining her shirt. "When you went down, I lost it." He brought his attention back to her face. "I had to get to you before it was too late. They were an obstacle standing between us. I wanted them gone, and in the next moment, they were. I couldn't hurt the soldier. He's like you—a victim who's been brainwashed and lied to." He shrugged. "I honestly don't know how it happened. One minute they were fighting us, the next they weren't."

Lauren wanted to ask more questions, but Amber drew their attention by standing. "Why don't we get into this more later?" Amber cautioned. "I think we need to go. Someone was bound to hear those gunshots. Our car is about two blocks away."

"Amber's right," Quinn said. "We do need to go."

"We can't just leave him here," Lauren protested.

"I can hear sirens," Gideon told her. "He'll be taken care of."

Gideon helped her to her feet. He took a moment to replace her ruined shirt, and the four of them took off. Within a few minutes, they were loaded in and driving away from the scene. Lauren leaned into Gideon's side where they sat together in the back seat.

"I was so scared I wouldn't get to you in time," he admitted for her alone. *"I could feel how far away you were. How close you were to never coming back."*

Lauren smiled up at him and reached out to lay her hand on his thigh. *"Never would have happened. Even when I saw Steven, and he held his hand out to me, I refused to go with him. I want the future you promised me. Once he knew I wasn't going with him, he told me to fight. And so I did."*

"I heard you calling out to me."

"I knew you would. Thank you for saving me."

"Thank you for not leaving me." He leaned down and kissed her.

16

Gideon saw love shining in her eyes. She had come back from the brink of death for him. If she hadn't started fighting when she had, he didn't know if she'd be sitting there beside him now.

For the first few moments he'd laid his hands on her, there'd been only a whisper of life left. Her strong will had saved her just as much as his gifts.

He felt emotionally exhausted. The rage he'd felt before getting Quinn's call had been replaced by the need to cause someone physical pain. To feel the impact of fist meeting face. Magic was great, but sometimes the physical exertion of a good fight just couldn't be beat for letting out some pent-up angst and hostility.

When that gunshot had rang out and he'd seen Lauren fall, his entire being had been filled with desperation and fear.

The men blocking his path to her had brought a fury that Gideon had never experienced before. He'd felt his power gathering and rising, and suddenly, they were just gone. When the soldier had started for him, Gideon had only spared him a glance, and he was down. His way to Lauren was clear.

"Everyone alright back there?" Amber took her eyes off the road long enough to catch his attention in the rearview mirror. She returned her gaze to the asphalt in front of them. "It got pretty crazy. I'm sorry we called you into a situation like that."

Gideon watched her in the mirror. "We're good. And I would have been pissed if you hadn't. You guys were in trouble back there."

"Still, I'm sorry." She drove for a ways before speaking again. "So...what you did back there. Vaporizing people, wiping minds. Do you do that often?"

"Nope. That was a first."

"How do you think it happened?" Lauren sat up and turned to face him.

"I was actually just thinking about that," he told them. "We all know our abilities are connected to our emotions. I think I just lost control. I was desperate to get to Lauren, and those guys were standing in my way."

"Is there any way to find out who he is?" Lauren asked. "He probably has a family out there somewhere looking for him."

"The police will handle that," Gideon assured her. "But I'll keep an eye on it, and if it looks like they run into trouble, I'll give them some help."

"How?" Amber asked.

"The coven knows who he is and where he came from. And we'll be seeing them soon enough."

"Thank you," Lauren smiled at him.

"Speaking of finding people," Quinn looked back over the seat, "were you guys able to connect with Melanie?"

Gideon pulled out his phone to check, just in case he'd missed her call. "Not yet. Her mother is getting in touch with her to have her contact us."

He started to put it back into his pocket when it rang. After a quick look at the screen, he hit the accept button. "Hello?"

"Hey, we're ready to beam out," Aiden said.

"Did you find Derrick's parents?" Gideon inquired.

"Yeah." Aiden took a deep breath that Gideon heard through the phone line. "It was like we thought. He has power. You're going to love this too—he can control minds. All he has to do is touch you, and he can manipulate what you think, feel, and see."

"I can understand how they might consider him useful to have on hand."

"Me too. We can get into the rest when we're all back at home base," Aiden told him. "Beam us up, Scotty."

"You are such an ass." Gideon laughed as he hung up the phone. He took a moment to find their signature in the ether and transported Aiden and Lindsay back to Marquand Manor.

"That was Aiden?" Quinn confirmed, turning in his seat to look at Gideon.

"Yeah. They were able to verify that Derrick has magic. He can control the mind with a single touch."

"Fuck," Quinn muttered.

"Yeah, that seems to be the consensus," Gideon shared.

Amber took one hand off the wheel and rubbed her head. "Wonderful."

Two hours later, they were pulling into the garage at the manor. Aiden and Lindsay were waiting for them in the library.

"Jack and Marissa not back yet?" Gideon asked. "Has anyone heard from them?"

"No," Aiden said. "Maybe someone was home after all."

Amber pulled out her phone and started dialing. Everyone waited for an indication that someone answered. There was none.

She hung up without leaving a message. "No answer." Her gaze swung to Gideon. "See if you can reach them telepathically."

He sent out a message to Jack. *"Hey, you guys okay?"*

"Yeah, we're good. You'll never guess what we found."

"What?"

"Not really what, so much as who. Alexander Mattison. We knocked on the door, and there he was," Jack told him.

"You captured him?" Gideon thought in shock.

"Don't sound so surprised. I've been known to take down a

perp or two."

"Did he try to use any of his magic on you?"

"I didn't give him the chance. I knocked him out pretty quick and tied him up. I also put a blindfold on him, since we don't what powers he has or how they work. He's still out cold."

"Smart move there. Aiden and Lindsay found out Derrick does have magic. He can control minds."

"Holy shit."

"Yeah, so watch yourselves. No telling what Mattison could be capable of doing."

"Will do."

"I'll keep this connection open. Let me know if you need anything."

"Yeah. All right."

Gideon relayed Jack's news.

"Son of a bitch. He found one of the seven," Aiden said excitedly. "Shouldn't we all be there to question him?"

"I think Jack knows what he's doing," his sister responded. "If anyone can get answers out of this guy, it would be him."

"I know," Aiden agreed. "You're right. I just didn't think we'd find one so soon."

"Maybe he can lead us to the rest," Quinn speculated. "And then to the leader."

"Well, while we wait for them," Gideon cut in, "Aiden, why don't you fill us in on what you found out about Derrick? I already told the others what you said on the phone, but take us through it again."

Over the next hour, they brought each other up to speed on their missions and added to the notes they already had. Gideon was glad that, other than a few shocked looks from Aiden and Lindsay, the incident with the men at the training facility passed without comment.

They'd just decided to break for food when Gideon got a heads-up. *"Inbound. About forty-five minutes."*

"Jack said they're on their way in," he shared with the others.

"He didn't say anything else?" Amber asked.

"No. Just that they were coming."

"Let's still move this to the dining room," Aiden suggested. "They can join us when they get here."

The group was discussing how best to locate the rest of the coven over cold-cut sandwiches when Marissa and Jack arrived.

Gideon thought they both looked tired and distressed.

"Well?" Amber demanded. "What were you able to learn?"

Jack sat heavily in the chair next to Aiden. He reached over and took Aiden's half-full bottle of beer and chugged what remained.

For once, Aiden didn't have a snarky comment. He, like everyone else, had deduced that things hadn't gone as planned.

Jack studied the empty bottle for a moment before he looked at the six faces staring at him. "Alexander Mattison is dead."

Gasps and muttered curses issued from around the table.

Lauren was the first to recover. "What happened?"

Marissa, who still looked a little pale, picked up the story. "He wouldn't talk. He wouldn't give us *anything*. We'd started to push him really hard, demanding he tell us about the other coven men. Where they were, what powers they carried, what their plans were. When he still didn't answer, Jack and I started discussing me trying to tap into his mind. He heard us and got extremely agitated—nervous. He shook his head over and over, and then he...um..."

She looked at Jack. She couldn't go on.

"He jumped me," Jack stated. "It turns out he could manipulate fire. He burned through the ropes and came at me. I drew my gun and leveled it at him, but he lunged and grabbed it. His hand was wrapped around the top. He must have been using his power to apply heat to it so I'd let go. The round in the chamber got hot, which ignited the gun powder, and it discharged. He was dead before he hit the floor."

He sat silent for a moment. "It all happened so fast."

Gideon was reeling. As were the others. He hated that his sister had witnessed what had to have been a horrific sight.

"One down, five to go," Aiden said. "We take out his coven and the leader will be defenseless."

"Let's not forget about his secret weapons," Gideon cautioned. "We have no idea how many kids he's kidnapped and brainwashed. From what we know of Lauren's training and what we saw out of that soldier today, they won't be easy to defeat. Worst case scenario, he uses them to stand between him and us."

"Gideon's right," Jack conceded. "He's had years to surround himself with powerful magic. And we're going to have to go through them to get to him."

Lauren stirred beside him. "But how do we even find the rest of them? It was just dumb luck that we had Alexander's address. And since he never told you where any of the others were, we're back to square one." She pushed her plate away in frustration. "With zero to go on."

Gideon reached over and put a consoling hand around Lauren's shoulders just as his phone rang. He looked at the screen. Blocked number.

He hit the little green circle. "Hello?" All eyes were on him.

"Is this Gideon Marquand?" a husky female voice asked.

"Yes."

"This is…ah, Melanie…Melanie Boone."

It sounded to Gideon as if saying her own name was foreign on her tongue. She'd probably been living under an assumed name all these years. He released Lauren and sat up straighter, listening intently.

"My mother said you were looking for me."

Gideon's eyes tracked around to everyone at the table. "Yes, Melanie, I am."

Upon hearing that name, everyone leaned in, their attention

focused on Gideon's side of the call.

"She said you were going to put an end to those men who hurt me."

"We are. My family and I are hunting them right now. That's why we need your help. We know you escaped from them. We were hoping you would talk with us, see if there's anything you might recall about your time with them."

"Oh, I remember every minute. And I'd be happy to share it all with you if it meant you'd wipe them off the face of the earth." Her voice was growing stronger, showing Gideon some of the strength and grit it had taken for her to get away and stay alive.

"That's our goal," he affirmed. "Is there a place you would feel comfortable meeting us? Like I told your mom, there's no worry about us being followed."

"Yeah, she said you could teleport." She paused. "Let me give it some thought, and I'll call you back."

"Okay. Thanks, Melanie." The call disconnected.

"She's going to help?" Lauren asked from next to him.

"Yes." He repeated their conversation.

"Let's just pray she has the answers we need," Amber added.

Before Gideon could speak, Lauren and Quinn both began to convulse violently in their seats.

Gideon shot to his feet. "Lauren!"

He barely caught her before her body writhed out of her chair. He took her into his arms and carefully lowered her down. He was only vaguely aware that Amber had screamed Quinn's name and was rushing to his side.

The sound of wooden legs scraping across the ceramic tiles was loud as everyone went to the ones downed by this mystery attack.

"What the hell is happening?" Amber's fear-filled eyes demanded an answer.

Gideon spared a glance under the table to where Quinn lay

much the same as Lauren. They were both unresponsive as their bodies jerked and shook. Blood began to run from their noses, ears, and mouths.

Aiden and Lindsay tried to help Amber with Quinn, as Jack and Marissa did what they could for Lauren.

They were dying. Gideon didn't know what it was, but something was killing them.

"Gideon." He barely heard her whisper, and his gaze flew to her face.

"Oh God, baby, tell me what's happening!"

"It hurts so much," she breathed. *"My head...my body...I can't..."*

The way her voice trailed off scared the shit out of him. *"You can! And you will!"* he urged. *"I'll make it stop. I promise."*

He didn't know how he'd keep that vow, but he'd do whatever it took. He couldn't lose her. Gideon reached for her head, his only thought to heal whatever damage was being done. He concentrated completely on finding the source of the seizures and pain.

But he found nothing. This wasn't a physical attack. It was mental. He went deeper, looking for any sign of what was causing her torment.

There. An echo of something malignant. Something evil.

He backed out and looked across the room. "Aiden, use your healing and search deep into Quinn's mind."

"What am I looking for?" Aiden asked, taking position.

"When I was trying to heal Lauren, I felt something. I want to know if it's the same for Quinn."

Amber jumped into action, ready to help. "What is it? What's doing this?"

"I'm not sure," he told her truthfully. "Something dark and unnatural." He swung his gaze back to Aiden. "You're going to have to go deep."

Aiden held his gaze for a moment and then nodded. He bent

to his task. It took him a little longer than it had Gideon, but soon he was confirming Gideon's findings.

"I see it."

"It has to be the coven," Jack theorized from where he held Lauren's legs, trying to stop her thrashing. "It's really the only thing they have in common."

"But how?" Lindsay asked, pressing down on Quinn's ankles.

"I don't know—a spell or something," Jack guessed desperately. "The coven must still have some kind of link to them. This has to be their retaliation for what happened with Mattison."

"Whatever it is," Amber wiped at the blood flowing from Quinn's nose, "it's killing them. We have to break whatever this connection is."

She turned and pinned Gideon with a look of pure determination. "You can do this. Find it."

"How?" He would do anything to stop this suffering.

"The astral plane," Amber told him. "You might be able to use it to track the spell back to the scumbags who are doing this." She paused, looked lovingly down at Quinn, and then returned her fierce stare to him. "But you're taking me with you."

"Me, too," Aiden stated.

"And me," Marissa added. "The four of us. Together. Marquand magic at it greatest."

Gideon nodded and gently slid Lauren into Jack's waiting hands. Across the room, Amber gave Quinn one final kiss before handing Lindsay the blood-soaked cloth. She stood, as did the rest of the Marquands.

Gideon, Marissa, Aiden, and Amber came together at the end of the table.

He looked at Lindsay and Jack. "Watch over them." With that, they clasped hands, and Gideon took them flying.

17

To anyone watching, they were standing immobile, eyes closed. But their consciousness was gone. Instead of focusing solely on their destination, Gideon held them in the ether, waiting until they found what they were searching for.

"Look at that." Aiden pointed to the black, undulating, tendril-like vines that speared into Lauren and Quinn's heads. As their bodies lurched and spasmed, the cord seemed to be sucking the life out of them.

Gideon looked up to where it had funneled through the ceiling. Amber was right. They could follow this right back to the source.

Blocking out what would happened if they failed, Gideon looked to the others. "You ready?"

They nodded. And with fingers tightly intertwined, they flew along the heaving and surging snake-like tentacle.

"This grayness isn't what I expected," Aiden said. "I was hoping that we'd be able to see…something. Streets, landmarks, anything. I'd hoped that once we'd traced this back to them, we'd finally know where they are."

"We'll find them with or without a road map," Amber told him, her voice sharp and resolute. "They won't get away with this."

"For now, let's just concentrate on breaking whatever spell this is," Marissa insisted.

Time had no meaning here. Gideon didn't know if they'd been trailing along this tether for minutes or hours. He hoped they wouldn't arrive at the other end too late.

They started to descend, and Gideon knew they were getting close. As they settled to a stop, they all looked around. The gray mists still blocked their sight, but Gideon swore he could hear something.

Now that they'd reached their destination, Gideon slowly, gradually, made their projections visible. The four stood hand-in-hand as their surroundings came into focus.

The sight that greeted them confirmed who was responsible. Five men in black robes gathered. One in a red robe stood off to the side. Watching.

The remaining men of the coven chanted and worked the spell that was killing Quinn and Lauren.

Their voices abruptly stopped when they noticed Gideon and the others. The leader snapped out the command to continue. They immediately obeyed.

Dropping his hood back over his shoulders, he turned to face their astral forms. "So we finally meet."

"Stop what you're doing," Amber demanded. "You're killing them."

"Oh, I know." He smiled, but it was cold and malicious. "You cost me one of mine. An eye for an eye. Too bad you came in astrally, or you could do something about it."

Gideon had seen the drawing, but only seeing this man in person could really convey just how malevolent he truly was.

"Why are you doing this?" Marissa asked him. "Why do you hate us so much?"

Gone was the cold master. In his place was an angry, seething man. He took one involuntary step forward. "You have something that should have been mine. The very fact that you exist is an affront to me. You should have never been born." His breathing was heavy and erratic, but he forcibly calmed himself before he said anything more. "Now, if you'll excuse me, you can see we're a little busy."

"No!" Amber shouted as he made a motion to return to his group. "Release Quinn and Lauren! Whatever you're doing, stop!"

"I take orders from no one. But you're welcome to stay and watch."

Gideon knew the time had come to take action. The longer this went on, the more Lauren and Quinn suffered. They may not be able to affect anything by touch, but they still had their magic. He tapped into his family's minds and showed them the words of the spell he'd just created specifically for this.

He started, and the others joined in.

"Marquand magic flowing strong in our veins

Gather and combine on this astral plane

Sever this cord that brings pain and suffering

Turn it back now on those we're uncovering."

The robed men faltered but pushed on. The Marquands held firm, shoulder to shoulder, and recited the words again.

After the fourth repetition, there was an audible snap, and the coven men dropped and started writhing on the floor, screaming.

"No!" the leader shouted furiously as he advanced on them. "I will kill each and every one of you! You will die an agonizing death!"

The satisfaction of seeing those bastards in pain was short-lived. Amber gave Gideon a look, and he knew she was as anxious to get back as he was. With the connection broken, Lauren and Quinn should be all right. But they needed to see for themselves.

Gideon didn't waste time on the return trip. They were back in the blink of an eye.

Jack was still sitting on the floor with Lauren in his arms. She was conscious but still ashen, the blood on her face and clothes a stark reminder that twice today alone, he'd almost lost her.

"Whatever you guys did worked," Jack told them. "Everything just stopped, and they started to come around."

Lauren was trying to sit up by the time Gideon reached her. "Hey, stay there. Relax. Don't try to get up."

He glanced over at Amber, and she was having the same conversation with Quinn. But like Lauren, he wasn't listening either.

As Gideon helped Lauren back to her seat, he happened to spot the ornate clock on the side table and was shocked to see that only a few minutes had passed. It had seemed so much longer.

Chairs were righted, and everyone sat to recover from the harrowing experience. Amber kept touching Quinn's face to reassure herself that he was okay. Gideon shared that sentiment. He couldn't keep his hands off Lauren. Marissa wet a couple of napkins in her water glass so the drying blood could be washed away.

Gideon brushed Lauren's hair back. "Are you okay?"

"Yeah." She took a deep breath. "What the hell happened?"

Once they'd explained about the tendrils linking them back to the coven, Quinn asked, "Is the connection gone for good?"

Gideon couldn't blame him for his concern. "Yes. The spell we used broke it and caused it to rebound on the coven. They were treated to the same torment."

"Did it kill them?" The hope in Lauren's voice was hard to miss.

"No," Gideon told her. "Unfortunately, we only had a fraction of our power in astral form. The most I could do was turn their own spell back on them. But hopefully, it will have caused enough damage to deter any more retaliation for a while."

"What do you think the coven leader meant when he said we have something that belonged to him?" Marissa asked.

"I wish I knew," Amber said. "I'd take it back to him and shove it right up his ass."

Aiden's snort of laughter broke some of the tension.

After moving to the parlor, Gideon insisted on doing a full body scan of Lauren and Quinn both, just to be sure there was no lasting damage and the link was indeed broken. He soothed sore muscles and took away any lingering aches from the brutal seizures they had suffered.

They were finally beginning to relax from the trauma when Gideon's phone rang. Taking it from his pocket, he saw that it again came from a blocked number.

"It's Melanie," he told the group.

"Answer it," Lauren said. "We need anything she can tell us."

Gideon accepted the call. She told him where she wanted to meet. In turn, he explained what he needed in order to teleport to her location.

After he hung up, they discussed the best way to handle her. They decided, so as not to overwhelm her, that only he and Lauren would go. He thought briefly about suggesting Marissa go in her place, but he already knew Lauren would fight him on it, since technically there was nothing wrong with her.

Gideon stood and reached out a hand to pull Lauren to her feet.

He wrapped an arm around her waist and swept the room with his gaze. "I don't know how long this will take. Don't feel like you have to wait. I'll let you know as soon as we get back."

"Good luck," Jack offered.

A beat later, they were standing in front of a tall woman

with shoulder-length dark brown hair. She also had a nice-sized baby bump.

Melanie rubbed her belly in that way mothers do and held their gaze. "As you can see, stopping these men is more important to me than ever now."

"Does your mom know?" Gideon asked, indicating her swollen belly.

She shook her head sadly and looked down at her baby. "No. I couldn't tell her. She'd want to be here with me, and that's just not safe yet."

"The baby's father?" Lauren wondered.

Melanie held up her left hand. "We're married. He knows everything. And that's all I'd like to say on that matter." She pointed at Lauren's chest before pulling the collar of her own shirt down. "I see we've met the same group of people."

"Yeah. It just took me a lot longer to get away from them."

Melanie's eyes saddened. "How long?"

"Twenty years."

Gideon sensed her cringe at the thought of being in that place for so long.

"I'm sorry," Melanie told her. "I thought a year was awful enough. I don't think I would have made it any longer than that."

She returned her focus to him. "So, what do you need from me?"

"We'd just like to talk with you about your time with them. If you have trouble remembering, I'd like your permission to look into your memories. I'm sorry if it feels like we're pushing, but I wouldn't ask if it weren't important."

The apprehensive look that came to her face was very similar to the one Lauren had worn when he'd broached the subject with her.

Lauren stepped forward now. "I had the same thought," she admitted. "I didn't want anyone to see what they'd done to me.

The idea of someone witnessing that was humiliating." Lauren looked over at him and smiled. "But Gideon is one of the good guys. He saved me. He helped me see that I did what I had to do to survive." Lauren returned her gaze to Melanie. "And that we survived is the most *important* thing. None of the rest really matters. You want to know something I just recently figured out?"

"Sure," Melanie nodded.

"If I hadn't been taken...if I hadn't lived through it...I would never have met Gideon. I wouldn't have a chance at a beautiful and happy future. I think you can say the same thing. If what you went through hadn't happened, would you be here, right now, married to a man you love, and pregnant with his child? I'm not saying what we went through wasn't truly horrendous, because it was. But it brought me, and you, to where we are today."

"You're right," Melanie admitted. "And if you really thought it would help, I'd let you look. But I don't think that'll be necessary."

She reached behind her, lifting the back of her shirt. Gideon tensed and wondered what she was doing. She made a move like she'd pulled something up and out of the waistband of her pants. When her hands returned, she was holding a spiral-bound notebook, one like you'd see in a student's backpack.

Gideon accepted it when she held it out to him. He shot a quick glance to Lauren and opened it to the first page. It was filled with the flowery script of a young girl. He read the first few lines and jerked his focus back to Melanie. She was grinning at him.

"But this is...How did you...?" Gideon was speechless as he realized just what he held in his hands. Lauren was looking at him, waiting for a clue as to what was written inside the book. His mind couldn't form the words to tell her.

"Apart from my water ability, I have a secondary power,"

Melanie admitted. "It didn't manifest until I hit puberty. I hated it. I thought it had ruined my life, so I didn't tell anyone. Then I was kidnapped."

"I don't understand," Lauren said. "What power?" She pointed to the papers in Gideon's hand. "What's in there?"

"If someone is touching me, I can read their mind," Melanie told her. "Every time they grabbed me, or beat me, or just brushed against me, I was able to see everything in their heads. That's how I was able to get away from them. I knew when and where my best chance would be. As soon as I escaped and felt safe enough, I bought that book and wrote everything down. I had hoped it would be useful someday."

Lauren stared at Melanie for a moment longer and then came to stand next to him. He flipped to pages randomly, and they both read what was there.

He returned his gaze to the remarkable woman standing across from him, grinned, and looked down into Lauren's stunned eyes. "We've got 'em."

Gideon thought about the madman who had just hurt the woman he loved, yet again. "What about the leader? Did you ever get a chance to read him?"

Melanie shook her head. "I had plenty of chances, but he's blocked."

"What do you mean, *blocked*?" Lauren asked. "He doesn't have any power."

"He wears an amulet," Melanie informed them. "It was given to him by the previous leader. It stops any and all magic from being used on him." She pointed to the journal. "It's all in there."

"Can we take this with us?" Gideon asked, still floored by her insight and what she'd done for them. "We'll guard it with our lives, I promise."

"Once you destroy them, burn it. I don't ever want to see it again."

Gideon went with his instinct and hugged Melanie. "Thank you so very much. You just shifted the balance to weigh heavily on the side of good."

He released her and stepped back.

Melanie grinned at Lauren. "You are one lucky woman. Enjoy that future. It looks amazing."

"I know," Lauren smiled in return. "And I will."

Startled, Gideon looked at the brunette.

"Hey, I warned you," she teased. "All it takes is a touch."

He laughed before turning serious again. "If you ever need anything, call me. And we'll let you know as soon as they've been handled, so you can share the joy of that baby with your mother."

Tears gathered in Melanie's eyes. "Thank you."

"Do you need help getting anywhere?" Gideon offered. "I can send you anywhere you need to go."

She smiled. "No, my husband is outside." She pulled a cell phone out of her pocket. "We've kept this call going the whole time. He's been listening to everything we've been saying." Melanie lifted the phone closer to her face. "Say hi, honey."

"Hey." A deep male voice came through the speaker. "Mr. Marquand, if you can do what you said and take away my wife's fears, I will be forever in your debt."

"We will," Gideon promised him. "And there'll be no debt to pay. This notebook she just gave us is more than we could have wished for. So consider us even."

"Come on then, hun. Let's go home," her husband said. "Let these people go do what they need to do."

"Be right out." Melanie ended the call, gave them a warm smile, and waved as she walked away. "Good luck."

Gideon turned to Lauren. In his hand was a large piece of the puzzle they would need to finally dismantle the coven. "Can you believe this?"

He still had a hard time accepting what they held in their

possession. This unassuming, college-ruled spiral notebook with the purple cover was going to bring down the men who had destroyed too many lives to count. How could something that looked so harmless hold such powerful information?

Melanie had held onto it for so long, waiting for the right moment—the right person—to use what it contained, to do what she couldn't.

"We've got to get started on this." Lauren's eyes were bright with anticipation.

"I know. Let's go. I'm dying to see what all is in here."

Gideon pulled her in close to his body and, with a thought, sent them home.

18

"That was fast. Was she able to give you anything worth the trip?" Gideon heard the doubt Jack was trying to mask.

"Yeah, you could say that." Gideon looked around the room. Six sets of eyes stared back at him, half of them some shade of green. His family had been through so much. They'd finally found their way back to one another, and now it was time to eliminate the threat to their futures, once and for all.

"Melanie provided us with more information than we probably could have gathered in a lifetime of searching." He opened to the first page. "Let me read you just a bit of what she gave us." He took a deep breath and started.

"I hated it when Warren came. He really loved what he was doing to us. His thoughts were always filled with pleasure and excitement. All he could think about was how fast he could get the video home so he could watch it all again. I think he got off on the pain and fear he inflicted upon us."

Shocked silence reigned when he stopped. Not a breath, not a movement, not a rustle of clothes could be heard. He chose another passage.

"Santino loves being second-in-command. He's secretly hoping he'll be chosen to be next. To that end, all his thoughts were consumed with doing anything he could to please his master.

"Didn't he take in that scrawny brat because it had been

demanded of him? I don't know who that is because that's the only way he thought of them. Maybe it's another kid like me. I know there are more of us.

"*When I heard Alexander's thoughts, he was hoping the nine he'd already collected would be enough. He'd been pretty proud of himself for finding just the right ones. I know they're gathering people like me—people with magic—for a purpose. It has something to do with a family of witches the master hates. I wish I could find some way to help them, or warn them.*"

"She has to be talking about us," Amber concluded.

"The way she wrote that, it sounds like she reads minds." There was amazement in Marissa's voice, but it quickly turned to confusion. "But I thought she only had the power to control water? Isn't that why they took her?"

"Melanie never told anyone she had a secondary talent," Gideon clarified. "She said it manifested shortly before she was taken. And similar to Derrick, it only works through touch. So every time one of these sons-of-bitches made contact with her, she got a full dose of whatever they were thinking."

"And wrote it all down." The gleam in Jack's eye told Gideon he'd gotten the ramifications of what was in the rest of the book. "I'm guessing she did this after she got away from them?"

Lauren nodded and picked up the explanation. "She said as soon as she felt safe enough, she started putting the journal together. She wanted to get everything down while it was fresh."

"Can I see it?" Jack took a step forward and held out his hand. Gideon turned it over, and Jack held it reverently for a moment before opening it and scanning through. All was silent as he skimmed the pages. "She mentions the powers each man has. I see names and locations of each soldier. Everything we need is here." He looked up and beamed. "Holy shit!"

"What about the leader?" Amber's eyes drilled into Gideon. "What's in there about him?"

"Not much, according to Melanie," Gideon admitted, leaning back against the front edge of the desk. He slid his fingers into his pockets. "Evidently, he wears an amulet passed down from one head of the coven to the next. It blocks magic from being used on whoever wears it. She was never able to read any of his thoughts."

"This fucker sure knows how to protect himself and hide in the shadows." Jack abruptly turned to look at Amber. "Did that drawing of him strike a chord with yours or Marissa's parents?"

"They said he did seem like someone they should know," Amber told him. "But they couldn't place him."

"Figures," Jack muttered.

"Before we get too discouraged," Aiden countered, "let's wait and see if Melanie was able to pick up something from the other men about him. Maybe at some point, one of them thought, 'man, that Joe Bob sure is a dick'."

Gideon laughed and shook his head. "Let's hope they did."

Over the next several hours, the four Marquand witches and their partners took turns reading excerpts from Melanie's journal. They took notes and discussed how each piece of information could assist them.

Some of the recollections were clearly seen through the eyes of a teenager. Especially the thoughts coming from Warren Newland. Gideon was almost grateful that Melanie's young mind hadn't grasped just how perverted he truly was. She'd known he was bad, but she'd missed a lot of the more vulgar references.

Gideon was looking forward to getting his hands on that particular son of a bitch.

"That's it." Marissa snapped it closed after the last passage was read.

"I am in awe of this girl," Lindsay announced. "To think of what she went through for a year. Then to have the presence of mind to put all of this down in writing." She turned to Gideon.

"I hope you told her if there is anything she ever needs to let us know."

"I did," Gideon nodded. "But all she wants is to go home, as most of us can relate to. She's married and pregnant, and hasn't been able to share any of it with her mother for fear that someone is still watching."

"We'll get her home," Quinn vowed. "We'll get them all home. We know who and where they are now. We can get them out of there and back with their families."

"That may be easier said than done," Jack warned, "minus Brooke Weston, who according to Melanie was enthralled like Quinn. And Cole Daniels, who we now know was the one Quinn and Amber ran into. That leaves four who will have been brainwashed and tortured like Lauren. And that's only if they didn't pick up more after Melanie got away. Those may be harder to get through to."

"We still have to try," Lindsay asserted.

"Agreed," Jack told her. "I just wanted to make sure everyone knew it wasn't going to be easy. Look at how long it took Gideon to break through Stacia to reach Lauren, and that was with round-the-clock contact."

"I could try to reach them in their dreams—find their memories of a happier time," Quinn offered, "like I did with Lauren."

"Wait. What? When were you in my dreams?" Lauren sat forward, eyes trained on Quinn. "I don't remember seeing you."

"I didn't make my presence known." Quinn smiled. "It was when Stacia had Amber's powers. We needed to know where they were kept. So I went in and...guided you to reveal where they were."

Lauren's brows furrowed. "Guided how? And you can do that? Manipulate dreams?"

"Yeah," he grinned. "And more."

"The birds," she guessed. "At the warehouse. That was you.

I was only told about your ability to absorb magic. That's why they wanted you so badly."

"Do you think they knew about the rest?" Jack's interest was piqued.

"I doubt it," Lauren told him. "If they had, they definitely would have found a way to use it."

"Their information seems to have some holes in it," Amber noted. "They knew about some of Quinn's powers but not all. They took Melanie for her water ability, but never knew about the touch telepathy. Someone either isn't doing their job, or they're purposely withholding some vital facts."

"Well, we know Mattison was in charge of finding and bringing in the chosen," Jack added. "But how did they know who had the powers they were looking for?" He looked to Lauren.

She shrugged. "I don't know."

"Jack," Gideon drew his attention, "what about Jared Howard? He's clairvoyant. And from what Melanie wrote, he's secretly disgusted by what the others have been doing—what *he's* had to do. Could he have done it? The abilities that were kept hidden were the same ones that ultimately enabled Quinn and Melanie both to escape. If it was him, I wonder if he'd be an asset to us. I think it might be worth checking him out first. If we can turn him to our side..."

"You could have something there," Jack agreed. "He may be working from within to hinder them. If he's willing, Jared may be able to get us the info we need on his boss. The most important being who the hell is he, and why the vendetta against this family?"

He stopped for a beat. "We need to keep in mind, though, that this is *all* speculation. We don't know for sure Jared Howard is the one sabotaging the operation. Until we're absolutely certain, we'll have to be very careful," he cautioned, looking around at everyone. "Because after everything that's happened today, they know we're coming for them. And they'll be ready for us."

~~~

After another hour of discussion, they decided to turn in for the night. Only Lauren, Gideon, Amber, and Quinn remained. Lauren was tired but thought it was time she had that talk with Quinn. They were linked in ways no one but them could understand. Today had only emphasized that point.

She was slowly coming to terms with what had happened to her by the coven's hands, but there were still a few things she had a hard time with.

What she'd done to Quinn being the worst.

She'd been responsible for his imprisonment for years. It had been on her order to dispose of him. Luckily, Amber and the others had found him and rescued him. If he had died, Stacia wouldn't have cared. But as Lauren, she would have been destroyed, knowing she'd been the cause of an innocent man's death.

The other was the scars. She just couldn't make peace with what they meant. It wasn't as bad as it had been, but deep down they represented a time when she'd given in. Maybe talking with Quinn would help her to understand, and finally put to rest her feelings of failure and shame.

Knowing the connection would be there, she looked to Gideon seated next to her on the couch. *"You go on ahead. I'd like to stay and talk to Quinn."*

He smiled at her in reassurance. *"I'll be waiting for you when you're done."*

"Thank you."

He leaned in to kiss her and then rose.

Amber and Quinn stood as well. "We're going to head up too," Amber said. "We'll see you in the morning."
~~~

Lauren's nerves made it impossible to remain seated. She got to her feet and spoke before she lost her nerve. "Quinn, I was wondering if I could talk with you for a minute?"

A brief look passed between him and Amber, and he nodded, turning back to Lauren. "Yeah, sure."

Gideon stepped up and looped his arm through Amber's. "Come on, Cuz." They started for the exit, but just before he cleared the door, he looked back over his shoulder and gave her a smile of encouragement.

Lauren could admit to being more than a little nervous. And now that she was here alone with him, she didn't know where to begin. She wiped her palms down the sides of her pants legs.

Quinn stood before her, relaxed, his thumbs hooked in the back pockets of his jeans. "Maybe it'll make it easier if I tell you I don't hold any of what happened against you."

Lauren was aghast. "But how can you *not*?" She'd been told he felt this way, but she still couldn't reconcile hearing the words from his own mouth. "I kept you caged and under a spell that robbed you of who you are. I exploited you and used you for my own personal gain."

"Let's sit." He motioned her to the couch beside him. Once they were both seated, he turned to her. His eyes were a deep ocean-blue now. When she'd held him captive, they'd been as black as death, an effect of the mind-control spell he'd been kept under. As he watched her now, his gaze was intent and serious.

"I want to ask you something. The person you are right now, sitting here—would *she* have done any of what you just listed out?"

"Oh, God no," Lauren exclaimed. "It makes me sick to know what I've done to you."

"That's why I can let go of it." He grinned a little. "But if Stacia ever shows her face again, we might have a problem."

Lauren couldn't share his humor and opened her mouth to

argue. He talked right over her. "Look. We both have a part of us that has caused pain and damage. But that man—the one who stripped all those witches of their powers—it wasn't me. Under the enthrallment spell, I was essentially someone else. As were you with Stacia."

"You didn't have a choice, though," she reasoned. "That spell deprived you of your free will. We made you...*I* made you do what you did."

"Did you have a choice but to become Stacia?"

"*Yes.*" And this was the point that still haunted her, no matter what Gideon, or her mother, or anyone else told her. She had made the decision to give in. To become what they had wanted. "I could have fought harder. Longer. I never should have surrendered. You didn't. Melanie didn't. Because of that, you both escaped them."

"Lauren—"

This time she plowed over his words of disagreement. "I know all the arguments. I was still a baby when they took me. You were basically an adult. I also know, and have come to believe, that if my life hadn't played out exactly as it had, I wouldn't be here right now with all of you. With Gideon. But—"

"No." His forceful, solemn tone cut her off. "No buts. Nothing that happened was *your* fault." He surprised her by grabbing her wrist and shoving the sleeve of her shirt up. "I know you think these hold a negative connotation. You think they speak of your weakness, but they don't. They're the proof that you beat them.

"Every single one of these scars is a symbol of your rebellion. Every time you fought against them, you gained at least one more. Look at how many there are. These aren't the stains of a coward...They're the badge of a fighter. You have them *because* you fought."

He laid his arm next to hers. His scars were more severe than hers, but she had countless more. "We beat them, Lauren.

They did *all this* to us, and yet here we are." Quinn took her hand in both of his. "I guess I look at this differently because of my Native American heritage, but I wear them proudly. They're a mark of my courage, my determination. They remind me every day that I was stronger than they were. And so were you. You may lack the blood to be Lakota, but you are truly a warrior at heart."

Lauren was speechless. She didn't realize tears were trailing down her cheeks until one slid into the corner of her mouth, and she tasted its saltiness. She made a move to wipe them away, but Quinn's hand was already there.

She looked at him with still-moist eyes. "I have to admit—I was dreading this talk. That's why it's taken me so long to come to you. I was afraid. But you've helped me more than I could have imagined, so thank you."

They both stood, and Quinn reached out to wrap her in a hug.

"I'm always here if you need to talk. See you in the morning." Quinn smiled and waved as he strode from the room.

"Good night."

She sat in the library for another few minutes, reveling in the new feeling of being unbound. Her heart felt so much lighter. Freer. The last weight that had been sitting in the pit of her stomach was gone.

Gideon's voice whispered into her head. *"Hey, are you ever coming up?"*

"I'm on my way."

Lauren stood up and headed for the door. She would take her happy, liberated self and put it to good use. Gideon wouldn't know what hit him.

19

The next morning dawned dazzling and radiant. Kind of like Lauren had been the previous night. Gideon had purposely closed the doorway in his mind he always held open between him and Lauren. He'd wanted to give her privacy for a conversation he knew would be hard for her. But judging by the mood she'd been in afterward, he'd wager a guess it had gone pretty well. Whatever Quinn had said to her must have been what she'd needed to hear. More of the shadows were gone from her eyes.

Gideon gazed over at her sleeping form. He watched the sunlight as it played through her blazing red hair. The strands glowed where they spilled out across the pillow. He could finally admit that maybe Fate had known what she was doing in pairing them together. He'd anticipated a rough road, and it wasn't smoothed over yet, but they were getting there. They were on their way to the future he'd seen.

Lauren shifted beside him. Long lashes fluttered and lifted to reveal beautiful hazel eyes.

"Hi." Her voice was low and sexy from sleep.

"Hi, yourself," he echoed.

She rolled into him, her hand sliding down his stomach and reaching for his already-hardening shaft.

"Good morning," she smiled, fondling him.

"Mmmm, I'll give you until forever to stop." Gideon leaned in and kissed her soft, agile mouth.

His hand roamed her body, from the base of her neck to the back of her knee. He loved the softness of her silky skin, especially first thing in the morning when she was at her most supple. Muscles usually toned and taut were yielding and pliant. She was warm and velvety to his touch. On the return trip up her sleek shape, his hand came to rest on her breast. He rolled the peak between his thumb and finger. As she drew in a quick breath, her hand tightened around him, and he groaned.

With his cock still held tight, she shifted, nudging him to his back. In one smooth motion, she came astride his hips and guided him deep into her core. His hands went to her narrow hips where his fingers dug in, seating her firmly against him.

The door in his mind flew wide, and he linked into hers, sharing magic and love, and so much more. Making love this way had shown them both new heights, the most intense being that he could feel her responses, and she his.

And it was because of that connection he knew to deny his urge to thrust into her over and over. The small, grinding circles she made with her hips had him hitting all the secret places deep inside of her.

As she rode him, Gideon reached up to squeeze and mold her breasts. She was driving him mad, and the need to move, to take over, was nearly more than he could stand.

When she finally lifted herself up and slid down him again, he thrust to meet her. The rhythm was set, and soon they were both cresting wave after wave of pleasure.

She collapsed onto his chest out of breath, her slight form a welcome weight.

They stayed joined as the sweat on their bodies began to cool. When he felt the goose-bumps rise on her skin, he wrapped his arms tightly around her and sat up. It took some doing, but he was able to stand and walk into the bathroom without having to let her go.

He strode to the shower and, one-handed, started the water

flowing. He stepped in and slowly immersed them under the hot spray.

Lauren sighed in his arms. "That feels so good." She drew back and kissed him. "Almost as good as you."

Gideon's recuperative abilities went to work, and making a quarter turn he pushed her back against the tile wall and began again.

~~~

Nearing the dining room a short while later, they heard raised voices. Walking through the doorway, they were assailed by a full-blown argument between Aiden and Amber. Lindsay and Quinn were both kicked back, letting them hash it out. There was no sign of anyone else.

Gideon had found out quickly that being Marquand meant your temper was immense and lighting fast. He'd learned the hard way to keep the worst of it under wraps. When your power was linked to your emotions, a bad day could go to hell in a heartbeat.

He listened with half an ear as he and Lauren crossed to the buffet and looked over the offerings.

"No!" Aiden shouted down the table at her. "You and Quinn are *not* going off on your own to look for the rest of the soldiers. Look what happened last time you ran into one."

"We handled it," Amber countered. Gideon glanced over his shoulder at her, and she wore a look of complete confidence.

"You had to call in reinforcements, for God's sake. And Lauren was shot," her brother reminded her as Gideon and Lauren, plates in hand, approached the table. "No. Wherever we go, we go in teams of four."

Amber's tone was exasperated as she sat forward, so her elbows rested on the table. "If we split into pairs, we can cover more ground. There are still five coven members, the leader,
~~~

and at least four soldiers out there."

Gideon showed Lauren to her chair and then seated himself.

"Yeah, and what about the guards?" Aiden asked heatedly, mirroring her move. "How many of them are stationed at each training center? Do *you* know that? *I* don't know that."

"We're witches, damn it!" She slapped the table with her flat palm. "We can take them."

Aiden's voice rose with hers. "Yes, *damn it*. We *are* witches, but we're not invincible."

Gideon took his own life into his hands and waded in. "For what it's worth," they both swung angry green eyes around at him, "I think Aiden's right."

"You *would*," Amber muttered at the same time Aiden barked, "Ha!"

"But," Gideon threw out to stop any further antagonizing words, "Amber poses a reasonable, yet flawed plan."

"Ha," Amber goaded and then stopped. "Wait. What? Flawed how?"

"We do need to put more effort into finding the soldiers, but—and this is where I agree with Aiden—we need to be smart about it. We don't go in alone. A minimum of four is a good idea."

Jack and Marissa strolled in at that point. "What's a good idea?" Jack asked on his way to the coffee carafe.

Gideon knew Aiden well enough to know he'd throw his sister under the bus, causing yet another battle, so Gideon started explaining before Aiden could get a chance.

"That no less than four of us should team up and go after the ones who were kidnapped. Amber was just volunteering her and Quinn to be a part of that team." Gideon grinned evilly at her. "And I think Aiden and Lindsay should be the other half of that group."

As expected, Aiden and Amber both shot him murderous looks. He felt a shift in the air and knew Amber was trying to use her magic on him in retaliation. Gideon dampened her power and arched a brow at her. *"Really?"*

She backed down with a huff. *"Jerk. You just wait."*

"Bring it."

A spark of humor flashed in her jewel-toned eyes, and she grinned.

Jack, unaware of the silent exchange, added his opinion to the original conversation. "That *is* a good plan. Those four can concentrate on that facet, and the rest of us can hone in on Jared Howard."

Thanks to Melanie, they knew the locations of the soldiers. All Aiden's team had to do was figure out where to start. After a brief conversation, it was unanimously decided they'd begin with Brooke Weston. Being enthralled like Quinn, they hoped that once the spell was broken, she would be relatively easy to deal with and accepting of their help.

The four left and went to ready themselves and the potion. Jack, Marissa, Lauren, and he remained. Gideon looked to where Jack sat drinking his coffee. "So how do we find Howard?"

Jack had obviously already thought this out, because he had an answer ready. "We go through the book one more time. Make sure we didn't miss anything. Pool all the data we have on him, and hunt him down."

"Can we do that in here?" Marissa asked. "I'm about tired of the library. And we can eat while we go over everything."

"Sure," Jack agreed, setting his mug aside. "I'll just run and get what we need."

Before Jack could fully stand, Gideon teleported the journal and all their other notes in from the other room. They landed in the middle of the table with a smack.

"Or Super Witch can just do that." Jack laughed and sat back down. "Show off."

Gideon laughed with relaxed humor.

Growing up, he hadn't let himself think about what he'd been missing by not having his family around him. If he'd allowed those thoughts and feelings to set in, he'd never have been able to do what needed to be done. So, he'd locked them down with an iron will.

But every so often they would fight back, and he'd wake from an intensely real dream with tears wetting his cheeks. On those occasions, he'd have to let the memories and wishes for something different fly free.

He'd give himself that day to feel the sadness of loss and loneliness. Then he'd push them back down and get back to preparing, readying for the day he'd reveal himself and return to his family to wage war.

What he hadn't taken into account, though, were people like Jack, Quinn, and Lindsay. People who'd taken up the fight out of love, loyalty, and generosity of spirit. These individuals his sister and cousins had chosen were a perfect fit into this family. Gideon would never have dreamed of the camaraderie and connection he felt with each one.

Jack, the brother he'd never had. Though he had not one magical bone in his body, the rough and ready PI certainly held his own in a crowd of witches. Gideon caught a glimpse of what the future had in store for his sister and her soul mate and grinned. Jack would need every one of those stalwart nerves to get him through the terrible-twos of a very opinionated and very magical set of twin sons he and Marissa would bring into the world one day soon. If he made it through that, he'd be able to handle whatever, or whoever, came after.

Quinn, the quiet warrior. Amber had chosen her perfect counterpart with him. Where she was quick to temper and prepared to battle, Quinn was settled and calm. Gideon knew he'd had to learn the hard way which wars to fight outright and which to combat with subtlety. What he'd gone through had not only strengthened his mind and body, it had brought him a greater sense of self. Quinn now knew he was part of a much larger world. A world of magic and spirit and nature. His connection to all three grounded him in a way he'd never been before. And when he finally took his grandfather's place as shaman, Quinn would become someone the tribes talked about for generations.

Gideon's thoughts turned to Lindsay, the little mother who had fought evil and won to save her child. A child who would grow to adulthood knowing she was loved and treasured by this big, boisterous family. As the years passed and more babies were born, no one would remember that Hannah Rose hadn't started out life as a Marquand. As the oldest grandchild, she would become ringleader to some of this family's most memorable stunts. And Lindsay would only be able to shake her head, because Aiden would have put Hannah up to most of them.

Lauren reached out and laid her hand on his leg under the table. *"Are you okay?"*

"Yeah. I'm good." Gideon turned his head to smile contentedly at her.

"Where did you go?"

"To the future and back," he told her.

"See anything good?"

Gideon swung his gaze to Jack, remembering the frazzled dad, and laughed. *"You could say that."*

"Anything you want to share?"

He sent her the image in his head and heard her silent laughter.

"Are those his and Marissa's kids?"

"Yup."

"Oh my. Do you think you should warn him?"

Gideon grinned. *"At some point."*

"Hey. If you two are done making googly eyes at each other, we've got some work to do here. Grab some paper, people," Jack teased.

"Or maybe not," Gideon sent to Lauren, making her laugh harder.

Half an hour later, Marissa's furrowed brow drew his attention.

"What is it?" Gideon asked her. "What do you see?"

"This memory Melanie pulled from Jared's mind, where she sees him standing at the water's edge, looking out into the distance. The piece of land he sees on the other side—I think I know where that is. I recognize a few of the landmarks he's thinking about."

"Where is it?" Jack set his own papers aside.

"It's a strip of Highway 31 between Acme and Traverse City. She hears him mention how brightly the whiteness of the fudge shop stands out against the green and grey of the surrounding setting." Marissa brought her gaze up. "If he's seeing that from across a body of water, that means he's out on the peninsula. Jared Howard is in Traverse City."

A sick feeling was growing in Gideon's gut. "I'm beginning to feel that we're being led around by the nose."

"Why do you say that?" Marissa asked.

"Think back on what we know about Howard," he told her. "He hates what they're doing and wants out. We're pretty sure he's withheld important information, causing certain aspects of this operation to fail. I'm beginning to think he saw all this playing out a long time ago and has done what he could, secretly, to put all the pieces in the right place. That he positioned himself in an area one of us would recognize, and planted that scene in Melanie's mind, knowing twenty years later, she'd show it to us and give us the clue we needed to find him. I think he's just been sitting back and biding his time."

"That's a pretty big stretch. You really believe he's orchestrated this whole thing?" The wheels of Jack's PI brain were working, sorting through puzzle pieces and putting them in place.

"I do," Gideon confirmed.

"Did you see him when you confronted them during the attack yesterday?" Lauren asked. "Did any of the men give any indication they knew you'd be there?"

"No," Gideon told her. "Aside from the leader, they all left their hoods up."

"So there's no way to know for sure until we find him. Great," Marissa sighed.

"How *do* we find him? We only have a general area," Lauren reminded them. "How will we know if we're getting close?"

"I'll bet if he sees us coming," Gideon told her, "he'll show us exactly where to go."

"Is anyone else freaked out about what we're blindly walking into?" Lauren asked.

"Oh yeah," Marissa confirmed.

Gideon and Jack both nodded in agreement.

"Good. I'm glad I'm not the only one." Lauren slid her chair back and stood. "Shall we?"

Gideon and the others followed her out. He caught up with her in the hall and wrapped his arm around her waist. "Are you worried about seeing Jared again?"

"Will it be the highlight of my day? No. I'll handle it, though." They walked in silence for a few steps. "I'll have to face all of them again at some point. But I'll do it if it means putting an end to them."

"Hey." He waited until she looked up at him. "You don't have to face them alone. Remember that."

The haunted look left her eyes, and she smiled a little. "I know. Thank you."

About an hour into the drive, Gideon got tired of the tense silence and decided to bust Jack's chops a little.

"Hey Jack, have you two thought about kids yet?"

Beside him in the back seat, Lauren snorted but tried to cover it.

Jack shot him a guarded look in the rearview mirror. "No. Not really. Why?"

Gideon purposely turned his head to look out the side window. He had to bite the inside of his cheek to keep the grin from spreading. "No reason. Just wondering."

Out of the corner of his eye, he saw Jack's head whip around to look at Marissa before focusing on the road again.

He drove without saying anything for a full thirty seconds and then exploded. "Damn it, Gideon! Why the hell would you ask me that? Did you see something about our kids?"

Marissa shifted in her seat to look back. "Did you really see something?" The excitement was clear in her voice.

"Just a snippet." He showed his sister the green-eyed blonde boys in her future.

"Oh my." Her smile was huge. "Really?"

"Yeah." Gideon knew not knowing was killing Jack, and he reveled in it.

"Someone better tell me what the fuck is going on," Jack demanded. "What did Super Witch see?"

Marissa laughed. "You'd better show him."

"You sure?" Gideon asked, just to poke at his brother-in-law further. "You think he can handle it? While he's driving? He might kill us."

"Gideon, I swear to God—I'm going to pull over, jerk you out of this vehicle, and beat you to a bloody pulp."

"All right, all right! No need to get violent." Gideon was laughing so hard, he could barely form the image to send to Jack.

When it landed, the car veered and swerved, making Gideon laugh even harder.

"Oh, hell." The portion of Jack's face Gideon could see in the mirror turned sheet-white. "*Two?*"

"Yup," Gideon gleefully answered. "Two. Twins. Boys. Identical."

"Shut up, Gideon. Now." The threat in Jack's voice didn't seem as dire while his face was still devoid of color.

Oh yeah, Gideon thought. *So worth it.*

20

Gideon was still enjoying the hit he'd struck when Jack slowed. He made the right turn onto the road which ran the full length of the peninsula. The car had barely straightened out when Gideon received their instructions.

"We need to make a right on Eastern Avenue, then a left on Birchwood," Gideon shared with Jack.

Startled grey eyes met his in the mirror. "He showed you that?"

"Yup. Guess he knew we were coming," Gideon answered. "Let's just hope it's not a trap."

Marissa twisted around to look at him. "Can you see anything about what we're walking into?"

"No. I may not need to touch something like you and Amber, but The Powers That Be still need to show it to me. I can't control when or what comes to me. Believe me, I've tried."

"We'll find out soon enough." Lauren's stiff shoulders told Gideon all he needed to know about her thoughts on that prospect.

They traveled another couple of miles when Gideon got the next set of directions. "Hang a right on Center. He said there'll be black steel gates on the left. Stop and hit the buzzer; he'll let us in."

"I so don't have a good feeling about this." Marissa sat forward in her seat, trying to see the entrance Gideon described.

It came into view about fifty yards ahead. Jack pulled in and stopped next to the box housing a single button. "Here goes nothing," he muttered as he tapped the control on the armrest to lower the window. He reached for the little white disc.

Before his hand was back in the car, the steel bars in front of them started to move. When there was enough room to fit through, Jack gradually accelerated.

He drove up in front of a large brick two-story house and parked. After shutting the car off, he leaned forward, and Gideon knew he'd pulled the pistol from the small of his back.

Gideon heard a click and then a scraping sound as Jack checked the contents of his magazine. With a quick snap, it was seated back into place. He racked the slide, loading a bullet into the chamber. A soft snick followed. The safety being engaged.

Like most guys, Gideon had watched his fair share of action movies. He'd heard the terms "locked and loaded" many times. But it wasn't until he'd met Jack that he'd found out what they actually meant.

Each person going into this meeting had their own form of weapon, Jared Howard included. Whether they would have to use them was anyone's guess. But they were all prepared to if needed.

Exiting the vehicle and walking up to the door was the hardest thing Gideon had done in a long time. Not knowing what was waiting on the other side had everyone's senses on high alert.

Gideon reached out with his magic, searching for any hazards, dangers, or traps. Finding none, he gave Jack a nod. Jack lifted his hand to knock, but the door swung inward before he could touch it.

A man, probably in his sixties, stood there waiting to usher them in. His hair was mostly gray with some of the original brown peppering through. He was short in stature, only five-six or -seven.

"I'm Jared Howard. I've been waiting for you."

Their group followed him down a short hall to a formal living room overlooking the manicured lawns at the rear of the property. Elegant furniture filled the space, but no one sat. The four of them stood facing Jared Howard, ready for whatever happened next.

"I can assure you I'm here alone. But please do whatever you feel necessary to confirm that." Because Gideon had already scanned the house, he didn't bother now.

Howard continued. "I've worked very hard, for a very long time, to make this happen." He looked at Lauren. "While you may have been under their control for twenty years, I have been stuck in that hell for much longer than that."

"Why?" Lauren positioned herself a few steps away from Gideon, her body loose and poised to react in an instant.

"I was a part of the old regime, you see." Jared crossed to the French doors and looked out. "I was power-hungry and arrogant and thought I could have it all. And we did, for a while." He turned his back to the view. "Then my master stepped down and this...this *monster* took his place." Disgust showed plainly on his face.

"He replaced most of the existing coven with others who were like him. He never found another clairvoyant as good as me, so he had to keep me around. I quickly became disillusioned by what he was planning." He slid his hands into his pockets, apprehensive now. "He talked of killing and destroying those who carried power." Jared's gaze took in Gideon and Marissa. "The Marquand family had always been his obsession, but when he started taking those innocent children...What he did to them. What *we* did to them." Jared shook his head. "I had no choice but to play along. But it just became too much for me. I started plotting and planning, and I waited for the day I could get out."

"Why not do something sooner?" Jack asked what they were all wondering.

"I've seen what he can do to those who cross him. And he has his other followers. They stay close and are loyal unto death, as you learned with Alexander. When I saw you," he turned his focus to Gideon, "I knew my time was coming. I'm not strong enough to stop them, but you are. You and your family."

Jared became reflective for a moment. "He may hate you, but I think deep down, he's also frightened of you."

"Why?" Marissa demanded. "Why does he hate us so much?"

Jared walked to a high-backed chair and rested his hands on the top. "With that damned medallion, I was never able to see any details concerning him. But I did hear a few things. It seems he feels the magic you all carry should have been his. That he is the rightful—"

Gideon felt a disturbance in the air, just as another set of French doors slammed open. He briefly thought about teleporting his family out but decided against it. This could be a chance to discover more. He turned to face the intruders.

"Well, isn't this just too cozy." The men they knew to be Warren Newland and Theo Zeeland stepped into the room from outside. They were followed by four henchmen. "Jared, Jared, Jared." Warren's tone was patronizing. "He is *not* going to be happy about this."

After the first startled recoil, Howard had remained unnaturally motionless and silent.

"What did you do to him?" Lauren stepped forward.

"I've taken away his ability to move or speak." Warren's brown eyes held contempt and hatred for the older man. "Can't have him spilling any more secrets now, can we?"

Theo issued an order to their men, his voice cold and hard. "Take that piece of shit out of here."

Two broke off and started towards the elder coven member.

Gideon felt the impact of Jared's gaze as it slammed into

him from across the room. With one last desperate thought, Jared sent him another piece of the puzzle. *Christopher.*

He tried to ask him what that meant, but he was out of time. Everyone knew what would happen to Jared if he were taken from the house. Gideon had to act now.

Just as the coven's muscle reached out to take hold of Jared Howard, he disappeared.

The newcomers looked around almost frantically. Gideon couldn't hold back the grin spreading across his face.

"Lose something?"

"Find him!" Theo barked out, and the same two men took off in search of Jared.

"That," Warren turned to Gideon, "was a very ill-advised move."

Jack's gun was already drawn and pointed at Warren's chest. "Take another step, and I'll drop you where you stand."

"Oh, I don't think you will," he taunted. "You see, I can turn your senses against you and make you see, feel, and hear anything I want. Or nothing at all. I can find your greatest fear and bring it to life. With just a thought, I can make you believe you're in the middle of a den of snakes, or trapped at the bottom of the ocean with no air. Have you ever watched someone die from fright? It's very...stimulating. Shall we try it?"

"Enough," Theo snapped. "We stop this, *now*." He flung Jack's gun across the room with a look. "Take him," he commanded, and the remaining two goons descended on Jack.

Marissa was at his side, ready and able to fight, so Gideon only spared them a glance. What bothered him more was the way Theo was eyeing Lauren.

"So, little Stacia has flipped sides. You always were more trouble than you were worth. I told him repeatedly to get rid of you, but he never would." The glint in Theo's eyes was one of utter loathing. "You're nothing, and I've been hoping this day would come. I've wanted to put you down for years." Theo reached behind his back and pulled out a long, thin sword.

Gideon turned to Lauren and saw she was prepared to meet the challenge, but he'd be damned if she were going to face this bastard unarmed. He knew she deserved this chance at retribution. So instead of stepping in to help, he conjured a matching weapon into her hand. The smile she flashed at him was pure Stacia.

He'd keep an eye on her, but with Warren still facing him, Gideon knew that's where his focus needed to be.

"I guess that leaves you and me." Gideon's tone was glib.

"And I'll so enjoy it," Warren sneered. "We've been looking for you for a long time."

"Yeah, I know. How'd that work out for you?"

Gideon felt his perception start to shift and knew Warren was trying to use his magic to disable him. The world around him began to fade away and in its place was nothing but darkness. Gideon quickly erected a shield around his mind. As he added and wove in intricate layers, the invasive force lessened, and the room came back into focus. The evil leer Warren wore slipped when he discovered Gideon was able to fight back.

The pressure on the outside of the shield increased, telling him that Newland had doubled his efforts. He'd probably never gone up against anyone capable of negating his talent. His natural inclination was to push harder.

Gideon wondered what would happen if he could turn Warren's own ability against him. Would it have the same effect on him that it did his victims? If he could somehow make the result permanent, Warren Newland would no longer be a threat to anyone. And one more coven member would be out of the way.

Gideon knew he had one shot at this. If Newland caught on to what he wanted to do, he'd just shut his talent down. Gideon needed him to keep it coming—the more power behind it, the better. To that end, he goaded the other man.

"Not the result you were looking for? I thought you were supposed to be this big, scary badass." Gideon recalled what they'd learned about this man. "What's the matter? Can't get it up if it's not an innocent young girl?"

If the look on Warren's face was any indication, the barbs landed with a direct hit. The amount of mind-altering magic being aimed at him amplified exponentially. If this plan was going to work, it had to be soon.

Gideon worked out all the different elements of the spell. They would have to be deployed simultaneously so Newland wouldn't have a chance to evade it.

One more push. "The master is going to be very disappointed in you. Maybe you and Howard can have adjoining torture chambers."

Warren actually growled as he threw everything he had at Gideon.

In that instant, Gideon triggered the spell. Three things happened as a result. The outer surface of his shield turned into a mirror. It completely engulfed Warren's mind and locked down tight, his magic on an endless loop, holding him forever in darkness. He stood now, his eyes sightless, his ears deaf, his mouth mute.

Where he and Warren's battle had been entirely mental, everyone else was engaged in physical combat. Concerned, Gideon immediately followed the sound of clashing steel to where Lauren and Theo were battling.

She was swinging her blade and pushing him back with maneuvers Gideon had only seen in movies.

His eyes ran over her body, searching out where she'd been struck by Theo's sword. None of the wounds seemed to be life-threatening. His gaze transferred to her opponent. He too had areas where blood had soaked through his clothing. She was giving as good as she got as they swung their weapons with all their might.

Gideon spared a glance at Jack and Marissa. They'd made quick work of the henchmen. Jack bent to retrieve his pistol and came to stand next to Gideon. "Do you want me to shoot him?"

"No, she needs this." Gideon knew it but still inwardly cringed every time steel sliced through the air. "But keep it handy, just in case." Even with as serious as the situation was, Gideon couldn't resist. "You know, I could probably come up with some kind of tether so you could hold onto that better." Gideon looked down at the gun in Jack's hand.

Jack scowled at him. "If everyone we ran into didn't have telekinesis, I wouldn't have a problem. You witches just have no respect for a man's gun."

Gideon's grin was short-lived when Lauren took a particularly bad hit. Blood instantly saturated the front of her shirt where Theo sliced across her stomach. It was all he could do to stand there. Beside him, Jack brought his weapon up in a two-handed grip. It stayed steadily trained on Theo's head.

He had to do something. As good as she was, she was at a disadvantage. This was the man who had trained her. He knew every move she would make and could anticipate it. Gideon was a heartbeat away from just taking the man out when a better idea popped into his head.

A scene from an action film he'd seen flashed into his mind. In it, two men were fighting much the same way as Lauren and Zeeland. The hero of the movie was cut and bleeding; he was close to losing when he struck out with a move the bad guy hadn't expected, winning the battle.

Gideon played the sequence over in his head. Could he send it to Lauren? Could she use it? It would be something Theo never saw coming, and it might turn the tables. *What the hell.*

"Try this," he sent to her mind as the images started to play.

She swept into the moves effortlessly, like she'd practiced them countless times. And as hoped, Theo was at a loss. He was left wide open, and she took him with a slash across the throat. He fell to the floor as his blood spilled, the strike fatal.

Lauren's breathing was deep and heavy as she walked into Gideon's arms, blade held down at her side. "Thank you."

"Are you badly hurt?" he asked her, gently enfolding her in his grasp.

"Stomach burns, but nothing I can't handle."

He cast aside her dismissal. He knew her tolerance for pain had been elevated by years of torture. What most would immediately run to the hospital for, she shrugged off.

Setting her back from him, Gideon lifted her shirt with one hand and placed the other on top of the wound across her midsection. A brief pulse of power had the bleeding stopped and the cut sealing closed.

Marissa stepped in close. "Where did you send Jared?"

"To his garage," Gideon explained. "I figured he'd take the hint and get the hell out of here."

"With everything he's done," Lauren said, "I'd hate to see him get off scot-free."

"We all would," Jack agreed.

Gideon continued to tend to Lauren until all evidence of her injury was gone. The rest would have to wait. They needed to go. They'd leave the others for the coven to find, so they'd know they were down two more members.

Gideon and Jack led the women out and into the car. Jack started it up and drove away. "By my count, that only leaves Mylos and Davis Sutter. And we still don't know who the brains behind the curtain is or where to find him."

"I think I may have something on that." Gideon relayed Jared's parting word before Gideon had teleported him out.

"Christopher," Marissa tested it out. "Do you think that's his first or last name?"

"Not a clue," Gideon told them. He reached out and pulled Lauren into his side. After kissing the top of her head, he asked her, "Do you remember ever hearing that name?"

She shook her head. "No. He was always just Uncle to me, and no one else ever talked to me about him."

"Even with the name, we're still no closer to knowing who he is." Jack made the turn onto Highway 31. "Do you realize how common a name Christopher is?"

"It's still something we didn't have before," Marissa reminded him. "I just wish Jared had been able to tell us more before they found us." She turned to look at him and Lauren. "The leader must have figured out Jared was working against him. Why else have him watched?" She glanced outside, but not before Gideon read the uneasiness in her eyes. "I wonder what he'll do to him if he finds him."

"Nothing good, I can promise you that," Lauren said.

They rode with their own thoughts for a few miles before Jack spoke. "I wonder why he thinks the Marquand magic should be rightfully his." He looked at Gideon in the mirror. "You don't have any other relatives, do you? Maybe a branch that didn't sprout from the witch side of the tree?"

"Not that I know of." Gideon thought about it. "My grandfather and grandmother were both only children. Ben and Conner were the only kids they had, and then there's us. I can't think of anyone who would think they would be related to us."

"We'll check out the family journals," Jack suggested. "Maybe there's a connection buried in there somewhere."

21

Lauren had been quiet during the drive back to Marquand Manor. When Jack pulled into the driveway, she took in the sight of the large house towering in front of her. She realized in that moment she missed Gideon's cabin on the lake. It had seemed like a prison for so long, but now she wished for its privacy and solitude.

It was a peaceful and tranquil place, and she needed some of that right now. She needed time to deal with the aftermath of having taken the life of someone she'd known since her childhood. It didn't seem to matter that he'd been responsible for making her life a living hell. Or that at the time, he'd been trying to kill her.

She had killed by the coven's order many times, but Stacia and her callousness were gone now, pushed back and dulled by Gideon's healing. Lauren's compassion remained, and no matter what Theo Zeeland had done to her, she couldn't just ignore the feelings his death had caused.

Jack parked in the garage and shut the engine off. Gideon opened the door and slid out. She followed, but as soon as she was standing, he pulled her in close. "You okay?"

Lauren had tried to hide what she was feeling. But she should have known better. He would always know. She looked up into his silvery-green eyes and shook her head.

"Tell me what you need," he whispered.

"The cabin. And you. Just for a little while."

He tucked her head into his chest and wrapped his arms tightly around her back. She heard and felt the rumble of his voice in his chest as he spoke to Jack.

"There's something we need to do," Gideon told him. "We'll be back in a couple of hours."

Jack didn't respond right away, and Lauren thought Gideon was probably telepathically explaining the situation.

"Yeah, sure," Jack finally answered. "See you in a bit."

In the next instant, Lauren heard birdsong and the sound of waves. They were standing on the porch of Gideon's house.

"I think I have something you'll like." He took her hand, guided her down the steps and around the side of the cabin. She'd noticed the enclosed gazebo when they'd reinforced the protection spells, but hadn't thought to ask what was in it. He tugged her along as he headed that way.

As they approached, the drop-down canvas sides began to rise. Revealed within was a large, churning hot tub. She followed him up the four steps and onto the decking where the tub was actually set into the gazebo floor.

He undressed her where they stood. Naked, she stepped down into the swirling water and submerged herself into heaven. She sank deep until the water covered her shoulders. The cuts she'd sustained earlier burned and throbbed, but she ignored them and waited for Gideon to join her.

His body was something to behold as he shed his clothes. Strong, firm, perfectly-toned muscles flexed as he lowered himself into the bubbling warmth. He fit against her effortlessly when he settled in behind her.

"How's that?" he asked her.

"Perfect." She relaxed into him and absorbed the heat of the water and the strength of the man holding her for several minutes.

"I can't seem to get past it." She knew she wouldn't have

to explain any more than that. He'd probably known all along what she was feeling but had waited for her to broach the subject.

"I can understand that. Taking a life shouldn't be easy. If it were, you wouldn't be the woman I've come to love."

"He was a terrible person. He hurt me and countless others. I shouldn't feel anything but relief that he's gone."

"I'm going to say something you're not going to like," he warned her. "But I want you to hear me out before you respond."

Lauren braced herself for whatever was coming. "Okay."

"In a strange way, these men were a part of your family."

If she hadn't given her word, Lauren knew the rebuttal would have burst from her lips. But she swallowed it down and nodded for him to continue.

"You thought Santino was your father. These men were his friends and associates. They were in your life every week for twenty years, and they were the only interactions you had during all that time. You developed relationships with each one, though not under pleasant circumstances. Those connections are still there, regardless of you knowing the truth about them now."

She gave serious thought to what he'd said. *Did* she think of them as family? He was right in that they were the only company she'd been allowed. And yes, she'd had a relationship with each one. They were her teachers, her trainers—her friends, for lack of a better option.

The sick feeling in her stomach began to settle as she finally acknowledged what these men had been to her. They *had* been a large part of her life, and she could be sad that she'd lost that. But they didn't deserve her loyalty or sympathy. She took a deep breath and when she let it go, the dysfunctional family of her past went with it, along with her guilt. She belonged to a real family now, one full of love, laughter, honesty, and trust. Her mother, Gideon, and the rest of the Marquands were the only ones who deserved her love and allegiance.

Gideon had just held her while she'd dealt with her emotions, but now his hands roamed her body. It took her a few minutes to realize what he was doing. The heat of the water masked the healing warmth of his magic. Each stinging cut receded to nothing under his attention.

When he'd seen to every last scratch, he tucked his arms around her waist again. "Better?"

"Yes. Thank you." Lauren tipped her head back and up at the same time her hand came up to cup the back of his head. A little pressure had him lowering his lips to meet hers.

They lost themselves in the moment, reveling in the touch and taste of each other. Slowly they ended the kiss, and Lauren settled back into the curve of his body.

"You never said what you did to Warren."

"I trapped him inside his own power." Gideon explained Warren's attempts to control his mind, and how that had backfired.

"I guess that's a fitting end to him. I can still remember what it felt like being trapped in a world of his making. I could never break free of it. Now he can't, either."

Lauren trailed her hands slowly through the water. "Uncle has to be shitting bricks right about now. If we count Jared, he's lost four of his coven members in short order. I'd bet he's scrambling to pull everyone he has left in close."

"Let's just hope Amber and Aiden can get to some of the soldiers before he does that."

Lauren gazed out over the edge of the hot tub and out to the lake. "How long can we stay here?"

"As long as you need."

She turned within the circle of his arms until she faced him. She ran her tongue over his bottom lip. "A little while longer, then."

~~~

They'd moved inside after making love. It was dark now, and they lay cuddled together on the couch, wrapped in a light blanket. Gideon had started a fire in the fireplace, the soft mood and flickering light soothing to Lauren's mind.

She was almost dozing when Gideon's body tensed behind her. She was immediately alert. "What is it?"

"We need to go," he told her, sitting up. "Something's happened back at the manor."

"Did you see it, or did someone call?"

"Jack put out the call. We need to go. *Now*."

The flames were extinguished, and they were both dressed before Lauren could even reach for her clothes. The power Gideon commanded was beyond belief at times. It was easy to forget what he was and the responsibility he carried because of that. She stepped into his arms now, vowing never to take that, or him, for granted.

They landed in the middle of the entryway to chaos.

"Why would they do this?" Mia asked no one in particular.

Ben and Conner were off to the side having a heated discussion about something. Amber and Lindsay were both pale and shaky. Quinn stood guard over both women.

"Is he still alive?" Marissa looked to Aiden as he emerged from the hall with Jack.

Lauren turned in time to see the small shake of his head.

"What the hell happened?" Gideon was as lost as she. Who were they talking about?

"We were just coming back." Amber's voice shook, and her face was ashen. "We found him lying in the road at the end of the driveway."

"Found who?" Lauren braced herself for the news.

"Jared," Aiden supplied, taking Lindsay into his arms.

Lauren looked up at Gideon and knew they were thinking
~~~

the same thing. He hadn't gotten away after all. The lackeys must have found him and taken him back to the coven leader.

"They dumped him out there for us to find," Aiden added.

"Why out in the road?" Lauren asked.

"Any closer and they would have triggered our protection wards and alerted us to their presence," Ben said as he approached the group.

"Where is he?" Gideon asked.

Lauren thought she could guess what he was thinking. And when his father spoke, she knew Ben had also surmised Gideon's intent.

"Gideon. There's nothing to be done. He's gone."

"Where. Is. He?"

Lauren looked over at Quinn. They alone had experienced the torment this man would have suffered at the hands of Christopher and his men.

"He's down the hall," Mia told him. "We moved him into a guest room."

Gideon turned and stalked off.

The last thing Lauren wanted was see what was left of the man who'd tried to help them, but she took off after Gideon anyway. When she caught up, she grasped his hand in hers and gave it a squeeze of reassurance.

Her first sight of the body lying on the bed made the bile rise to the back of her throat. He resembled nothing of the man they'd seen just a few hours before. His face was swollen, bruised, and cut to ribbons. The congealed blood staining his tattered clothes told her the rest of him had been given the same treatment.

Gideon stepped up to the bed. He bent and placed his hands on either side of Jared's head. Minutes passed, but nothing happened. No healing power on earth was going to restore this man to what he'd been.

But Gideon wouldn't give up. He pushed himself so hard

that Lauren began to worry about him.

She approached him and laid a hand on his back. "Gideon, you have to stop. There's nothing you can do."

Lauren thought he'd brush off her touch, but he just dropped his hands to his sides.

"In spite of what he'd done, he didn't deserve *this*," Gideon said wearily.

"No one does." Lauren squeezed his shoulder consolingly before coaxing him out. "Come on. Let's get you cleaned up."

He let her lead him out of the room and across the hall to the bathroom. Once his hands were washed clean of blood, Lauren stepped into his arms. It was hard to believe that only a few short minutes ago, they'd been relaxed and content. Then all hell had broken loose.

"Let's go find out what the others know," Lauren said as he released her.

They turned and headed back. The front hall was empty now, but the clamor of voices told them the family was gathered in the parlor.

Solemn faces met them when they walked through the door. Amber held a tumbler of a dark, tawny-colored liquid. She still looked shaken, but some of her color had returned. Quinn sat close to her, maintaining physical contact.

Lindsay and Aiden were also taking comfort in each other. Lauren imagined finding a sight like that would throw even the sturdiest of people.

Both sets of parents were seated off to the side. The men looked pissed off, while the women cast worried glances at their kids.

Marissa sat close to Amber, opposite Quinn. Jack had stationed himself at the window, looking out over the front drive. When he heard them come in, he turned.

"How did this happen?" Gideon demanded.

"We had no clue he was out there," Conner started. "We

didn't know anything about it until Amber and the others rushed in, shouting."

"What if they come back?" Lindsay's voice still trembled.

"They won't need to come again," Jack said flatly. "They delivered their message."

"I wish we would have found him sooner," Becca said. "If we had, maybe we could have saved him."

"They never would have allowed that," Lauren said sadly. "He was dead before he got here. Jack's right. He was meant to be a message. This is what'll happen if you cross us."

"I'm going to do more than cross them." Jack's voice had gone ice-cold. "I'm going to wipe out every fucking trace of them."

"But to do that, we still need to find them." Quinn stood and joined Jack. "We struck out. Every training facility we found was empty."

Lauren slid her gaze to Gideon. "He's gathering his troops. Just like we thought he would."

"Yeah, making it harder to hunt him down." Gideon, too, moved to align himself with Quinn and Jack. "But we'll find him. He won't be able to hide behind them for long."

Aiden stood and crossed the room to stand with the other men. "When we're done with him, he'll have nothing."

The four men stood as one unit. Tall and proud and furious. Lauren studied them. They hadn't known each other long, but the bond they shared had been forged in battle. Each one would go down fighting to protect their loved ones, as well as each other. In appearance, they couldn't have been more different. But in ideals and virtues, they were of a like mind. They made a striking and fearsome group of warriors.

Jack turned thoughtful. "Since he's retreated and pulled everyone in with him, I think we're going to have to come at this from a new angle."

"What do you mean?" Amber sat forward, drink clasped between her hands.

"First of all, how does he move so many people around?" Jack asked. "We know each member of his army was housed in a separate location. And if Mattison and Howard were any indication, the other coven members are the same. That's a lot of folks to get from point A to point B."

He pinned Lauren with those steely eyes. "How did they travel from one soldier to the next? And how was Quinn transported? When he was brought to you, how did they bring him?"

"By helicopter," she told him.

"What about a sea plane?" Marissa drew everyone's attention. "We had to take one to get to Quinn. Alexander Mattison and Jared Howard both lived on a large body of water. I wonder if the rest of the coven does as well. A sea plane would make getting in and out a lot easier."

"I don't know anything about a plane," Lauren said. "I only saw the helicopter."

"I'll get a search started for registered helicopters *and* sea planes," Aiden offered.

"Start with the upper half of Michigan and the UP," Jack told him. "That seems to be their area of concentration."

"Yeah, all right," Aiden agreed.

"Wherever he's holed up," Ben added, "it's some place large enough to house all those people. Before he started losing members, there were over a dozen of them, coven and soldiers both."

"And if this Christopher resents the Marquands for taking power away from him," Conner put in, "I'd imagine he'd want bigger and better than we have—show us he's more worthy." He caught Jack's attention. "Look for a setup that's...I don't know...*more* than we have here."

"That's good," Jack nodded.

"Does that name mean anything to any of you?" Gideon asked the room in general.

"No," Ben returned. "Jack told us what Jared said, but we can't think of anyone by that name."

"What about Jared?" Marissa asked. "What do we do there? We can't just leave him here."

"I'll take care of him," Gideon promised.

"It's late," Mia said, standing. "And it's been a very wearisome day. Why don't we all try to get some rest? We'll come back tomorrow with clear heads."

A short while later, the parents left. Lauren expected everyone else to follow, but no one moved.

"Why does it seem like we're always playing catch-up?" Aiden asked, discouraged. "Just when we think we'll find that last piece, it's ripped out of our hands."

Lauren took this moment to broach a subject she didn't know if anyone else had thought of. "We may have a way to get ahead of them."

All eyes turned to her. "We have a member of the coven lying just down the hall," she reminded them.

"He's dead." Amber set her empty glass aside. "He can't tell us anything now."

"I think he can," Lauren countered.

"How?" Jack stepped closer, intrigued.

"One of you could try to get a vision from him," Lauren explained.

"Off a dead body?" Revulsion tinged Marissa's voice. She snapped her gaze to Amber, looking for backup.

When Lauren looked to the other woman, it appeared Amber might be considering it.

Marissa turned to Jack. "I'm sorry, but I am not touching a dead body. Amber or my brother can do it."

"I think it'll work best if we all do it together," Gideon answered, dashing his sister's hopes.

"Why?" Marissa asked him. "You're the Super Witch."

Gideon grinned at his sister's reluctance, and Lauren was

glad to see a smile on his face. He'd taken what had happened to Jared really hard. But that little lightening of his mood gave her hope that he'd be able to move past it.

"I *could* try on my own, and I'd most likely get something," he told her. "But if all three of us did it, we'd probably get *more*."

"No…" she trailed off, and then muttered, "damn it," when she saw the determination on Gideon's face.

They all retraced the steps Lauren and Gideon had taken earlier. They were a somber group walking through the door of the bedroom. Gideon, Marissa, and Amber took their positions next to the bed. Lauren, Aiden, and Lindsay rounded it to stand on the opposite side. Jack and Quinn stayed as close to their women as they could get without actually touching them.

Gideon stood with the women on either side of him. Amber was at Jared's head, and Marissa was near his feet. Gideon took their hands in his. "Each of you will have to touch him."

Lauren saw a shudder pass through Marissa, but she reached out a hand and laid it on the toe of Jared's sock-clad foot. Completing the circuit, Amber rested hers on his shoulder. All three closed their eyes.

Lauren wasn't sure what to expect. She'd never seen anyone have a vision, let alone three working together. She looked at Jack for some guidance, but he only shrugged, conveying that he wasn't sure what was going to happen either.

They all stood quietly and waited. Time seemed to slow to a crawl. To Lauren, it felt like hours had passed. She sent a quick look at Jack, but his eyes were trained on Marissa, just as Quinn's focus was completely centered on Amber, waiting for a sign.

Just as she was surely about to go out of her mind, Gideon opened his eyes. Both women stumbled back a little. Jack and Quinn were there in an instant to support them.

"Wow." Amber sounded weary but awed. "Are your visions always like that?"

"Yeah, pretty much." Gideon smiled at her. "A little more intense than you're used to?"

"Intense is the right word. Wow," she repeated. "Easier on the way in, but holy cow."

Marissa was wiping her hand down the side of her pants leg. "How do you sort through it all? It comes so fast. It was like falling into a slipstream of information. Everything was everywhere. All at once. "

"I've never known any other way," Gideon explained.

"Man," Marissa said. "How about we not do that again? My head is still spinning." She looked up at her brother and sent him a small grin. "Tell you what. You can keep your super powers. I'll stick with my own measly ones, thanks."

Gideon laughed.

"Hello?" Aiden drew their attention. "In the dark here. What did you see?"

"A lot," Amber told him. "Let's head back to the other room, and we'll walk you through it."

"What about him?" Lindsay motioned to the body on the bed. "Is it okay to just leave him here?"

"Yeah," Amber said. "Aunt Mia put a spell on the body to make sure it doesn't...change."

Lindsay nodded and fell in behind the others as they all went back to the parlor.

22

Once they were all seated, Gideon launched into what they'd seen. "It started with Jared's early life in the original coven—a group of men bent on living large and taking all they could. Our family popped up on their radar when Jared had a vision of Grandfather being the one to end their lifestyle. That's why they killed him."

"So it wasn't to stop your magical line like we thought," Jack clarified. "It was only because he was in their way."

"Yup," Gideon nodded. "Pretty messed up. And that's why our parents didn't really hear anything else out of them for a long time."

Marissa picked up the story. "That's when Gideon came to their attention. Once they saw what he would become, they decided they wanted that for themselves. Which, like Gideon said, was why they sent Roanik after us."

Amber took up where Marissa had left off. "We jumped forward a few years to when a young Christopher was brought in to learn the ways of the coven. Even then, for whatever reason, he carried a deep hatred for us. Since the coven still wanted what we had, the old leader decided he could use that hate to his benefit and started to groom him. We watched as Christopher came into his own and eventually took over. And just as Jared told us, he brought in new people to replace the old. So, twenty years ago, when he had everyone in place, he changed the game plan."

"Because of his loathing for us, instead of merely acquiring our magic for himself," Marissa broke in, "he wanted to destroy us. But we were already gone, so he had to bide his time. With the help of Howard's visions, he found the people he needed and started to build his army. When Grandmother died, he set his plan in motion. Jared was privy to Christopher's rages every time we bested him. With each defeat, he descended deeper into darkness. Madness."

"This is all great," Aiden said. "It fills in a lot of holes. But none of that is really helpful to finding and stopping him."

"No," Gideon agreed. "But what we saw next may be."

"And what was that?" Quinn asked.

"The compound where Christopher lives," Gideon answered.

"You saw where he is?" Aiden's tone was brusque as he came up off the couch. "Why the hell didn't you lead with that? That's what we've been searching for. Let's go."

"Because we still don't know exactly where it is," Gideon told him. "We have the layout, but not the location."

"So how does that help us?" Aiden said dejectedly.

"When we *do* find the location, we'll already have a plan of attack in place," Jack chimed in. "We'll know where every building and every possible point of entry is." He turned his attention back to the three who saw the vision. "I need a detailed drawing of that compound from all of you. I want to know where each structure, tree, and rock is on that property. The more we know, the better prepared I can make us."

~~~

An hour later, Gideon stood over the body of Jared Howard. This time he was by himself. He'd told Lauren to go on up to bed. That he needed to do this alone.

"You and your cronies killed my grandfather to keep your
~~~

way of life. You set this course into motion with your greed," Gideon told him. "You stole thirty years away from this family in your insatiable hunger for more. And you saw nothing wrong with what you were doing as long as it benefitted you." Gideon turned and walked to the end of the bed before bringing his gaze back to the man lying there.

"I guess I should be thankful that, in the end, you chose to do the right thing. You made it possible for a few of the people they'd taken to escape." Some of the anger he was feeling slipped out. "And it's for that reason alone I'm not sending you into the deepest pit to rot." Gideon took a deep breath and pulled it back in. "No matter what I feel, no one deserves to be hurt this way."

Gideon closed his eyes and sent what remained of Jared to the county morgue. Someone would find the body and do what needed to be done. But he was finished with him.

He swung around to leave when a vision filled his head. Scenes and people sped through until he understood what The Powers That Be were telling him. He immediately teleported himself upstairs and urgently knocked on the door.

Aiden answered, dressed only in his jeans. "Gideon, what's going on?"

"We have to go. *Now*. Your mother's in danger."

Gideon grabbed Aiden's arm, and they were instantly inside a small, darkened house where a woman slept, unaware of the threat against her.

Aiden tore off down the hall. Gideon followed, knowing they didn't have much time. He crossed the threshold of the bedroom two steps behind Aiden. The other man bent over the bed and gently touched the woman who had raised him.

"Mom," he whispered. "Mom, wake up."

"Aiden?" Her voice was groggy, but she must have heard the urgency in his tone. "What's wrong? What is it? Where's your shirt?"

Gideon stepped forward. "Ms. Covington, I'm Gideon— Aiden's cousin. We haven't met yet, but we need to get you out of here. There are men coming for you, and I'd rather none of us be here when they show up."

"Men? What men?" she asked, even as she was fighting the blankets to get out of bed.

"We don't have time now. Aiden will explain when we're all back at Marquand Manor."

But Gideon had no intention of making the return trip. He'd be here waiting for them when they came. They'd be expecting a defenseless woman. What they'd get was a pissed off witch. With a thought, he sent Aiden and his mother away, and then prepared to exact some revenge of his own.

He quickly readjusted the bedding to make it look like Joann was still sleeping there. It wouldn't fool them for long, but it would give him the time he needed to get the jump on them. When he was finished, he crouched in a corner of the room where he would be out of sight but could still see the doorway.

His senses were wide open, searching for whomever Christopher had sent, when Lauren's voice whispered in his head.

"Gideon. You've got everyone scrambling here. What's going on?"

"I saw that they were making a move on Aiden's adoptive mother. I had to act fast."

"That's fine, but why did you send Aiden back? You shouldn't take them on alone."

"I'll be fine."

"No doubt. But you don't need to do this by yourself. If you don't want Aiden there, bring me over. I'll help."

"Lauren—"

"Gideon, you either teleport me right now, or I'll make you regret it to your last breath."

He could only smile, because he knew she could. *"All right.*

But be prepared to fight. I don't know how many there will be."

"Fine." How was it that women all over the world, no matter what language, could take that one word and make it mean so many different things? This particular time, the meaning was clear. She wasn't at all happy with him.

In the next moment, she was crouched next to him. He saw that she'd brought the sword he'd given her during the last battle.

The sight of her with that weapon stirred something in him. He was about to tell her she reminded him of a particularly hot fantasy he'd always had of a certain petite actress from a sci-fi TV show he used to watch, but a shift in the air caught his attention.

"Here they come."

She nodded and steeled herself.

Two black-clad figures came through the door and into the bedroom. One of them raised an arm, and Gideon saw a gun pointed at the mound of bedding. The sound when it fired was different than a normal pistol. There was just enough light for Gideon to make out the shaft and tuft of feathers sticking out of the blankets. A tranquilizer dart. They'd meant to drug Joann and take her back with them. *Sorry to ruin your night, boys.*

As the two men approached the bed, Gideon and Lauren readied themselves to spring into action. They'd taken no more than a step, when another person dressed all in black entered the room. Gideon had a moment to react, but was unprepared for the bolt of energy that hit him square in the chest.

What the fuck? He staggered back and into the wall.

While he fought for breath, Lauren charged ahead and took on the newcomer. Gideon pushed to his feet to give her some help. He was still shaky, but he knew his healing would kick in soon enough.

His head finally cleared just as the first two into the room came at him. He sent a burst of magic their way, which froze them in their tracks. Gideon set his sights on Lauren and the assailant she was engaged with. He figured this was the person who'd shot him with the blast.

Before he could reach them, however, another figure stormed through the door, making a total of four men sent by the coven. Gideon had had enough. Throwing his hands out wide, he immobilized the entire room, which saved the life of the energy thrower. Lauren's sword was only an inch away from the throat of her adversary.

He walked over and slid the blade from Lauren's hand and then released her. Her body followed through on the deadly swing, but there was no weapon to slice deep.

"What the hell, Gideon? I had him."

"I know," he told her. "But I figured Joann wouldn't appreciate a puddle of blood on her bedroom floor." He handed her back her weapon. "Plus, this one," he stepped in front of the dark figure, "has magic, making him one of the soldiers."

Gideon turned on the lights and took a good, hard look. He reached up and removed the hood covering the head of her rival.

"Son of a bitch," he muttered when muddy brown hair tumbled down and black-as-night eyes met his. "Brooke Weston."

"The other one like Quinn." Lauren looked up at him. "We have to help her."

"And we will. We'll take her back to the manor, give her the potion to counter the enthrallment, and see what happens."

"What about these wackos?" Lauren nodded towards the other three goons.

"I have an idea there." Gideon smiled and thought the chief of police would be quite surprised to find these guys in his holding cell come morning. He didn't know if they'd be held once found, but at least they would be out of the way in the meantime.

Once that task was complete, Gideon accompanied Lauren and Brooke back to his family's home. He made sure to keep her neutralized until they could undo the spell she was under. What happened after that would be anyone's guess. He just hoped her mind hadn't been too damaged by the coven.

They appeared in the entry and, even though it was the middle of the night, a group of people were there waiting.

Marissa came forward. She spared a fleeting glance to the statuesque person he'd brought home before looking up at him in concern. "You okay?"

"Yeah. Is Joann all right? I didn't have time to tell her about the teleporting. I just had to get her out of there fast."

"She's fine. Aiden explained it to her. He's getting her settled in." Marissa smiled. "He's pissed that you sent him home and stayed behind."

Gideon grinned. "I knew he would be."

"Why did you?" Jack came to stand next to Marissa. "And who's this?"

"Brooke Weston," Lauren told them.

"She was leading the team they sent in to grab Joann," Gideon disclosed. "So I grabbed her. I'm hoping once we give her the antidote, she'll answer some questions."

"Did you know she'd be there?" Amber asked.

"No. In the vision, I just saw men entering Joann's house. I knew I had to get Aiden and get in there before that happened. I also knew he would want to stay if I told him what I had planned. Then I was sure Joann would put up a fight, knowing her son was going to be in harm's way, so I took the choice out of their hands altogether and sent them both home. I intended to see what I could learn from whoever was coming. We still need a lot of answers, and I thought this was a good time to look for some."

"You shouldn't have taken that on yourself," Marissa warned.

"That's what I told him," Lauren huffed. "I was able to talk some sense into him, and he teleported me in to help."

"You talked some…" Jack reached out and grasped Lauren's hand, lifting it for his inspection. He studied her fingers for a moment before speaking. "Yup. Wrapped up nice and tight, right there." He pointed to Lauren's pinkie.

Marissa and Amber choked back a laugh.

"You are such an ass." Gideon scowled at Jack, but he had to fight the grin that threatened. "Anyway, let's give this girl the potion and see where we stand."

"I don't think we should do that in the house," Lauren cautioned. "No one knows what she'll do when she comes out of this. She knocked Gideon on his ass with her magic. She shoots out energy bolts or something. Is there another building on the property somewhere? Something isolated?"

"She knocked him…" Jack smiled at Gideon. "This just keeps getting better and better."

Before Gideon could wipe the grin off Jack's face, Amber stepped between them. "There's a potting shed out back. My mother still uses it, so if she causes any damage, it'll have to be fixed."

"Sounds perfect. I'll teleport her and myself out there. You guys grab the potion and meet us."

"I'm going with you," Lauren stated.

"All right." Gideon tucked his hand into hers and then touched Brooke. Just before they left the house, he heard Jack cough, and he swore it sounded like "whipped." He was laughing as they reappeared in the potting shed.

"What?" Lauren asked.

"Nothing. Jack was just giving me a hard time."

"What was that with my hand?"

Gideon forgot sometimes that she hadn't grown up as the rest of them had. She'd missed out on a lot. There were many nuances of speech and social interaction she'd never had the opportunity to learn.

He reached out and pulled her into his arms. "He was just commenting on the fact that you have me wrapped around your little finger."

"What does that mean?" Her hazel eyes studied him.

He leaned down and kissed her. "It means that I will do anything you ask."

She leaned her body into his. "Anything, huh?"

He nuzzled her neck. "Anything."

Lauren cupped his face in her hands and looked up into his eyes. He instantly dropped the glamour. She smiled. "I think I might like having you wrapped around my finger."

Gideon wanted to sink into that hot mouth, but he could hear the others coming. "We'll have to pick this up later. We're about to have company." He looked over at Brooke. "Well, more than we had."

"Can she see anything?" Lauren asked him. "Is she aware at all?"

"No," he shook his head. "I made sure she was under completely. I didn't want to take a chance on her zapping me again, or anyone else, for that matter."

His sister and cousins walked in with their significant others. Marissa was carrying the small vial which would free Brooke from the black spell that was currently holding her captive. Gideon took it from his sister and approached the motionless woman.

He turned back to the group behind him. "I'll have to unfreeze her for the potion to take effect. Keep alert."

They nodded and spread out around the room. He swung back to face the soldier. He grasped her chin and applied some pressure to open her jaw. Lifting the bottle, he poured the tea-like liquid into her mouth. He waited until it had all flowed down the back of her throat and into her stomach.

Gideon glanced at the others. "Be ready."

He backed away, and as a precaution, erected a shield around her. Hopefully it would withstand her power long enough that they could talk to her.

Gideon released her. She came up swinging, her last memory of Lauren's sword coming for her neck.

"Brooke!" Gideon tried to get her attention. "Brooke Weston!"

She stilled, looking at him warily.

"Easy. No one is going to hurt you." Gideon kept his voice gentle and non-threatening. He also sent waves of calm into her mind.

Which was a mistake. She felt the intrusion and took it as an attack. "Stay out of my head!" Her words were followed by a blast of power. Thanks to the barrier, Gideon knew it wouldn't hit him. But Amber didn't know that and froze her again the moment she made a move at him.

"Shit. She's pissed," Amber said.

"Her eyes are still black," Quinn noticed. "Didn't it work?"

Taking a better look, Gideon turned back to the group. "It did. They're just naturally dark. A deep, chocolate brown. You'd have to be closer to see the difference."

"Gideon, can you communicate with her telepathically while she's like this?" Lauren asked. "It might save us all some time and trouble."

"That's a good idea," Jack agreed. "And we won't have to dodge her power. If it knocked Super Witch on his ass, I don't want any part of it."

"Wait. What? She landed him on his keister?" Aiden was obviously getting a kick out of that news, too. "Oh, that would have been fun to see."

"Do you both want to go to hell?" Gideon pointed at each man. "I can send you there, you know."

Neither Jack nor Aiden had the sense to take him at his word. They just stood there with stupid grins on their faces.

"Boys, boys," Amber waded in. "As funny as it would be to watch you all go at each other, we have something a little more pressing here. Gideon, *can* you talk to her and try to explain what's happening?"

"Yeah, I should be able to."

"Then do it."

He gave Amber a dirty look just for good measure, and then turned back to face Brooke. He hoped he could get through to her.

"Brooke? Can you hear me? My name is Gideon. No one is going to hurt you."

He waited for a response. None came.

"Brooke?"

"Get the fuck out of my head!" she shouted. *"I will tear you apart when I get my hands on you. Hurt me all you want, I won't do anything you say. You all can go fuck yourselves."*

"We're not going to make you do anything," he told her. *"We took you away from the ones who were hurting you. We just want to help you."*

"I can't see. Why can't I move? What have you done to me?" Her voice rose with each question.

"For everyone's protection, I've immobilized you. If you can promise not to attack us, I'll release you. Then we can talk."

"Us? We? How many of you are there?" Distrust still laced her thoughts.

"Right now, there are eight people here with you. They're all members of my family. And I can promise you that none of them is here to harm you."

"How do I know you're telling the truth?"

"I guess you can't. You'll just have to trust me."

She was silent for a moment. *"Let me go. Please."*

The last word was said as if through gritted teeth. Gideon figured that word didn't come easy to Brooke Weston. But at least she was making an effort.

Gideon looked at the others. "I think she's ready this time."

Still, they all tensed, waiting to see what Brooke would do.

"Okay. I'll release you. But just stay calm," Gideon told her as he released the magic binding her.

When she could, Brooke looked at each person spread out around her. "Who the hell are you people?"

"Like I said, my name is Gideon. We're here to help you," he repeated. "And we're hoping you can help us, too."

"Help you, how?"

"The men who were using you—we're looking for them." Marissa said.

Brooke's dark brows snapped together. "Using me? What do you mean, using me? They snatched me from where I was crashing and threw me in a locked room."

"What happened after they took you?" Lindsay asked.

Suspicion laced Brooke's features. "Nothing. They came every day and demanded that I work for them, but I told them to fuck off. They left."

"Brooke," Quinn stepped forward, "when were you taken?"

"I don't know. Maybe six months ago."

"What was the date?" Quinn clarified.

"Sometime in early February."

"What year?" he asked carefully.

"What you do mean, what year? This year. 2006."

Gideon's anger spiked. Those fuckwits had kept her locked in nothingness for *seven years*. This poor girl had no idea she'd lost so much of her life. At least he could take comfort in the fact she didn't remember any of what they'd made her do.

"Why does everyone suddenly look like they've swallowed a lemon?" Brooke demanded. "Someone better tell me what the hell is happening."

Over the next half hour, they brought her up to speed with what was going on and how long she'd been missing.

She was holding tough, but Gideon could see that she was in shock.

"Do you have any family that would be looking for you?"

Lindsay asked her.

Brooke was willfully fighting off the emotions swamping her. "No. I don't need anyone. I can take care of myself."

"You were living on the streets," Quinn stated.

"Yeah, so what?"

"Why were you on your own at thirteen?" Quinn asked.

"Look, I can handle it." Brooke became nervous. "With my power, no one messes with me. If those stooges hadn't drugged me, I would have gotten away from them."

Gideon noticed she still spoke like a thirteen-year-old street kid. It would take her a while to reconcile that she was twenty-one now. She'd lost a whole third of her life to the blackness of the enthrallment spell.

Like Quinn, who had also lost great spans of time, Brooke would never remember those years. Which didn't bode well for getting the answers they needed. Under the spell, she wouldn't know if she'd been to the compound or not.

But what about before that? If she was right on the timing, she'd been with them for six months before they'd put her under.

Gideon looked to her now. "After they took you, what do you remember? At some point, they transferred you from Idaho to Michigan. Do you remember anything about the move?"

"It goes in and out. I think they kept me drugged, but I do kind of remember being in a vehicle. I woke up a couple of times, and I could see the metal floor and side walls. They were..." She waved her hand in an up and down motion, trying to describe the texture.

"Corrugated?" Jack asked her.

"Yeah," Brooke said, pointing at Jack. "Yeah, like that."

Jack looked at Gideon. "They must have had her in a cargo van."

Gideon nodded in agreement before turning back to Brooke. "What else do you remember?"

"There were old fast food bags and garbage all around me. I remember seeing this one piece of paper. It was for one of those hunting places or something. It had birds and dogs and men with rifles. At that moment, I'd really wished I'd had one of those guns. I would have blown their fucking heads off."

"Did you see a name?" Jack guided her through her memory. "Do you recall what the place was called?"

Brooke fought to bring the memory back. Gideon was about to suggest they try the memory merge again when she finally spoke.

"It was a weird name. Wy-something. Wy-something Lake."

Aiden pulling his phone from his pocket drew Gideon's attention. He was obviously searching the internet.

"Too many possibilities for Wy-something Lake," Aiden said. "I need more info."

"Try adding in Michigan," Jack told him.

Aiden's thumbs flew as he made the adjustments. "Bingo," he announced. "Wycamp Lake. It's a hunting club in northern Michigan."

"Yeah, that's it. Wycamp Lake," Brooke confirmed.

"This could still be nothing," Jack cautioned. "It doesn't mean that's where the compound is. But I think it's worth checking out."

"Look. We're all exhausted," Amber interrupted. "I think we've gotten all we're going to get tonight. It's been a long and very trying day. Let's get some rest and hit it hard tomorrow."

She crossed to where Brooke was standing. "Come on. I'll show you where you can sleep."

Gideon and Lauren fell into bed a short while later. He pulled her in close and breathed in the scent of her. He was asleep in moments.

23

Morning arrived only a few short hours later. Gideon rolled to his back and rubbed his hands over his face.

"It can't possibly be morning already," Lauren mumbled beside him.

A huge jaw-cracking yawn racked Gideon's body. "Unfortunately." He curled his body back around hers and enjoyed the warmth of her skin. "When this is done, I want to go back to the cabin and not get out of bed for a month." He nuzzled her neck. "Nothing but you and me for weeks on end."

"Mmm, I'd like that," she sighed at the thought.

He kissed his way up to her ear and took the lobe between his teeth. He reached for her mind and was met with a preoccupation about what they'd learned from Brooke last night. Gideon resigned himself to the fact that his morning wouldn't be starting the way he'd hoped.

He wrapped his arms around her waist and held her.

"Do you think we'll find them today?" she asked into the silence.

"I don't know. Like Jack said, this Wycamp thing might be nothing. But just the fact that it's here close by, tells me it may mean *something*."

"It could mean everything," she speculated.

"Yes, it could," he agreed and rolled naked out of bed. "And if I'm going to be of any use finding that out, I need a shower and large quantities of caffeine. Come on. Let's get to it."

Forty minutes later, showered and somewhat more awake, they walked into the dining room. Jack was seated at the table, a cup of coffee clutched in his hands.

"Where's everyone else?" Gideon asked as he filled his own mug.

"I don't know. Marissa was still in the shower when I left." Jack grimaced. "I have to say—dude, your sister is *not* a morning person. She about took my head off when I spoke to her this morning. It might be a good idea to let her get the first shot of caffeine into her system before you say anything to her."

"Noted," Gideon grinned. He and Lauren rounded the table and took the two chairs that had become theirs. He looked down the table at Jack.

"I'm really hoping the hunting camp is somewhere near the compound. It'll just mean we're getting that much closer. What do you think?"

"After studying some satellite images this morning, I'd say it might be pretty close," Jack told him.

Gideon's cup stopped halfway to his mouth. "What did you see?"

"Wycamp Lake is perfect for his needs." Jack went on to explain. "It sits in the middle of nowhere. From what I can tell, very few people live on the lake. And even though it's quite shallow in spots, a float plane could get in and out of there with no problem."

"Any sign of his compound?" Lauren sat forward in her seat.

Jack shook his head. "No. The canopy is too dense. But I did see an open area not far away that looks like it could accommodate a helicopter. I wish we could take a closer look around."

"Why don't I teleport us in?" Gideon suggested. "We can scope it out. Find out if there's anything there."

"That's what I was thinking, too," Jack said.

"Just the two of you?" Lauren's tone told Gideon she didn't like that part of the plan.

"We're just going to look around," he said.

"Then the more eyes you have, the better," she argued. "Isn't that what you said when you were searching my memories? "

"This isn't the same. If the compound is there, it's there. It'll be hard to miss."

"What'll be hard to miss?" Amber asked as she and Quinn came in.

"Gideon and Jack want to take off to Wycamp Lake to search for the coven's base," Lauren told her.

"No less than four—I thought that was the rule," Amber reminded them. "You guys threw a bitch-fit when I suggested splitting into pairs to cover more ground."

Marissa, Aiden, and Lindsay walked in on the middle of Amber's rant.

"The more people we have tromping through the woods," Jack reasoned, "the higher chance we have of being seen."

"Who's planning on tromping through the woods?" Aiden stopped and looked at those already seated.

"Jack and Gideon," Amber shot out. "They think they know where Christopher's base is."

"You're not going without me." Marissa looked at her fiancé and crossed her arms.

Gideon didn't know how this had gotten so out of hand. What should have been a simple discussion of recon had escalated into a full-blown argument over who would go and how many they needed.

Lauren was in his face stating her point when a shrill, high-pitched whistle split the air. All discussion stopped.

"I have a suggestion," Quinn said into the silence he'd created. "We can get the intel we need, and no one will have to go anywhere near the place."

Gideon was intrigued. "How?" he asked.

"I can ask a friend for help," Quinn told him and went on to clarify. "I have the ability to connect with and see through the eyes of any animal." Quinn glanced at the white eagle feather he wore at his waist. "I'll ask my brother eagle for his assistance. He can fly over the area in question. If there's something there, we'll see it."

"That's brilliant," Gideon smiled.

Half an hour later, they were all outside on the patio, seated on various chairs and benches. Quinn chose to sit on the ground with his legs folded underneath him. He closed his eyes, took a deep breath, and went still.

Minutes passed before he spoke. "He'll help us. We're going now."

Gideon would love to know what it was like to fly with an eagle. Taking a chance, he lightly brushed against Quinn's mind, seeking permission to fly with them.

In the next moment, the world opened up to Gideon. Blue sky above, earth beneath. He gasped as he experienced something so majestic and so beautiful it was indescribable. They soared on the air currents for what seemed like hours before the eagle gave another powerful sweep of its wings.

Terrain gave way to water as they flew. Gideon sensed a shift in Quinn's and the eagle's minds and, before he knew what was happening, they dove. Gideon held his breath as the bird of prey took them to within inches of the water's surface, wing tips just brushing the waves with every downward push.

He heard Quinn's laughter in his mind. Gideon didn't know if this was Quinn's idea or the eagle's, but he didn't really care. This moment was one he would never forget.

Their guide gave a giant thrust with his wings, and up they went to skim the tops of the trees. Minutes later, he started to make large circles over the same area. Gideon surmised they'd reached their destination.

He put the joy aside and concentrated on the landscape

below. He could feel the communication between Quinn and the eagle, but he couldn't hear it. He trusted that Quinn would let their friend know what they needed.

Sure enough, he flew in under the treetops and started a search pattern guided by Quinn. It wasn't long before they saw the tall concrete fence. They traveled alongside it for a good distance. It seemed to stretch all the way around whatever was inside of it.

Quinn must have been as eager to see what this fence was hiding as Gideon. They soared over the top, and Gideon knew they'd found what they were looking for. This was the place he'd seen in the vision. The coven's secret lair.

The eagle flew over outbuildings and paths. Gideon saw people moving about. A few looked up at them, but none would know they'd been found. The bird swooped in and perched on a branch of a tall tree. It looked to be almost central to everything going on below. It gave them a three-hundred-and-sixty-degree view of the property.

Gideon took note of everything, from the men patrolling with fierce-looking dogs, to the soldiers training in a large, open area.

What he didn't see were any of the coven members. They had to know Brooke's mission had failed. Where were they? What were they doing? What were they planning next?

Gideon sensed their time was up here. He silently gave his thanks to the eagle and pulled himself out of the link.

Quinn came back a moment later. He looked over at Gideon.

"That's something else, huh?" Quinn smiled as he stood and stretched out stiff muscles.

"I'll never forget that as long as I live," Gideon told him truthfully.

"Wait," Amber said. "You went with them? Why?"

"Are you kidding?" Gideon grinned. "I had to know what it was like to fly with an eagle."

"How was it?" The wonder in Marissa's voice said she would have loved to experience that, too. The looks on everyone else's faces said the same thing.

"It was unbelievable." Gideon tried to put into words what he'd felt. "The power, and the speed, and the freedom." He looked over at Quinn. "Skimming over the water—was that your idea?"

"Yeah. I thought you'd enjoy it."

"Oh, yeah. The whole thing was amazing. Be sure to tell him thank you for me."

"Did you see anything?" Jack brought the conversation back around. "Was it there?"

"It was," Gideon told him. "Just where you thought it would be. It looks just like the vision we had. One thing we didn't count on, though, was that he has guards patrolling with big dogs."

A thought occurred, and he looked over at Quinn. "Could you communicate with those dogs?"

"I haven't tried," he admitted, "but I don't see why not. I should be able to handle them."

"So, now we know where he is," Aiden said. "We know the layout. I say we make some plans and go in and take him down. For good."

"Not yet," Jack cautioned. "I think we can all agree we want them stopped, permanently. To make that happen, we need to have all the information available to us. We can't have any surprises. And no one is sneaking away. I suggest we keep an eye on the place for a few days. Learn the schedule of the guards and find out where everyone is located on the property. We know there are several different buildings, but we don't know what, or who, is in them. I want to know everything about this setup before we go in."

"I can keep an eye on things, Jack," Quinn offered from where he stood behind Amber's chair.

"I'd take you up on that, but I think I have a better idea." Jack looked at Gideon. "How's your teleporting precision?"

Gideon had no clue what was up Jack's sleeve. "Why?"

"I was thinking you could pop into a few of the trees overlooking the base and plant some video equipment. That would give us a bird's-eye view of everything going on in there."

"That sounds like a good plan," Amber interrupted. "But they probably have wards in place to tell them if anyone gets too close, like we have here."

"We could test it out," Lauren said. "Gideon could start out some distance away and see if it triggers anything. If not, he moves closer."

"This is all assuming Super Witch can land on a tree branch," Aiden teased.

"Bite me," he told Aiden, grinning. Inside, he was just hoping he *could* land on a tree branch. As he'd told Lauren, he and trees didn't have a good history. But he'd never admit that out loud in front of these guys.

Instead he shot back, "I could always practice with you. I'll teleport you to the tallest one I can find—see if you land okay."

Aiden laughed. "I'll pass, thanks."

Lindsay shook her head, and it reminded Gideon of the flash of her future he'd seen. She'd better get used to Aiden's antics, because she would be dealing with them for years to come.

"If you two are done," Jack cut in, "we need to add in the details from Quinn and Gideon's fly-over. Then I want to take another look at the maps for exact placement of the cameras." He looked at Gideon. "Lauren's plan is sound. See how close you can get without being detected. If we can't get close enough, we'll have to figure something else out."

Humor flashed in Jack's gray eyes as he dropped his voice to a whisper. "But you might want to try it out here first. Maybe something low to the ground."

Now it was Gideon's turn to shake his head. *Family.*

~~~

Lauren stood back and watched as Gideon popped himself into trees around the manor. It made her uneasy that he'd be going on this mission without her. She knew they didn't need to be connected at the hip, but up until now they'd always worked as a team, watching each other's backs.

She, better than anyone, knew Gideon could take care of himself. But she'd just feel better if she were there to make sure nothing happened to him. This time it would be Quinn who held his safety in his hands. As Gideon worked his way closer and closer, Quinn would watch through the eyes of another animal friend for a reaction from the inhabitants of the coven's lair. If Gideon's proximity caused any alarms to sound or people started to scurry, Quinn would relay that information immediately.

Before she could reconcile her feelings with the situation, Gideon materialized beside her.

"I think we're good to go," he told her. "I should be able to do this without killing myself."

Lauren knew he was kidding, but it didn't help her anxiety at all. What if something did go wrong? She was trying to come up with a way to tell him how she felt when Quinn approached.

"You ready?"

"More than," Gideon told him. Taking a moment, Gideon concentrated, and he was suddenly standing before them in head-to-toe camouflage.

Quinn once again sat on the patio. As soon as he'd established a connection with whatever animal he'd chosen, he told Gideon to go for it.

With a quick grin and a wink, Gideon blinked out of existence. All Lauren could do now was wait for him to return.

After half an hour, she discovered she sucked at waiting. She was ready to tear her hair out and needed a distraction
~~~

from her thoughts.

Motion to her left caught her eye. Margaret, with Hannah in her arms, was walking slowly down the garden path.

Up until now, Lauren hadn't spent much time with her mother, and none at all getting to know her niece. Seizing the moment, she turned and followed them. She caught up just as they stopped to look at some flowers. Margaret looked over at her.

"Hi, honey. We were just enjoying the beautiful day."

"Do you mind if I join you?" Lauren asked.

"Not at all. We'd love it."

They walked for a little ways before Margaret spoke again. "How goes the hunt? I heard you were getting close."

"Yeah, we are. Gideon is attempting to set up cameras around their base, so we can get a better idea of what goes on in there."

"That's good," Margaret said. "Sounds like this will all be over soon."

"Let's hope." They'd reached a wooden bench shaded by a large tree. Lauren sat and watched the grass and flowers wave in the slight summer breeze.

"What's the matter?" Margaret asked from where she'd sat down beside her.

Lauren shook her head. "Nothing, really. It's just driving me nuts that I'm not there with him."

Margaret turned her head to look straight at her. "Do you think he's in danger?" There was a hint of concern in her voice.

"No more than usual," Lauren was quick to reassure her.

Her mother visibly relaxed. "So what's the problem?"

"I'm just having a hard time sitting back and doing nothing. I'd feel better if it were me watching his back."

"Who is?" Margaret fussed with the blanket surrounding Hannah's little head, pulling it up around her ears.

"Quinn."

Satisfied all was good with the baby, Margaret looked back to Lauren. "And you don't think he'll protect Gideon?"

"It's not that," Lauren told her. "Quinn's strong, steady, and more than capable." She stopped.

Her mother studied her closely and nodded. "But you don't fully trust anyone but yourself. And Gideon."

Lauren whipped her head around, surprised that Margaret had been able to put into words something that Lauren was just figuring out. "How did you…"

"Lauren, it's only natural for you to have issues with trust," her mother consoled. "You have been lied to over and over again. People you thought you could rely on have repeatedly betrayed you. Used you. You were stuck in a brutal hell for a very long time. You had only yourself to count on until Gideon pulled you out. From what you've said, he's been there for you ever since."

"One of the first things he ever told me was that he'd never lie to me," Lauren confided. "He never has. Even when it wasn't what I wanted to hear, he's always told me the hard truth."

"He's earned your trust. And more. He's been there whenever you needed him. You and he have formed a tight bond. It only stands to reason you'd want to be there when, or if, he needs you. Plus, when someone you care about is taking risks, you worry. You want to do whatever you can to protect them."

Lauren heard a note of something in Margaret's tone and realized that she, herself, was probably causing her mother some sleepless nights.

"I'm sorry," Lauren told her.

Curiosity flashed in Margaret's eyes. "For what?"

"I didn't understand until now how what I'm doing may have affected you. You must feel this way every time I leave to confront the coven."

"I'll admit it's difficult," Margaret said. "But then I remind myself that as bad as it was for you growing up, it prepared you for what you're doing now. I just have to have faith that you'll come back each time."

Margaret reached out and cupped her cheek. "And you have to believe that Gideon will, too."

Some of the tension in Lauren's shoulders lessened. She brought her hand up to place it over her mom's. "Thank you."

"You're welcome, sweetie." Margaret smiled tenderly.

Lauren released her mother's hand and dropped her gaze to Hannah.

"Would you like to see your niece?"

"Yeah," Lauren admitted, "I would."

Margaret sat Hannah up in her lap, supporting her back and head. Lauren was a little surprised when bright blue eyes met hers. She bent forward a little and touched the baby's hand.

"Hi, pretty girl."

"Hi, Aunt Lulu," Hannah's little voice spoke inside her head.

24

An hour later, Lauren had gained enough nerve to actually hold the baby. And that's how Gideon found them.

"Beautiful." His softly-spoken words brushed against her mind. When she looked up, he wore a soft smile.

"What?" she asked him.

"You, there, holding her. I've seen that. Only it was our child sleeping on your chest."

Lauren returned his smile and asked him out loud. "How did it go?"

"I was able to place the four cameras Jack wanted. He's working on setting up the feed for them right now. We should have live video shortly."

"Well, then," Margaret stood and reached for the sleeping Hannah. "I'll just take this little one inside and let you two get back to work."

Lauren got to her feet also and wrapped Margaret in a hug. "Thank you."

Margaret kissed her cheek. "I love you."

When she turned and left, Gideon stepped in close and took Lauren into his arms. His mouth caught hers, and she fell into the heat and magic of his kiss.

They were both breathing heavily when the embrace ended. She looked up into the vortex of his eyes. In them, she saw arousal and need and something else. She saw a yearning. A desire she understood. One for family, and home, and life itself.

"We'll have all that," she told him, running her hand through the silky hair at the back of his neck. "We'll have everything you saw, everything you showed me."

He leaned in and kissed her again, a gentle confirmation of the future they were fighting for.

His arms were still wrapped tightly around her when he raised his head. "We should probably go see what's on the video feed."

Lauren heard the reluctance in his voice and felt the same way. "Yeah, probably."

They remained there for another few minutes, and they both laughed. "Come on," Gideon grasped her hand and pulled her towards the house, "before someone comes searching for us."

Lauren thought they'd be heading to the library. But when Gideon bypassed the doors, she had to ask. "Where are we going?"

"To the theater room."

There was no way she could have heard him right. "Did you say *theater room?*"

"Yup." He made a turn and led her down another long hallway. "Evidently they have a large movie screen set up back here. That's where Jack has the video from the compound coming in."

Lauren was speechless. She followed along, but her mind was still trying to fathom a whole theater set up inside of someone's house.

The first thing she saw when they opened the doors was a very large screen on the far side of the room. It was split into four sections, and each one showed a different view of the coven property. Each panel was as large as the TV she'd seen at Gideon's cabin.

The room was softly lit with lights that hung on the side walls. They were turned down low enough so as to avoid glare on the screen, but bright enough she could still see clearly without running into anything. Looking around, there were rows of reclining chairs. She counted three rows of ten. There was seating for thirty people in here.

Behind the last row was an open area, and that's where everyone was gathered. They were all standing and watching what was happening on the far wall.

"A little overkill, don't you think?" Gideon asked Jack.

He laughed. "Hey, I didn't even know this was here. Ben suggested it. He said a computer monitor was too small for what we were doing. And then he brought me here."

Aiden turned to Amber. "You grew up with a whole freaking theater in your house?"

Amber smiled at his jealous disbelief. "I had some pretty awesome birthday parties."

"I would say so," Aiden muttered and grinned. "I am so watching Jaws in here."

"Well, you'll be doing that all on your own," Lindsay advised. "That movie scared the crap out of me. I still refuse to get into any kind of water where I can't see the bottom. The first time something ever touched my leg, you'd see me running on top of it."

Aiden wrapped his arms around her and nuzzled her neck. "I'd protect you."

"Yeah." She pushed him away, laughing. "I don't think so. You're still on your own, buddy."

Everyone laughed at Aiden's hurt expression.

Jack was still smiling when he explained how this would work. "We're going to take shifts. And for the next few days, we're going to watch everything these people do. Whoever is on duty will make notes of anything that happens. Hopefully a pattern will emerge, and we can use that to our advantage.

"Aiden and Linds offered to take first watch. That way they'll be done when it's time to put Hannah to bed. Then Marissa and

I will take over." Jack consulted his notes. "Gideon and Lauren after that, and Amber and Quinn last. We can always mix it up, too, but I want at least two in here at all times. Three hour shifts. I think that's the most we'll be able to take of staring at those screens before going nuts."

Beside her, Gideon pulled his phone out and noted the time. She glanced at it to know what time they'd have to be back. In the meantime, she wanted another look at the journal they'd gotten from Melanie.

If they were going in swinging, she wanted to know all there was to know about the soldiers she'd be facing off against. They'd all received the same training as she. If there were weaknesses to exploit, she wanted to know them.

When they were walking down the hall again, she relayed her thoughts to Gideon. Everything they'd gathered was kept in the library, so that's where they headed.

Gideon positioned himself in the corner of the large sectional while she retrieved the book. When she approached, he patted the space between his open legs.

She eyed him skeptically. "I want to read through this, not snuggle with you."

"Why can't we do both?" He grinned and patted the seat again.

Still not sure it was a good idea, she sat in the V of his thighs and rested back against him. This was so *not* how she was used to preparing for battle.

Gideon wrapped his arms around her waist, and Lauren gave him a stern look over her shoulder.

The look he gave her back was one of pure innocence. She didn't believe it for a minute but opened the journal to the first page.

Gideon proved that he too had been reading along when he pointed out a section about a soldier named Timothy.

"It says here he has super strength. He may be the one we

have to be most careful of."

"Why?"

"His ability would be the hardest to neutralize. The others—their magic comes from the mind. They manipulate their powers with thoughts. His strength is always just *there*."

"Good point."

As she flipped to the next page, she felt the hair on her neck being pulled aside. "What are you doing?"

"Your hair was tickling my face."

Lauren had read no more than a sentence when she felt Gideon's lips at her nape. It sent a shiver through her system. "Gideon, we're working here."

"I know," he said between nips. "Continue on."

She tried to read the next line, she really did, but what he was doing was fogging her brain. The journal fell to her lap, and she tilted her head to the side to give him better access.

"I thought you wanted to read that." She actually felt his grin against her skin.

"I knew it wasn't a good idea, sitting like this."

"If you really want me to stop," he ran his tongue along the rim of her ear, "I will. I'll let you get back to your research."

Lauren reached up and grabbed a handful of hair at the back of his head. She turned and tipped her head back far enough to look up into his eyes before pulling his head down to meet hers. The last thing she saw before their lips met was molten heat.

They sank into the kiss. Lauren shifted around until she was lying stretched out on top of him.

A sound from the doorway startled her, but Gideon held her tight. "It's okay," he whispered. "It's only Jack."

She turned now and sat up next to Gideon. He pulled her into his side. "I guess that's the price of living with a big family. No privacy," Gideon joked.

Jack came in to stand at the other end of the couch. "Hey, if you wanted privacy, you should have at least closed the door."

Humor sparked in his gray eyes. "Aren't you a little old to be caught making out on the couch?"

Gideon laughed. "You're never too old for that." He winked at Lauren and returned his focus to Jack. "Were you looking for us?"

"No," Jack said, moving to the desk. "I just wanted to go over a few things again."

"Yeah," she nodded. "That's why we came here, too."

Jack arched a brow at her.

A heated flush threatened to ride up her face. She'd never been embarrassed in her life, but then again, she'd never had anyone tease her before. "We *did*," she asserted, searching around her for the journal. It was under Gideon's hip, and he wasn't budging to make it easier.

She gave him a dirty look. "Move."

Gideon smiled and lifted the right side of his ass off the papers. She lifted it for Jack to see.

"We were reading through this again, looking for weaknesses in the other soldiers."

He let the matter of what they'd been doing drop. "Did you find any?"

"A few," she told him. "But we also found what could be a problem. Gideon and I were discussing Timothy. We think he's going to be the one to give us the most trouble."

"Why is that?" Jack asked.

She explained what Gideon had told her. "A straight-up brawl won't get us anywhere with him. And I'm kind of worried that his strength will allow him to fight through any powers we might throw at him. Melanie noted that it didn't matter what Alexander or the others did; Timothy could usually withstand it."

"Yeah, but he's never met Super Witch here," Jack said. "My money's on Marquand magic."

"Still, we need to be prepared," Lauren cautioned.

"I agree." Jack sat behind the desk. "Which is what brought us in here. So, was there anything else you noted about the soldiers?"

They spent about an hour going over everything Lauren thought was pertinent to the battle to come. Afterward, Jack gathered up his notes. "I'll take these, so Marissa can look them over before we do our shift."

When Jack was gone, she looked over at Gideon. "Do you really think any of this will help us to defeat the coven and put a stop to Christopher?"

"Yes, I do."

Lauren wished she shared his confidence and certainty.

~~~

A few days later, surveillance was finished. Jack decreed they had all they were going to get. The whole family was now gathered to come up with a plan of attack.

Gideon thought back over their recent days of observation. It had passed in a blur of black and white images. And mind-numbing boredom. Three hours in a stretch may not have seemed like much, but staring at a large screen, watching people mill about, had become excruciatingly endless.

However, the long hours had served their purpose. They now had detailed notes on the comings and goings of every guard, every soldier, and every coven member living within the ten-foot-high walls. Christopher had been the hardest to track. He'd held to no schedule, and his ventures outside of the building had been sporadic. He'd shown up on camera a few times, but mostly had kept himself sequestered away. He'd rarely left the main house at the center of the property, his actions in there anyone's guess.

Gideon looked around at the fourteen people seated around the dining room table—all the Marquand witches and their
~~~

respective partners, plus Joann and Margaret, who refused to be left out of the plans their loved ones were making.

The only ones not included in this discussion were Hannah and Brooke. Hannah was upstairs asleep. And Brooke was probably still fuming about being left out of the fight.

Gideon's mother and aunt had taken her under their loving wings. They'd begun to catch her up on everything she'd missed. Her time trapped within the enthrallment spell had robbed her of much of her teenaged years.

Brooke had argued that she owed the coven for what they'd done to her, but Mia and Becca had managed to talk her out of going. This mission would be dangerous. Even though she'd been skillfully instructed, her training had been learned while she'd been unaware. They couldn't take the chance that she'd get into trouble and not know how to get out of it.

"I know we all want a hand in bringing these guys down," Jack began, drawing everyone's attention, "but I don't think we should go in en masse."

"Before you go any further," Conner interrupted, "you can cut your numbers by four. As much as it kills me to admit, this fight is for the current generation. I, my brother, and our wives will remain here. We'll do what we can from a distance."

"Are you sure?" Jack asked.

Conner smiled. "Jack, don't pretend you weren't trying to think of a polite way to gently ask us to bow out."

"Sir, I wouldn't—"

"Jack," Conner stopped him, "make your plans."

"Yes, sir."

25

They'd done all they could to get ready. Preparations had been made and studied endlessly. The sun had set hours ago, and it was finally time to put their plan into action.

Just seven gathered in the library now. This was the invading force that would take down the coven. Gideon looked at each one in turn.

Jack—the rugged PI. Prepared to risk his life for love and loyalty. Marissa—a witch with a late start; she'd embraced it fully and had grown in so many ways. Amber—tough and formidable, but she also possessed a big heart. Quinn—his life's path hadn't been easy, but it had given him the tools he needed to become someone who would do great things. Aiden—the reluctant witch. It took fighting for the lives of those he loved to fully accept who he was. Once he had, his life had become complete.

And finally Lauren—the single most important person in his life. He hadn't been sure about Fate's plan for him, but now he couldn't see his life without her in it. She'd become his everything. The damaged and broken woman had become fierce, independent, loving, and funny. Gideon had known once the two sides of her nature merged, she'd be a force to be reckoned with. And she was.

She would give him a run for his money for the rest of their lives, but he wouldn't have it any other way. She was his.

Forever.

Movement at the doorway brought Gideon out of his thoughts. He turned to see both sets of parents. They'd be staying behind, but had come to offer last words of encouragement.

Those said, Gideon and the others were headed out the door when a vision rocked him.

In it, he saw an old man tied to a chair. His head had fallen forward, his limp gray hair hanging down, covering much of his face. What Gideon could see was bruised and bloodied. He wasn't sure how he tied in to the war they'd wage tonight, but he was fairly certain he did.

He didn't recognize the man, but maybe one of the others would know.

"Incoming." That was all the warning he gave before broadcasting the images he was seeing into the minds of Jack, Marissa, Aiden, and Amber.

They gasped and Amber supplied the answer.

"That's Charlie. Who did this to him?" she demanded.

Gideon remembered him, but it had been over thirty years since he'd seen him. Charlie was a very good friend of the family. He and Gideon's grandmother had been best friends for decades.

Hearing Amber's angry words, Ben and Conner swung around, worry etched on their faces. "What's happened?"

Gideon replayed the vision for them.

"Son of a bitch!" Ben turned to Gideon. "Is this happening now?"

"Yes."

Jack spoke up next. "We'll have to split up. We can't just leave him there."

"No." Conner stood. "You guys go after the coven as planned. We'll get Charlie."

"That'll work," Jack nodded. "But be careful. It's probably a trap."

"No doubt," Ben agreed.

"Wait." Gideon stopped them as they turned to run for the door. "I can get you there a lot faster. I'll teleport the four of you into Charlevoix. When you have him, send out a call. I'll bring you all home."

"No," Ben shook his head. "We'll take the lift there, but we'll make our own way home. You'll have too much going on to mess with moving us around."

Gideon saw his logic. "All right. You ready then?"

All four heads nodded. They grasped hands, and with a thought Gideon set them down at the marina. It was only a few blocks from the restaurant Charlie owned. The rest was up to them.

"You know this was the coven's doing," Amber said. "But why would they go after Charlie? He has nothing to do with this."

"To get at us," Marissa speculated. "Anyone who knows the Marquands knows that Charlie holds a special place in the family."

Gideon looked at Lauren. "Did you ever hear anyone mention Charlie before?"

"No." She shook her head. "I researched him as a part of my assignment on you and your family, but they never said anything specific about him or made mention of any particular plans for him."

Beating old men may be low on the coven's atrocities-committed list, but this last ploy showed they'd stop at nothing to hurt *everyone* connected to the Marquands.

"We need to stop these fuckers once and for all," Gideon growled in disgust.

"Let's do this." Aiden stepped forward as the others nodded.

The plan was for Gideon to strategically drop them into the compound. Quinn would be stationed close to the kennels. After he did his thing there, he'd make his way to Amber and Aiden, who Gideon would put near the guard's quarters. The three of them would then neutralize that threat.

Jack and Marissa were to take the last two coven members, Santino Mylos and Davis Sutter. Through video footage, they knew the two men stayed in a small structure at the rear of the property, probably where the coven had done most of its dirty work.

That left the soldiers to him and Lauren. Once all of Christopher's people were taken care of, they'd converge on the main house and the man who'd wreaked such havoc on all their lives.

To maintain contact with everyone, Gideon would hold open the link in their minds so they could relay information telepathically.

He looked at Jack and Marissa, got their ready signal, and then they were gone. Gideon waited to hear from Jack.

"All clear."

Quinn was next. At his quick nod, he disappeared.

When Aiden and Amber were dropped into position, Gideon turned to Lauren. "You ready for this?"

"Oh yeah."

This battle would not be easy. The ones they were facing off against were as skilled and deadly as Lauren herself. It was going to take all they had to take them on.

Gideon grasped her hand and teleported them to the back side of the building where the soldiers slept.

They were crouched down in the heavy shadows. Gideon listened to see if he could hear any indication that their cover might be blown. There was nothing.

"The dogs are my best friends. They won't make a sound," Quinn said through the connection. *"Moving on now."*

Lauren started creeping along the side of the building, Gideon right behind her. When she stopped suddenly, he almost ran into her.

"Problem," she said in his mind. *"The door's open."*

On high alert, Gideon and Lauren approached. After a quick scan, she disappeared inside. She was back in just a few seconds. "It's empty."

"Shit," Gideon muttered. This wasn't good. He wondered if anyone else had located their targets.

He got his answer in the next breath. *"Uh, Gideon, guard's quarters are cleared out,"* Aiden said.

"Same here," came Jack's reply. *"Mylos and Sutter are gone."*

Fuck. Gideon turned and looked in the direction of Christopher's house. "What do you want to bet they're all in there waiting for us?"

"That would be my guess."

Gideon paused to do some quick thinking.

"Okay. Here's what we're going to do. Quinn, go back to the kennels and release the dogs. Bring them with you to the rear of the main house. Jack, you and the others meet up with Quinn and wait for my signal."

"What are you going to be doing?" Jack asked him.

Gideon looked down at the woman beside him. *"Lauren and I are going to walk right in the front door."*

"Gideon, are you fucking nuts?" Aiden shouted in his head. *"You can't just stroll in there. He'll kill you both!"*

"I don't think he will. Not right away, anyhow. I want some answers from him, and I think he may just be arrogant enough to give them to me."

"Our magic won't work on him," Marissa reminded them all. *"Not as long as he wears that amulet."*

"I know, but thanks," Gideon sent.

He brought his gaze down to Lauren. "Do you trust me?"

Her hazel eyes stared up into his. "Yes," she said without hesitation.

Gideon cupped her face in his hands and leaned in to kiss her. "I love you."

Lauren smiled. "I love you, too."

Together they ran in the direction of the two-story brick house in the center of the sprawling property. When they reached the front door, he raised his hand to knock. It was thrown open, and Gideon was staring down the barrel of a pistol. Another was trained on Lauren. By the size of the holes aimed at them, Gideon would guess they were both .45 caliber.

The goon on the left jerked his gun twice to the side, indicating he wanted them to go in that direction. Gideon placed his hand on Lauren's back and followed the guard's directions until they entered a large living area.

The four soldiers were stationed around the room looking intent and ready. Mylos and Sutter, the last two members of Christopher's coven, stood together on the right side. And Gideon counted eight guards spaced out around the perimeter.

The man bent on destroying Gideon's family sat, drink in hand, in the center of the room. The high-backed leather chair he occupied looked more like a throne than a regular seat.

He appeared unconcerned with what was happening as he swirled clear liquid around in the short tumbler in his hand. In a quick motion, he brought the glass to his mouth and shot it back. He then set it aside. The snap of it hitting the table gave away his temper.

"Did you think I wouldn't know you were coming?" Christopher asked. "That I wouldn't know the rest of your loathsome family is waiting nearby?" He turned to the soldier closest to him. "Find them and kill them."

The soldier gave a short nod and then pointed at the only female soldier with a motion to follow. Before turning to leave, he held up one hand and circled it in the air. All eight guards broke off and followed them out of the room.

Shit. Gideon sent a warning. *"Heads up, guys. Ten headed your way. Two of them soldiers."*

26

Gideon cast a quick look at Lauren. This was the first time she'd seen the men she'd believed to be her father and uncle since learning the truth. He wanted answers, but he'd take his cue from her for now. If she wanted to confront the men who had ruined her life, Gideon would stand behind her.

"Stacia." Christopher turned his attention to her. "I'd wondered where you'd gone. I had thought they may have killed you that night."

"My name is *Lauren*. Lauren Donnelly," she told him with twenty years' worth of anger and resentment glowing in her hazel eyes. "You took that away from me. You and your band of psychos."

She moved a couple of steps closer to him. Gideon sent her a word of caution. *"Watch yourself."*

"I helped you to reach your full potential," Christopher crooned. "Carl Donnelly couldn't see what was right beneath his nose. But we saw it and honed it. You should thank us." His tone had turned hard and cold. "You would have never become what you are if you'd stayed with that fool. *I* made you. I made all of you into what you are."

"You made us killers!" Lauren shouted. "And mercenaries. You robbed us of our youth, our families, loving homes. You tortured us and abused us and brainwashed us." She took another step closer and yanked the sleeves of her shirt up. "I'll have to wear these scars for the rest of my life. They'll act as a reminder every day of what you did to me. If you weren't hiding behind that amulet, I'd give you a taste of what power really feels like by snapping your neck."

Christopher had the audacity to smile at her, tauntingly.

Lauren grinned in return. "Yeah, go ahead and hide. I may not be able to use my power on you, but I *can* do this."

The throne-like chair Christopher was lounging in flipped violently backward.

The two remaining soldiers surged forward. Gideon gave them a shove that sent them tumbling across the floor. They were up again a moment later and zeroed in on him and Lauren. Until a signal from their leader stopped them cold.

They watched as Christopher slowly got to his feet. There was rage simmering in his eyes. Lauren had just bested him in front of his followers, and he was furious.

Gideon thought it was time to shift Christopher's focus and moved to put himself in the coven leader's path.

"Hey!" Gideon snapped out, trying to draw Christopher's gaze. "Since you're being so forthcoming, how about answering a few of *my* questions?"

Christopher's scathing look remained fixedly on Lauren. Gideon thought he'd have to up the ante to pull the lunatic's notice when he swung around to face him.

"What is it you want to know, freak?"

"Why is it that you hate my family so much? Did one of us kick your favorite puppy?" Gideon knew he was goading him, but he thought it might be the best way of getting some answers.

Gunfire erupted outside, and a wholly-satisfied smile spread over Christopher's face.

"It's a shame, really. I was so hoping that I would be there when you Marquand witches got what you deserved. Oh, well. At least I have the pleasure of knowing that no one is coming to your rescue now."

Gideon held his anger in check. "You seem to have us exactly where you want us, so answer the question. Why are you doing this?"

Christopher slowly crossed to where Gideon was standing and stopped right in front of him. It was gratifying to know he had to look up to meet Gideon's eyes. "Why am I doing this? Well, let's see. It could be because the magic that flows through your veins should have been mine. That *I* am the rightful heir to all that power. You know, none of this would have been necessary if my father would have just married Sofia all those years ago. They would have had me, and I would have been the recipient of all the gifts you carry."

"Why would my grandmother have married your father? Who the hell is he?" As soon as the words left Gideon's mouth, he knew. "Charlie."

"Yes, *Charlie*," Christopher sneered. "I," he pounded on his chest, "should have been the child of Sofia Marquand. Not that weak cow that raised me. God, she hated them. Hated that they'd made a fool of her with their relationship. A relationship that should have produced me, instead of those matching bookends she called sons. None of you should ever have been born. And that's something I mean to rectify here and now."

Christopher swung back around, and at some unseen sign, the two remaining soldiers sprang into action.

Lauren backed far enough away, so that she could move unhindered. Gideon had just turned to face his opponent when he felt something happen to his senses. Sounds around him became muffled, his vision dimmed, the connection with his family was gone, and his body seemed weighed down. It was as if someone had thrown an excessively heavy blanket over him.

He looked around to see if he could find why this was happening. His gaze landed on Mylos and Sutter across the room. Gideon's mistake had been forgetting they were there.

This is where the magic Christopher utilized came from. And right now, they were chanting something he couldn't hear.

Gideon tried to use his power, but there was nothing there. Whatever they were reciting was hindering his abilities. Before he could figure out what to do about them, the soldier was upon him.

Muscle memory from years of fight training took over. He swung out with a right cross and connected with a hard jaw. His hand exploded with pain. His opponent smiled and advanced on him. Using both hands, he slammed them into Gideon's chest, sending him flying backward. In that instant, Gideon knew he was facing Timothy—the one who possessed super strength.

He sent a quick look over at Lauren's attacker. Gideon knew as soon as he saw the youthful face who she was up against. Derrick.

"Don't let him touch you!" Gideon shouted to her. "Mind control."

"Yeah, I kind of figured that out already," she returned as she backed away from the soldier.

Gideon couldn't spare any more of his attention. Timothy was hauling him up off the floor. With his powers under Mylos and Sutter's control, Gideon knew he was in trouble.

Would any of them make it out of this alive?

All thought stopped when Timothy plowed a fist into Gideon's side. He actually heard his ribs break. The pain was almost unbearable and stole the breath from his lungs. Gideon dropped to the floor, gasping.

Lauren uttered a short cry. Gideon swung his head around to see Derrick holding her against his body, his bare hand wrapped around her throat. He looked directly at Gideon as he whispered something in her ear.

She transformed right before Gideon's eyes. Derrick had gained control of her mind.

Shit.

"Ah yes. Nicely done, Derrick. You've brought Stacia back to me," Christopher cooed before turning his smugness on Gideon. "I know I shouldn't have favorites, but she has always been special to me. As soon as I saw her, I knew she'd be perfect." He transferred his gaze back to Lauren. "I named her myself. Stacia means resurrection, you see. And *I* brought her forth from the ashes of her former life."

He nodded at Derrick, and the soldier released his hold on her. Before backing away, he unsheathed a long black blade from his thigh and handed it to her. "Well, my dear. Make Uncle proud, and kill that abomination."

Gideon had a moment to see Timothy and Derrick both return to flank Christopher. But all his attention needed to be centered on Lauren. As she stalked him, he slowly got to his feet, his arm braced around his ribs. This was who she'd been when he'd first brought her to his cabin. That deadly warrior was the person he was looking at now.

He had to get through to her again. He had to bring her back.

The clatter of feet drew everyone's attention to the hall. Five people came storming into the room, their clothes torn and bloody. But they all looked ready and fit for battle.

Gideon quickly caught Jack's eye and yelled, "I'll handle this! Take Mylos and Sutter out!"

He didn't have time for any more than that as the woman he loved bore down on him with lethal intent in her hazel eyes.

"Lauren," he tried, each word a knife in his side, "Lauren, you need to hear me. Derrick's magic has control of you. You have to fight it."

She shook her head and adjusted her grip on the blade Derrick had given her. "All I have to do is kill you."

Gideon backed up a step with each one she took towards him.

"Running scared?" she taunted. "Really? *You*?" Another

foot closer. "What's the matter? Afraid of hurting poor little Lauren? Well, you don't have to worry. That gutless wench isn't here anymore. It's just me now." She slowly stalked him a few more paces and smiled sadistically.

"This isn't you." Gideon retreated further. "You don't want to do this."

"Oh yeah, I do. I *really* do."

Before he saw it coming, she used her powers to toss him backward and into the wall. The impact must have driven the splintered edge of a rib into his lung. All of a sudden, he couldn't breathe. It was a struggle just to bring oxygen into his body.

Gideon started to get light-headed. In a daze, he looked around and saw the rest of his family still fighting to stop the others. He could do no less. Watching them bolstered his resolve. Gideon refused to let Christopher get away with everything he had done to them, as well as countless others.

For the first time ever, Gideon uncaged his full temper. For all they had lost. For all they stood to lose here. He gave in to everything he'd ever kept bottled up, and as the wrathful storm of fury and hate filled him, he allowed it to completely take over.

The atmosphere suddenly crackled around him as his revulsion and outrage fought against the spell the coven was using to disable him. His blood heated, and power surged as his magic returned. The muted feeling vanished, and Gideon was restored to who he was meant to be. As he rose to his feet, his internal injuries healed instantly, and he was whole and healthy once again.

He stared down at Lauren, but under Derrick's command, she had no fear of him. She was still ready to battle him to the death.

But neither one of them were dying here tonight.

Before she could strike out at him again, Gideon vanished and reappeared behind her. He quickly disarmed her and spun her around to face him, wrapping his arms around her. She struggled against him, but he held firm and dropped the glamour masking his eyes. With his mind, he speared his way into hers and showered her with memories of who she was.

He showed her happy moments she'd shared with her mother and with Hannah. He reminded her of what she meant to him and what he meant to her. Gideon replayed the visions of the future he'd shared with her once before.

He drowned her in the love that now surrounded her.

She stared deeply into the swirling green until the tension slowly drained out of her. "Gideon?"

He eased his grip, and as recognition dawned, he put the glamour back into place.

"Welcome back, baby."

"What happened?"

"Derrick took control of you," he answered.

"Oh." She rubbed her head. "I remember he got his hands on me, and then nothing." A look of panic creased her face as she turned worried eyes up to him. "Did I hurt anyone?"

"No, you didn't. I got you back."

Gideon became aware of the silence surrounding him. He and Lauren looked up to find their family standing over what remained of Christopher's crew.

Santino Mylos had taken a direct hit from one of Aiden's fireballs. He was a smoldering heap on the floor. Davis Sutter had a neat, round hole in the center of his forehead—Jack's handiwork, by the look of it.

The soldier Derrick was backed into the corner, two snarling dogs holding him prisoner at Quinn's order. Timothy, the super-soldier, was being subdued by Amber. Well, sort of. He'd fight through her freeze power, and she'd have to render him immobile again.

"A little help here?" she asked. "I can't keep doing this. He's getting out of it faster each time."

Gideon added his power to Amber's, and all movement ceased. For good measure, he froze Derrick too until they could figure out what to do with them. Gideon had an idea, but it would take more thought and time than he could afford right now.

Finally, he turned in search of the one responsible for all of this. "Where's Christopher?"

Aiden was the first to spot the open door. "He must have slipped out while we were fighting."

"He is *not* getting away." Gideon stepped away from Lauren and turned towards the same exit. "He couldn't have gotten far."

Still riding the wave of power he'd released, Gideon took off out the door. He knew the others would be right on his heels. They ran down a long corridor. At the other end was another way out. Gideon pushed through, and they spilled out onto the back lawn. He could see Christopher running up ahead of them, clearly headed for the sea plane docked on the water there.

Gideon formed a thought and heaved the ground beneath Christopher's feet, sending him sprawling.

The four Marquand witches advanced on him, Quinn, Jack, and Lauren spreading out behind them.

His prey got to his feet and turned to face them. "You can't touch me." He reached into his shirt and pulled the amulet out. He let it hang against his chest in full view, his shield against punishment for his crimes. "As long as I wear this, you can't do a damned thing to me! No one can."

"You're done, Christopher," Gideon called out. "Your coven is no more. Your soldiers are gone. You have nothing left."

"Oh, I don't think so. I still have a few secrets up my sleeve."

The sea plane exploded into a ball of fire. Gideon looked over at Aiden to see him grinning. "Oops. Looks like you'll have to find another ride. *If* you can make it past us, that is."

Water escape thwarted, Christopher started to move towards

the woods. He must have a way of getting past the wall. And that meant another means of escape. Gideon thought he probably had a helicopter waiting in the clearing they'd seen.

Gideon became aware of a large shadow emerging out of the darkness behind the coven leader. It slowly began to split apart, revealing eight separate beings. They formed a line between Christopher and the safety of the trees, the rumble of low growls their only warning.

"I wouldn't try it," Quinn advised him. "Take one step, and I'll release them. Believe me, I'd like nothing better than to turn them loose on you and watch them rip you to shreds. To destroy you like you've destroyed so many. But you know what? You missed the mark with us. We're stronger than you. We've beaten you. You are nothing now."

Even though Christopher had nowhere to go, he continued to boast, a look of pure disgust on his face. "You haven't beaten me! I'll recruit more guards and soldiers to aid me, and I will come for you again. I won't stop until every last one of you is dead!"

"No," Amber said. "This is where it ends. You've tormented my family long enough. You've taken too much from us, and there will be no more. We are whole again, because you couldn't break us. And you won't break Charlie, either. He'll survive this. He'll survive you. We'll see to that, because we love him."

"Before I'm done with him, he'll know what his choices cost him." Christopher sneered at her. "His selfishness deprived me of my rightful inheritance." He paused and looked at the four of them standing there. "And don't think I've forgotten about Ben and Conner and their cunt wives. I have some special plans set up especially for them. And you can do nothing to stop me."

The wind rose, and leaves and debris pelted the coven leader where he stood. Gideon could feel the energy surging from Marissa. Leaves and branches swirled and dove. Christopher's head snapped back as they slapped him in the face. His arms flailed, trying to stop the stinging strikes.

Deciding to join the action, Amber conjured rocks and pebbles to add to Marissa's assault, pelting them all over Christopher's dodging and twisting body.

Their attack was more degrading than if they had smashed him over the head. Each slap and stone thrown was a demeaning and mortifying humiliation.

Gideon saw when Christopher's hold on sanity broke and knew the time had come. The man was crazy and couldn't be left to hurt anyone else.

"Rissa, Aiden, Amber—I'm going to need your help," Gideon sent to his family.

"You have it," his sister replied without pause.

"What do you need?" Aiden asked.

"Everything you have," he told her. *"For what I have planned, it's going to take all of us."*

They stepped forward to stand with him, aligning themselves shoulder-to-shoulder, Marissa on his left, and his cousins on his right. Gideon opened himself up and felt the power they were channeling into him. He drew it in and let it build until one massive ball of energy beat in his chest. Gently, carefully, he molded it and shaped it into a sharp and deadly arrow, nocked and ready to fly.

Gideon marveled at the magic of his family. Alone, he was strong. But combined together this way, the power of the four of them was transcendent.

With his senses wide open to accept the massive amounts of energy funneling from his family, he felt another force— foreign, but pristine and dazzling in its own right.

Radiating from behind him was the brightest, most iridescent star he'd ever seen. And it was coming from Lauren. This was why they had needed her. Not for the information she'd provided them. But for this.

With heart and mind healed, Lauren was able to accept the

love she deserved, allowing the resplendent fire within her soul to shine through. The once-broken child stood whole, her past and future merged—finally the woman she was meant to be.

He reached out to her now. *"Lauren, baby."*

"Gideon, what are you doing?"

"I need something from you."

"What? Anything—it's yours."

He sent her a visual of what he was seeing and heard her gasp.

"What is that?"

"That's you, love. It's what we need to end this forever.

"How do I share it with you?"

"Just open yourself up to me, and I'll do the rest."

When Gideon brought Lauren's brilliance into his body and joined it with Marquand magic, he started to glow from within. Her white-hot radiance fused with their magic, fortifying the arrow and bolstering its strength.

Christopher was still oblivious to the fact that he had no place to go and no hope of escape. As he continued to taunt them, he spread his arms out wide, baring his chest. "Do your worst. Nothing can stop me. I am invincible!"

"Wanna bet?" Gideon muttered under his breath and then let loose the arrow. He watched as it flew true and found its target a moment later.

The shaft of pure white magic struck the amulet square in the center. It shattered into a million shards before exploding into dust. With nothing left to protect him, the bolt continued on its trajectory and tore into Christopher's chest.

He stared down at the hole Marquand magic had ripped through his torso. Christopher's eyes tracked back to Gideon and those who stood with him. Stunned disbelief filled his expression before it all faded away, and he dropped to the ground, dead.

EPILOGUE

Five years later

Gideon found Lauren seated on that same wooden bench tucked underneath the tree as she snuggled the young infant to her chest. Sunlight filtered down through the leaves, leaving her flawless skin radiant in a yellow strapless sundress. This time, as he'd seen so long ago, it *was* their child asleep in her arms.

"There you are." He sat down next to his wife of four years and gazed lovingly down at the infant she cradled. "Did she pass out while eating again?"

"Yeah." Lauren smiled down at their daughter. "She's nothing like Steven was. He'd eat until I thought he'd explode." She laughed. "I was so glad when he was finally weaned."

Gideon stared down at this little human he and Lauren had made in love. Megan was two months old already. And their son, Steven, had just turned three.

It seemed to him as if a lifetime had passed since the night their lives had finally been able to begin.

His parents had fought hard to rescue Charlie. Christopher had left six men behind to watch and guard his father until he could return to finish the job. The four elder witches again proved why this family had survived for so long. The four of them were a power unto themselves. Gideon would put them at his back anywhere, anytime.

Once they had gotten Charlie back to the manor, Conner had healed the wounds he'd sustained. After that, he'd told them who had been behind it all. Christopher had been there when Charlie had been grabbed and had ordered him beaten. He'd raged at his own father for not having given him what should have been his.

Come to find out, after Charlie's wife had disappeared with their son, she'd spent years filling his head with lies and poison about his father and the Marquands. She'd continued to warp him until her death, shortly before the coven had found him.

Charlie had taken it all extremely hard. The knowledge that his own son had terrorized them for so many years caused him to suffer greatly. He'd felt such guilt and shame, he had cut himself off from them for a long time.

There'd been a time they hadn't been sure he'd make it through, but they'd stood by him, letting him know, over and over, that none of it was his fault. They'd made sure he knew they still loved him, and that he was an important part of their family. Slowly, over many months, he'd started to come around.

Though he still had moments where it brought him down, he'd mostly put the whole awful experience behind him. He'd gone back to his restaurant and poured his soul into surprising his patrons with his delectable dishes. Over time, and as more babies came, Charlie started spending less time there. Now, whenever they saw him, there was always at least one of the little ones with him. He'd taken the role of honorary great-gramps to heart.

All the children loved Charlie, and he them.

Marissa and Jack had married that winter. Those twin boys Gideon had seen, Charlie and Jason, had arrived soon after that. They were four now and ran Jack ragged. Gideon laughed to himself. Even after the chaos of the twins, Jack had had the guts to get Rissa pregnant again. They were expecting another son in a few months. That kid would be no slouch, either. They'd have their work cut out for them, just as they always did.

Aiden and Lindsay hadn't waited much longer than Jack and Marissa to get married. Shortly afterwards, Aiden had legally adopted Hannah. To honor her birth father, they'd added Donnelly as a middle name. When Hannah was four, they'd welcomed Cami into the world. Hannah loved her baby sister, and now that Cami was a year old and mobile, the two were inseparable. Aiden was quietly freaking out at having two daughters. Gideon had ribbed him mercilessly, asking what he'd do when they started noticing boys and wanting to date. That had all come to an abrupt stop when he'd had a daughter of his own. Now he understood Aiden's anxiety.

Amber and Quinn had just celebrated their fourth wedding anniversary. Their son Logan was two, and Amber was pregnant again, due around the same time as Marissa. They lived most of the time on the reservation with Quinn's family, so he could train with Samuel to take his rightful place in the tribe.

That night hadn't been easy on any of them. Gideon had later learned exactly what had happened after Christopher's men had found his family outside of the compound.

It had been a pitched battle that had left seven of the guards dead, one unconscious, and two soldiers contained. The good guys hadn't come through unscathed, either. Amber had suffered a dislocated shoulder, and Quinn had taken a bullet to the thigh. The others had wounds too many to count. Aiden had healed it all before they'd charged into the house to fight all over again.

There *had* been some good that came from that awful night. The four soldiers who'd been there with Christopher, as well as the fire-thrower from the warehouse, were all back with their families again.

Since learning he could wipe minds, Gideon had decided to

do what he could for the rest of the soldiers. After some fine-tuning, Gideon was able to erase only the time spent at the mercy of the coven. They all had lost years of their lives, but at least they were home and happy. He'd even done what he could to remove the scars from their ordeal.

Melanie, too, was home and content. Gideon had called her mother as soon as they'd returned. He hadn't given any thought to the hour, knowing she'd want to know it was over and could bring her daughter home.

They still received letters and pictures from them from time to time. The last one had been news of the birth of Melanie and Scott's third child. Her mother was reveling in being a grandma.

Brooke had ended up staying with them and had become a member of the family. In the time she'd spent with them, she'd caught up on everything she'd missed in both life and school. Three years after being rescued, she'd legally changed her last name to Marquand. She was attending college and had a new boyfriend she'd yet to bring home. Gideon figured she was scared her adoptive older brothers would frighten him off. Which was a good possibility.

Gideon smiled. He, Jack, Quinn, and Aiden took their rolls very seriously. They all swore they'd read the Big Brother Handbook and had committed it to memory.

The sound of kids' excited laughter pulled Gideon out of his thoughts. He brought his gaze back to Lauren's. "We'd better head back to the party. It sounds like it's getting crazy. You ready?"

"Yeah. Has Hannah opened her gifts yet?"

"No, she was waiting for you and Megan."

"Wow. That had to be hard for a five-year-old. We'd better go before she sends her horde after us."

As the eldest grandchild, Hannah was indeed the leader of the pack. Her five younger cousins followed her around as if she were the center of the universe. On any given day, it took all of the adults in the family to contain the trouble six magical kids could create. And more were on the way.

His parents and aunt and uncle were in heaven. They finally had the houseful of kids they'd always wanted. When everyone came home, like now for Hannah's fifth birthday, there was never a dull moment.

All the kids had become pros at being teleported back and forth between houses. Gideon was always on call to shuttle one or two of them somewhere. But he still refused to send Aiden and Lindsay to any kind of island, deserted or otherwise.

Gideon stood and then reached down to lift his daughter out of his wife's arms. He offered Lauren his hand, and when she took it, he pulled her to her feet and into him, his hand lifting to cup the side of her face. He thought of the white fire he'd found in her that night so long ago. He'd never seen it again after that night and probably never would again, but he knew it was there. He smiled down into her hazel eyes, dropping the glamour on his own.

He'd never gotten around to telling anyone else about this little quirk of his magic. It remained a private part of his and Lauren's connection. Gideon leaned in and took her mouth with his, making promises he fully intended to keep later.

Since the grandparents were in charge of all the kids tonight, Gideon planned on enjoying a little adult time with Lauren back at their home on the lake. He slid his hand down the silky-smooth and unblemished skin of her arm and entwined his fingers with hers.

"Uncle G! Aunt Lu! Are you coming?" Hannah's bubbly voice carried all the way across the yard.

Gideon thought of all he'd seen and grinned. Oh, the adventures this next generation of Marquand witches would have.

Together, he and Lauren walked back into the loving chaos

that was their family.

Dear readers –

Thank for taking this journey with me and the Marquand family. I hope you laughed with them, cried with them, and cheered them on. Who knows, maybe someday down the line we'll visit with them again and find out what's going on with the next generation. I'm sure Hannah and the others will be getting into some kind of trouble.

I have a few new things in the works, look for updates on my website: mishamckenzie.com. There you can also find a link to my twitter account and my Facebook Author page. I would love to hear from you.

And whatever you happen to be reading, whether it's me or someone else, please take a moment and post a review on your favorite online blog or retailer.

Thank you and Happy Reading!

Misha McKenzie

Misha McKenzie has been an avid reader since learning how at four years old. Countless books later, she still loves to immerse herself into the lives of the people within those pages. After graduating high school, she went on to earn a degree in Business Administration, married her high school sweetheart, and had two beautiful boys. At thirty years old, while working as an office manager for a construction company, a family of witches began to brew, and The Magic of the Heart Series was born.